PRAISE FOR *A CALAMITY OF MANNERINGS*:

'This book is bliss.' HILARY MCKAY

'What an absolute hoot! Set in 1924, and galloping with coming-of-age giddiness, and the promise of parties and life-changing romance, Joanna Nadin's *A Calamity of Mannerings* simply brims with vim.' *LOVEREADING4KIDS*

'Flawless. Fabulous.' RACHEL DELAHAYE

'If Louise Rennison had written *I Capture the Castle* it would be this book. Witty, totally charming and proper laugh-out-loud-several-times-on-each-page funny, it's just a joy from start to finish and I felt sick with envy over the writing.' LAURA WOOD

'A real roaring 20s romp of a read. Delightful.'
WRD ABOUT BOOKS

'A storyline that tips a cap at *Love in a Cold Climate*, *I Capture the Castle* and even *Bridgerton* make this a must read for ages 16–106!' CATHY CASSIDY

'So much fun! So clever, with such wonderful characters who I can still feel breathing and squabbling around me. I kept on guffawing with laughter.' NATASHA FARRANT

HAVE YOU EVER WONDERED HOW BOOKS ARE MADE?

UCLan Publishing is an award winning independent publisher specialising in Children's and Young Adult books. Based at The University of Central Lancashire, this Preston-based publisher teaches MA Publishing students how to become industry professionals using the content and resources from its business; students are included at every stage of the publishing process and credited for the work that they contribute.

The business doesn't just help publishing students though. UCLan Publishing has supported the employability and real-life work skills for the University's Illustration, Acting, Translation, Animation, Photography, Film & TV students and many more. This is the beauty of books and stories; they fuel many other creative industries! The MA Publishing students are able to get involved from day one with the business and they acquire a behind the scenes experience of what it is like to work for a such a reputable independent.

The MA course was awarded a Times Higher Award (2018) for Innovation in the Arts and the business, UCLan Publishing, was awarded Best Newcomer at the Independent Publishing Guild (2019) for the ethos of teaching publishing using a commercial publishing house. As the business continues to grow, so too does the student experience upon entering this dynamic Master's course.

www.uclanpublishing.com
www.uclanpublishing.com/courses/
uclanpublishing@uclan.ac.uk

*For my mum, who taught me to love funny women,
and in memory of Joe Roberts, whose thoughts on class,
and loan of books on Soho helped shape this idea.*

Birdy Arbuthnot's Year of 'Yes' is a uclanpublishing book

First published in Great Britain in 2025 by
uclanpublishing
University of Central Lancashire
Preston, PR1 2HE, UK

Text copyright © Joanna Nadin, 2025
Cover illustrations copyright © Anna Morrison, 2025

978-1-916747-65-4

13 5 7 9 10 8 6 4 2

The right of Joanna Nadin and Anna Morrison to be identified
as the author and illustrators of this work respectively has been asserted in
accordance with the Copyright, Designs and Patents Act 1988.

All rights reserved. No part of this publication may be reproduced,
stored in a retrieval system, or transmitted in any form or by any means,
electronic, mechanical, photocopying, recording or otherwise,
without the prior permission of the publishers.

Set in 10.5/17pt Kingfisher by Becky Chilcott.

A CIP catalogue record for this book is available from the British Library.

Printed and bound in Great Britain by Clays Ltd, Elcograf S.p.A.

Birdy Arbuthnot's Year of 'YES'

JOANNA NADIN

uclanpublishing

'Soho isn't a place, it's a state of mind.'
(Anonymous, 1959)

DECEMBER 1959

SATURDAY 26 DECEMBER

11 A.M.

I write this sitting in the kitchen sink. Or, rather, I tried to, but the sink is perilously small and slippery, the ceramic draining board is horribly cold, and I was just wondering whether or not to run the hot water lest I get chilblains when my mother walked in. She said at eighteen it was high time I grew out of all that 'Cassandra Mortmain nonsense' and in any case she needed it for scrubbing potatoes as Aunt Barbara (ambitious, bunions) and Uncle Roy (obsessed with war and golf) are coming for lunch, so please go and do whatever it is I was doing in somewhere more suitable, i.e. the dining room. I was about to point out that I am barred from the dining room (for reasons I cannot be bothered to explain here but suffice to say I vehemently disagree with) but I could tell she was in no mood to brook argument (her lips go inexplicably thin) so I have come upstairs to my bedroom and she has gone back to doing something inventive with mince.

So, in actuality, I write this sitting on lavender candlewick, whilst wishing, yet again, that my life were more novel-like.

I shouldn't even mind if it wasn't *I Capture the Castle*, however attractive moving to a dilapidated mansion in East Anglia might be; I'd settle for anything disaffected and preferably French – like Cécile in *Bonjour Tristesse*, perhaps. Sadly there is no chance of torrid poolside affairs in Surbiton, where private swimming pools and disaffection are regarded with the same suspicion as are exotic pets and ambitious hair. Instead I am constrained by complete mediocrity. Even my name – Margaret – is average (Princess Margaret notwithstanding, as she is a goddess amongst women). Why can I not be a Calypso? A Viola? A Genevieve?

It could be worse, I suppose. I could be a civil servant (John, my brother) or a dentist (Daddy) or be engaged to Trevor Phelps (Felicity Higgins, my best friend). Not that I wouldn't mind a boyfriend of some sort. But that sort of thing is difficult when one is a) plain b) prone to mishap and c) under my mother's jurisdiction. Also there isn't a single boy in all of Surrey with whom I would deign to hold hands, let alone engage. Felicity insists Trevor's friend Colin is a 'catch', but I told her there was nothing 'catching' about clerking for a solicitor and keeping bees. Besides, settling for the boy-next-door (even if he does live three streets away) is so very Surbiton. Even my parents met in more interesting circumstances, i.e. on a train to St Austell – she on a day trip; he on the annual Arbuthnot holiday – which is practically romantic.

Perhaps I shall meet someone when I get to university.

If I get to university. Cambridge entrance is a month away and I am woefully ill-prepared. If I was to get Freudian about it, I should say that it's because I am avoiding what I know will, at best, only lead to more tedium and, at worst, abject failure. But Freud is barred in this house along with all forms of fortune telling (Mummy says horoscopes are for the 'mentally weak') and Cliff Richard (Daddy is averse to his hair) so I shall just surmise that I am not an Oxbridge sort. It is just a shame Mummy doesn't agree. Though I suspect it is only because she regrets never being able to go to university at all on account of being poor and from Cornwall. Daddy effectively rescued her from a life of butchery (the family business, not murder) in Bodmin so I suppose Surbiton, for her, is almost Hollywood.

The upshot of which is that I should be revising this very minute, i.e. trying (for the umpteenth time) to finish *Mrs Dalloway*. But, I ask you, who wants to read about the elderly and their depressing dinner parties? I get enough of that at 43 Magnolia Road when Mummy and Daddy have the Tredegars (two doors down, amateur dramatics) round. Although Mummy doesn't worry about fetching flowers as they are an 'unnecessary extravagance', especially where the Tredegars are concerned. I'd rather read about Virginia Woolf herself, who led a far more thrilling existence. Anyway, my point is (which I admit I struggle to stick to, and which again does not bode well for university interview) that instead of studying I am writing this journal, which is number one in my New Year's

Eve resolutions. And yes, I know it is far too early, being a week away, but John gave me the notebook (which is a dear thing – emerald leather with my initials embossed on the cover) for my Christmas present yesterday along with the pen from Mummy and Daddy (the most gorgeous Osmiroid – a dark marbled navy), and my Cassandra Mortmain dreams were instantly renewed, much to Mummy's chagrin.

Oh, heavens! The doorbell has just gone so I suppose I shall have to put aside the rest of the resolutions until later, put on my out-to-please face, and brace myself for Aunt Barbara and Uncle Roy. One can only hope they have not brought Julian (ten, knows too many facts) with them. He makes Mrs Dalloway seem a welcome guest.

7 P.M.

It is a miracle I have survived lunch unscathed, if not exactly scot-free. And though I do not entirely blame Julian, his presence did not help in the slightest. I concede it started off well enough – all seated at the table listed yesterday's presents, and there was much 'Oh, lovely!'ing etc. etc., although what one would want with a pair of bellows (Aunt Barbara) or an icon of the Virgin Mary (Julian) remains to be proven. But conversation swiftly turned, as seemed inevitable, to my 'Future', a word I always imagine spoken with a menacing capital 'F', as if it is something one must regard with the same trepidation as one does bears or the clergy. Aunt Barbara asked if I had given any more thought to Hull University, which is her alma mater, and where she met Daddy's brother Uncle Roy. At this my mother's lips thinned again – I believe she regards anywhere north of Watford as some sort of No Man's Land, marked on the map with 'here be dragons'. On top of which, she does not consider Uncle Roy in any way a good match, given his weak knees. I said I had indeed given thought to Hull, but did not add that the thought was an enormous 'no, thank you'. Julian then began to list facts about Hull (the fishing industry there was started by monks; something about phone boxes) none of which were in any way encouraging, at which point Mummy, who was quite red-faced by that point, snapped, 'She'll be going to Cambridge, like . . . like Charles Darwin, so all this fish talk is moot!' I did not dare dissuade her from this conviction. Nor did Daddy, who seemed inordinately interested in his Brussels sprouts throughout this exchange (he only mustered the gumption to speak when the conversation turned, as was inevitable, to the state of the eighteenth hole at Sandown).

Julian, however, was decidedly vocal. 'Vladimir Nabokov went to Cambridge,' he said. 'Also Lord Byron.'

This risked a further outburst as my mother regards them both with the same air of suspicion as she does Freud, so by way of a distraction I said I really should get back to my revision, as Mrs Dalloway wouldn't read herself (though I heartily wish she would). However, Aunt Barbara then seized on the opportunity to grill me in the form of a quiz, i.e. Who fought in the battle of the Boyne? Why is a horse measured in hands? How many ounces in a gill? I had to admit I did not know the answers to any of these (unlike Julian) but said I did not think any interview at Girton, if I got one, would consist of a general knowledge competition. Aunt Barbara said it pays to be prepared for anything and I should brush up on my capital cities, heraldry and semaphore as well. I did not answer that one for fear of being sent to my room, appealing though that was. Thankfully they left soon after dessert (yesterday's pudding heated up with custard, and the stilton that Daddy insists on buying every Christmas and then no one eats and so it will be thrown out looking even bluer come Easter) citing perilous weather conditions on the Richmond Road (it is drizzling).

It is unfair that my brother no longer has to suffer through these affairs, which I said, and which earned me another black look from Mummy even though I waited until everyone had left. It is because John's wife, Gloria, is pregnant, which is usually a useful distraction for everyone, but she is currently afflicted with piles, which means she has to sit on a rubber ring, which John insists is the wrong sort of distraction, and so they are excused from social events (bar immediate family) until the 'situation below stairs' improves.

On the bright side, I am back on the lavender candlewick, having refused Mummy's offer of a turkey sandwich for supper (she will be trying to palm these off on us for weeks; it is the same every year. It is a wonder we had hot lunch in the circumstances) and am attending to my resolutions. So far I have:

1. Finish *Mrs Dalloway*.
2. Do something with hair. I am never going to get anywhere in life with mousy brown hanks that lurk around my face like curtains. Even Felicity has started using curlers. Though the overall effect is less Jackie Kennedy and more Mrs Weedon from the Post Office, but at least it is an improvement on looking about twelve.
3. Pass Cambridge entrance.

Though, the more I stare at it, the more unappealing number 3 seems. I don't want to go to university; I want to LIVE (with capitals!). I want a life more like the fictional ones I keep reading about and less like the actual one I seem destined for – the dull suburbs, the safety of university in a honey-bricked city, then back to the suburbs to marry a Clive or a Colin and waste said education by having children who will repeat the process all over again. The question, though, is *what*? What does the alternative look like? I can hardly run away to join a circus in the depths of January. Besides, I feel sorry for the poor lions, and acrobatics are not my forte. I have still not recovered from the week we did box vaults in PE, though the less said about that the better. It will be a miracle if I'm even able to have children.

Perhaps God (or Allah or Mohammed – I am trying to be open about these things. Mummy says hedging my bets will not stand me a better chance of getting into heaven, but I say why not try?) will give me a sign. Yes, that is it. I will scratch the Cambridge thing and change it to:

3. Live, to wit: look out for a sign from 'God'.
4. If no sign by Friday, then buck up and revise.

That looks much better. Oh, I feel ready for a turkey sandwich after all! Though I shall continue to eschew the stilton. I feel only bad things can come from eating blue cheese. Not even God would stoop to that as a sign.

10 P.M.

I have had a thought: what if God (or Allah etc.) has been sending me signs all along and I have been too head-in-my-book to notice? What if now, he, or she (like I said, I am hedging all bets) is sitting back on their comfy chair with a cup of tea, saying, 'Well, my girl, I gave you umpteen opportunities and you refused all of them. Didn't even blink'?

I blame Mummy. She has always said I should stop looking for intrigue where there is none, e.g. the time I thought Daddy was a spy. I asked him outright and he said no. Only, being clever, I said, 'That is precisely what a spy would say,' and then went to investigate his study while he was playing nine holes with Mr Tredegar. Only, the golf got rained off and he reappeared just as I was dismantling a scale model of a navy frigate in a bid to find a secret transmitter and bellowed, 'For heaven's sake, I'm not a bloody spy! I wish I was.' And Daddy never swears unless he is mortally injured, or Surrey have lost at cricket, so now I just feel a bit sorry for him being a dentist. Perhaps that is why he understands me – he probably had bigger dreams than Surbiton, unlike Mummy, for whom it is the peak of achievement.

There is no alternative: I shall have to take matters into my own hands and just alter the course of my own existence. Be my own fate! I shall start saying 'yes' to things. Mummy says no to everything – or, rather, 'No, I don't think so' – and look where that has got her. Admittedly she no longer has to wee in an outside lav or use the public baths once a week but still, that was because of the 'yes' she said to Daddy all those years ago, so I think, in a roundabout way, I have just proved my own point. Thus:

1. Say 'yes' to everything.

That should do it. Yes (that word again!), by the end of this week, the course of my very existence may well have changed. I could have married a prince, or become a spy myself, or joined the circus after all (this one very much depending on there being some sort of emergency circus set up on Hampton Wick and Mummy actually allowing me to attend). At the very least, it will please Felicity, who has been begging me to double date on New Year's Eve with the terminal Colin, but as long as he doesn't propose or ask me to do anything untoward, it will be an 'experience' and, in my new fate-embracing guise, I am all for those.

WEDNESDAY 30 DECEMBER

11 A.M.
So far the plan to embrace fate by saying yes to everything has not worked out entirely in my favour, i.e. I seem to have ended up:

1. Working on reception at Daddy's dental practice all day yesterday and the day before, because Mrs Peabody (aggressive hair, once met Harold Wilson in Debenhams), who usually does it, has had an incident with a turkey bone and Mummy refuses to step in these days because:
a) she doesn't suffer people gladly, and
b) she says the waiting room is a hotbed of gossip, and she is above that sort of nonsense.
2. Agreeing to mind Julian a week on Friday, which usually I would refuse given that the last time I babysat he spent most of the evening detailing the stages of gestation

in various farm animals and then beat me at chess four times in a row, which is humiliating from a ten year old.
3. Eating some of the wretched stilton, which pleased Daddy no end but, as predicted, resulted in bad things, because I had the most frightful dream about badgers and woke up in the small hours yelling for help, which woke Mummy, who is now in one of her moods.

On the bright side, at least Felicity hasn't proffered up Colin again yet so I am excused that experience. And, as a result of her mood, Mummy is refusing to go with Daddy to some matinee in the West End that he won tickets for in the golf club tombola. She pointed out (quite reasonably) that if someone was giving away tickets then it must be a terrible show in the first place, but Daddy says he can't *not* use them in case Gordon Rawlingson, who is golf club captain, is at the matinee and observes the empty seats (our pair were not the only tickets on offer). The upshot is that Daddy then asked me to go and of course I had to say 'yes'.

Partly, all I want to do right now is lie down in a darkened room and try to bury (metaphorically) the badgers, but in the spirit of positivity, I shall muster and lug myself up to London with Daddy. In any case, Soho is at least more interesting than Surbiton. Not that Mummy agrees.

'It is a square mile of vice,' she said. 'You will be lucky to come out with your purse intact. Or your morals.'

'Perhaps we shall meet my namesake, Princess Margaret,' I said, given she has been spotted on Berwick Street on more than one occasion.

'All the more reason not to go,' said Mummy. 'She's terribly reckless. And, how many times – she is not your namesake!'

'Nice try, Birdy,' said Daddy (which is his nickname for me, and which I grew out of about ten years ago, but he will not relinquish it however much I beg him). 'Come on. We can have lunch at Lyon's if you shake a leg.'

And so I have shaken a leg and we are off in a jiffy. Mummy has given us strict rules, i.e. under no circumstances am I to:

1. Speak to anyone foreign in case they try to traffic me overseas.
2. Speak to any men with overly shiny shoes (she is convinced this is the hallmark of a gangster or, possibly worse, jazz musician, when, really, wouldn't they be too busy with their guns and trumpets and such to worry about brogues?).
3. Speak to Princess Margaret, unless it is to point out that the last birthday portrait of her is far too racy and she is letting the side down. I did not bother to ask which side this was, as I suspect that would place me 'not on it'.

Anyway, all of these have only succeeded in making the whole thing more appealing. Perhaps I *shall* meet Princess Margaret, or a gangster, or even a jazz musician! And if I don't get trafficked overseas, I shall at least have escaped the rest of the hideous stilton.

7 P.M.

Something extraordinary has happened.

I shall cut to the chase, because there is nothing journal-worthy at all about the drive to the West End (traffic average) or lunch at Lyon's (eggs on toast, also average) or even the play itself (a perfectly passable version of *Measure for Measure*, though why anyone would choose to stage it is unfathomable as it is not Shakespeare's best, what with all the dull nunnery business). First: the Pippin! For that is the name of the theatre, tucked away on Beak Street, and barely a sliver of a building. Mummy would have hated it, with its peeling paint and missing lightbulbs, and sandwiched as it is between a 'men's bookshop' and Soho's own version of the Moulin Rouge. But for me, the slight shabbiness and the dubious neighbours just add to the glamour. But that was only the beginning: the shell of it, if you like. The meat – the real, extraordinary thing – was inside and came much later. The meat was, incredibly, a girl. And *what* a girl! The sort whom, you know from merely glancing, is the kind to launch ships; a veritable Helen! But I am getting ahead of myself. For I still haven't explained how, exactly, we met.

After the curtain had come down on the less-than-impressive Shakespeare, there I was, standing in the queue for the lavatory (unisex; I shan't tell Mummy, and anyway it was at Daddy's insistence, as he didn't want to have to stop on the way) behind a slab of a man in a Homburg hat when I heard a voice.

'You!' it yelped, in a tone not far off Princess Margaret (if she were picking a hockey team), and someone snatched at me.

I snapped round, fully expecting to be met by royalty, but instead was greeted by someone infinitely more dazzling. She was almost six foot tall – taller than Daddy, anyway – with blonde hair in disarray, her forehead a sheen of perspiration, and green eyes wide with something approaching panic. But the sort whom you know, in more fortuitous circumstance than a lavatory queue, could make Grace Kelly appear lacklustre.

'Me?' I questioned, despite the fact she still had her substantial hand wrapped around my comparatively scrawny upper arm. (I am unused to being chosen – even in hockey, when it is always Felicity and me as the very last dregs.)

'Yes, you. Are you free tomorrow?'

I stared back into her eyes, my pupils by now, I assume, as ink black and enormous as hers. 'I ... that is to say ...' I thought quickly. Was I free? On New Year's Eve? I supposed I was, given I still hadn't heard from stolid Colin or even Felicity, and the alternative was an evening at home with Mummy. They have been invited to the golf club annual cheese and port party but have turned it down. Or at least Mummy did ('no, I don't think so') when Daddy suggested it. And, wasn't I committed by my very resolutions to say yes to things? So, 'Yes,' I said, hesitantly. Then, emboldened by the feel of the word on my lips, blurted it again, emphatically and with an exclamation mark: 'Yes!'

'You absolute doll!' She yelped again and gave me the sort of crushing hug Grandma Arbuthnot is renowned for, before releasing me and looking hard into my eyes again. 'You'll need to be at the stage door at six sharp though. Can you do that?'

'I . . . Yes,' I repeated, mesmerised as I was by that emerald stare – as bewitching and emphatic as any cat's.

She grinned then for the first time and I saw how wide her smile, how guileless. 'You're a lifesaver.'

'I am?' I asked, naively.

'Well, figuratively,' she confirmed. 'Six, yes? Ask for Charlie. That's me,' she added, before I could even conjure up some cad of an actor, or a dour stage manager.

I didn't give her my name – I didn't have time, because before I could open my mouth to mumble an apologetic 'I'm Margaret' she was off, bustling past the rest of the queue, one hand waving above her head as she went. So shocked was I, I clean forgot to go the lavatory at all. It was only when I had to ask Daddy to stop at a public convenience at Clapham Junction that I realised I hadn't even thought to ask what, exactly, I was saying yes to. Still less whether or not I'll be able to pull it off, but I shall come up with something. And by tomorrow.

Lawks! This is all terribly exciting. More thrilling, indeed, than when I thought Daddy might be a spy, because Soho is not vice, it is wonder! It is bright lights and dark corridors and Promise! Promise! Promise! And tomorrow I shall, for a few hours, in some as yet unknown way, be part of it. I just have to persuade Mummy to follow suit with a splendid 'yes' of her own.

THURSDAY 31 DECEMBER

9 A.M.
I have barely slept; the bedsheets as rumpled as I feel, my night restless with thoughts of Charlie, and to what she might be inviting me. What if it *is* vice? Or, better, what if *she's* a spy and is recruiting me too? Although why the Secret Service would consider the Pippin a hotbed of potential is rather far-fetched, I suppose. No matter, it is all moot unless I get there. To wit: I have formed a three-point plan of action, the gist of which is 'lie'.

1. Practice the art of persuasion and convince Mummy to change her mind about the Cheese and Port party. This way Mummy will have at least two glasses of something to cope with Beryl Tredegar and won't notice if I am a smidgen tired tomorrow. Given I was briefly vice-president of Debate Club, I feel this is not beyond the realm of possibility.
2. Claim I am going out with the horrible

Colin et al after all, and must leave for
Felicity's at four fifteen to get ready.
3. In actuality, catch the 4.40 from Surbiton to
Waterloo, and run from there to the Pippin,
then do the same in reverse at curtain down
to catch the last train home, whereupon I
shall undress and be in bed before Mummy
and Daddy are even home.

It is not exactly failsafe, but I feel it has potential. And if it doesn't work, I shall just have to put Plan B into action, which is to shut myself in my room claiming I have fallen foul of the blue cheese again, and then shin down the drainpipe as if I'm in a mystery novel – which has an appeal all of its own! One of them has to work, as I feel sure I am destined for a life of adventure, or at least one with more interesting decor than bland Anaglypta.

10 A.M.

I am on tenterhooks! There is no 'yes' yet from Mummy, but Daddy is definitely on side re: point 1, and I am almost sure Mummy will be too, come lunch, given my six-point argument:

1a) It is traditional to *do* something on New Year's
Eve, and that something is not sit in the lounge

and discuss whether cabbage is preferable to kale as an accompaniment to steak and kidney pudding (answer: neither; the entire meal is a war crime) or if it is wise to leave Bob Foster's wisdom teeth in for another six months because in all likelihood the emphysema will have got him by then anyway.

1b) Even *I* am going out, so I will not be there to adjudicate any disagreements that arise from said cruciferous vegetable/dental discussions.

1c) Gordon Rawlingson is bound to be at the party and what if he notices Daddy's absence and leaves him out of the crunch match against Kingston in February as some sort of punishment? (This was quite the act of genius, I think, as Daddy has gone on about nothing else for three months – since Derek Fenton defected and got recruited onto the Kingston A Team).

1d) This time next year they will probably be babysitting for John and Gloria so this is their last chance ever to have a festive night out.

1e) Aunt Barbara and Uncle Roy have taken Julian to visit his maternal grandparents somewhere up North and therefore will *not* be there.

1f) Mummy can take the stilton and surreptitiously sneak it onto the buffet table and no one will be any the wiser and we will be blue-cheese-free a good two months earlier than usual.

The only downside is that I am now briefly incandescent that Miss Boreham (sinister spectacles, smells of camphor) blackballed me from Debate Club (I skipped a meeting because Felicity said she saw Elvis Presley in Bentalls, only it turned out to be Tommy Rawlingson – son of Gordon; equally annoying – with an inadvisable hairdo), as it is evident that I could persuade even the most rational of thinkers that white is black and vice versa. I almost hope that tonight *is* my recruitment into MI5 as it is clear I would be excellent at subterfuge and possibly negotiation in a hostage crisis.

2 P.M.

It is a 'yes'! Albeit a tentative and qualified one, i.e. they will arrive at seven and leave by nine and Daddy is not to get squiffy and/or:

1. Invite the Tredegars around for dinner again.
2. Challenge Gordon Rawlingson to a four-ball.
3. Challenge Gordon Rawlingson to an arm wrestle, staring competition, or game of anything.

4. Try it on under the mistletoe.

Also, I am to make up for tonight's absence with a full day of Cambridge entrance prep tomorrow.

Daddy is pleased as punch and has promised none of the above will happen. I do not entirely hold out hope that he will stick to these but, as Aunt Barbara would say, 'not my circus, not my monkeys'. No, my circus is the 4.40 to Waterloo. It is Soho. It is the Pippin theatre and whatever fate awaits me there!

Now, what to wear? I had my best dress on yesterday (a rather drab navy thing, with a Peter Pan collar that makes me look like a stray from *Malory Towers*) so I am left with school uniform (definitely not), a red sweater festooned with snowflakes (again, no) or the black crepe I wore to Grandpa Goggins' funeral.

It will have to be the black. It will give me an air of mystery, I think.

4 P.M.

Daddy asked if someone had died and Mummy said, 'Well at least Colin won't be trying to ravish you,' which was harsh, and I said so, and also that Audrey Hepburn wore black all the time and look at her being imaginarily ravished by everyone, including Daddy. At which point Daddy told me to stop talking, which on reflection was probably for the best.

Anyway, I am off, so wish me luck, dear reader (whomever you may be), for, the next time I write, I hope to be saying 'yah boo' to revision and Cambridge for ever, and 'yes!' to the brand new decade, for I shall likely be a spy!

JANUARY 1960

FRIDAY
1 JANUARY

7 P.M.

I am not a spy.

I am not anything, other than the same plain Margaret Arbuthnot I was yesterday, still facing a future of university, still stifled by suburban mediocrity – and quite literally too, given I have been shut in my room all day as punishment with only a penitent's lunch of cream crackers and margarine to sustain me through the tedium of *Beowulf*. I make quite the pitiful sight, what with all the pointed sighing I am doing. Not that Mummy is swayed. She says I should have thought of that before I betrayed her trust to 'play at Jezebel'. I said I was hardly a murderer or prostitute, but that has only earned me further punishment, i.e. a week's grounding. I suppose I should explain myself, starting at the beginning, though I fear this will only make me all the sadder as it kicked off with such promise.

There was not a single hitch in my masterplan to escape Surrey for London. I left 'for Felicity's' on time and without question from my parents, caught the train, which, for once, was not held up by a rogue goose or cow on the line, and arrived at Waterloo with an excess of time to reach the Pippin. And, oh! Beak Street on New Year's Eve was a sight to behold: the pubs and clubs lit up and shimmering; girls in furs and every shade of sugared almond; men in hats and spats and London Fog. How I longed to be among them, giggling and drinking, even – a Campari, perhaps? Or, no, an Advocaat snowball! Daddy has one every Christmas Eve and lets me have a sip and it is quite the most sophisticated thing I have ever tasted. But of course I had a job to do, a place to be, and be there I was: at the peeling, red-painted hatch of the Pippin.

I was greeted there by someone of indeterminate gender – I say greeted but they were asleep on the counter (how, in that racket, is unfathomable) – who, upon waking, informed me they were 'Doris', 'full-time doorman, and part-time chorus girl'. I did not bother to enquire as to the logistics of this as, frankly, I suspect that in Soho anything can happen and frequently does. I merely asked after Charlie, and was sent along a dim-lit corridor to 'wardrobe'.

'You came!' she yelped on seeing me, then turned to a tall, dapper man with greying hair. 'See, Val? Didn't I tell you it was all tickety-boo?'

I felt my heart jink, like a March hare. What was tickety-boo? Who was Val? But I didn't get the chance to ask as, upon seeing me, he just gave me a quick up and down, said, 'She'll do.'

Again I opened my mouth to protest, but Charlie gave

another yelp, and this Val character disappeared back down the corridor in the sort of hurry Mummy is in when she thinks she may have left the oven on.

'I . . . what will I do for?' I finally asked, as Charlie turned to me again, her eyes as bright as Piccadilly neon.

'You—' She stopped herself. 'What was your name again?'

'Oh, Margaret,' I told her, and not without a flash of embarrassment. 'Margaret Arbuthnot.'

But if Charlie found it laughable, she didn't let it show. 'You, Margaret Arbuthnot, are the Pippin's newest wardrobe-mistress-come-usherette, and I am the Pippin's newest Isabella!' She actually squealed at this, her blonde hair bouncing in a halo around her delicate face. 'You'll help dress everyone, and then at the interval, you'll go out and sell peanuts and sweeties. No choc-ices because the freezer packed up three weeks ago and neither Val nor Rollo can afford to fix it.'

Val? Rollo? Who were these exotic men? But again, questions for later because there was something far more pressing to grapple with. 'I'm . . . dressing people? By which, I mean . . . men?'

'Well, and me. But yes, mainly men. Although in Doris's case it's moot.'

'And they'll be . . .' – I had to say it – 'undressed as well.'

'Oh, not completely. They have to wear underwear since an incident with some sparklers. Not that it should bother you. After half an hour, one penis is much like any other. They sort of merge into a single, non-specific thing. Like . . . a third ear, or a sixth digit.'

'Right,' I replied, unconvinced.

She frowned. 'You have seen a penis, I take it?'

I said nothing, awaiting hoots of derision. But came there none.

'Right,' she said. 'Well, I can't say I blame you. Anyway, I'll be around too. We've only one dressing room currently because the other was flooded – the freezer, you see. Bridget always dresses in here, which is half the reason she's stormed out. She's cross with not getting a room to herself, amongst a hundred other things. Her loss is my gain, though.' At that she squealed, Bridget being the ex-Isabella I assumed.

'So I do both?' I checked again. 'Usherette and . . . dressing.'

'I know. Hellish, but that's theatre for you. Not enough money to pay for a full crew and so everyone mucks in double. Equity hasn't cottoned on yet. Anyway, thank your lucky stars it's not summer. Sweatier they get on stage, the worse it is for me.' She shuddered. 'Or, well, *you* now.'

I jinked again. 'Wait, this is . . . this is a job? A proper job? A . . .' – oh, crikey – 'permanent job?'

She frowned. 'If you want it? Six nights a week until the run ends in Feb. Matinees on Wednesdays and Saturdays, but Doris sometimes covers those for me if I'm sitting.'

Sitting? I didn't ask about that either. 'I . . . It's just—'

'Oh please don't back out now. Or at least not tonight.

When I said you were a lifesaver, I meant it. This *is* a life or death situation. *My* life. My *career*. I've waited months for this break and now she's finally flounced out so as first understudy I get to take the lead.'

'And second understudy?'

'Well, that's Doris. They barely know half the lines, and, well' – she paused then, tactfully, said, 'they're not the most believably nunnish of people.'

'Quite.'

'So you'll do it?'

I felt myself shimmer. 'I'll do it!'

But at that she handed me what looked like an outfit from the revue bar next door – a sort of velveteen playsuit with shorts that I could see would barely skirt her buttocks. Even on me they'd be far above the knee and, as for the neckline, it was so low as to be obscene. Had she been wearing this the day we met? I pondered and realised with horror that she had.

'I . . .' I began.

'I know. But the punters love it and you'll be behind a tray anyway. If anyone does try anything, rap them on the knuckles with this.' She handed me a ruler. 'I keep it among the ice cream,' she added needlessly.

There was nothing for it. I was here now; I had to help her, if only for the evening. And so, with considerable flinching, I climbed out of the funeral dress, and into the . . . well, I don't know what to call it, except to say thank heavens I am on the stickish side. Charlie, in contrast beside me, was disrobing from a wildly interesting shift dress, itself far above the knee, into the voluminous habit of a bride of Christ.

'Can you possibly fix my wimple?' she asked. 'Bridget's head is as child-sized as the rest of her and this is far too tight.'

I looked down at the skirts of the habit, which were dangling foot above the floor. 'Of course,' I said, edging towards Charlie. But as I did, an extraordinary woman – all lips and cigarette and choking perfume – burst in.

'What the devil do you think you're playing at?' she demanded, stubbing her cigarette out on the sink. 'And who' – she gave me the same disconsolate up and down that Val had – 'is this?'

Even under the wimple I could see Charlie had turned scarlet, and not just at the tightness. 'B–Bridget?' she stammered. 'But you said . . . you said you'd left.'

'I know. Convincing, wasn't I?' Bridget expertly arched an expertly plucked eyebrow (an act I tried to mimic immediately and probably only succeeded in looking even madder than I did already). 'Which is why I'm lead and you're' – she flapped a hand at me – 'one of them. What is she even doing now?'

I stopped arching.

Bridget shook her head and turned back to Charlie. 'Get out of that now, and if you've stretched it there'll be hell to pay. But, ha!' She smiled tightly. 'That will be your problem, won't it, *wardrobe*?'

I won't go into the rest of it, but Charlie was back in her shift in minutes and I was ham-fistedly sewing up a rent where the habit had torn after all. Once Bridget was dressed again, she flounced out, a trail of cigarette smoke and perfume trailing in her wake like a cartoon cloud.

Charlie sighed – so expansively it put my own efforts to shame.

'I suppose I should go home,' I said, realizing, as the words left my mouth, that I didn't actually want to, despite the muddle.

Charlie frowned again. 'Oh, do stay. You can keep me company. And you might as well keep that on now.' She nodded at the outfit. 'At least this way both jobs will be done properly.'

And so I did. I sold only two Fry's bars and a single bag of peanuts before curtain up, but I managed to do it without bungling the change, or getting groped once, which was pleasing in itself. As soon as the five-minute call went up I scooted back to wardrobe and Charlie.

'I did it!' I whooped. 'And no wandering hands!'

Charlie, beaded with perspiration, having waved off the last of the tunic-clad chorus boys, sunk into a battered red chair, and patted the one next to her. 'I like you,' she said, as I sat. 'You're funny. Val says I'm funny but I'd rather be tragic and damned.'

'Oh, me too!' I agreed. 'Who's Val?'

'Valentine. The man you met earlier? Tall. Minor aristocracy. Owns this place. Though God knows for how long.' She smiled, pulled a cigarette from a packet stuffed up her sleeve and offered me one.

I declined. Proximity to eleven men and their penises was one thing but Mummy really would have a conniption if I took up smoking as well.

'So where are you supposed to be tonight?'

'Oh.' I felt myself deflate slightly. 'On a date with someone called Colin.'

'Oh dear,' said Charlie, mirroring my deflation. 'That doesn't bode well. One can't fall madly in love with a Colin.'

'Quite,' I replied.

'And other than that? What does Margaret Arbuthnot do all day?'

I perked, if only at the knowingness. 'I fill in at Daddy's dentist surgery when Mrs Peabody is off. The rest of the time I swot,' I told her.

'For . . . ?' she asked, blowing a wreath of smoke up into the musty air, where it seemed to dance in a vast shaft of artificial light.

'Oh, Cambridge entrance. Worst luck.'

She shrugged. 'My aunt and uncle – well, *sort of* aunt and uncle – went there. And now he's a doctor and she a Member of Parliament, so it can't be all bad.'

'It's just . . .' I rooted for the right words. 'Not what I had in mind.'

She smiled. 'Oh golly, nor I. Not that I'm clever enough.'

'Oh, I don't—'

'No, really,' she cut in. 'I was terrible at school. Not bright at all. But then, nor am I dull enough to suffer the alternative. The kind of life mapped out for debs . . . Or would-be-ones,' she added wistfully.

I wanted to ask her about that, of course, but worried it might be needling a sore spot. Instead I said, 'You're ambitious, then?'

'Of course. Aren't you?'

'Very,' I said.

'Then we'll get on splendidly!'

I didn't ask why that would matter, given it was just one evening, and over sooner than I had hoped. The two and a half hours plus interval (fourteen Fry's bars; sixteen bags of peanuts; one hand on buttock, swiped away with a deft flick of ruler) seemed to positively flash by, and within what felt like barely minutes the curtain was down, the theatre emptying out onto Beak Street.

'Thanks awfully,' said Charlie as we hung costumes back on racks amid the banter of the chorus boys, all of which Charlie brushed off with a roll of her eyes, which hit its mark as sharply as the ruler. 'You can have half my wage of course.'

I brimmed. 'I should be paying you,' I said. 'Tonight was the most fun I've had since my cousin got his head stuck in the railings at Kew.'

At that, she hooted. 'I knew I liked you,' she said, then fished in her pocket (pocket! Her dress had pockets!) and opened her purse. 'Bother. I've only got half a crown,' she said. 'Here, take that and I'll have to owe you the other.'

I nodded, staggered to have any pay at all, given the circumstance. She pressed the coin into my hand. 'I suppose you've got to run off?'

I snapped to. 'Crikey, the time! My train leaves at half past.'

'Your train?'

'Oh, didn't I say?' I shrunk a little. 'I live in Surbiton.'

'Surbiton?' She repeated in disbelief. 'That's practically... the West Country.'

I didn't correct her on her geography, merely nodded and apologised.

'How ghastly.'

I nodded again, then, grabbing my coat and bag, rushed after her along the dim-lit corridor, to Doris and the stage door. It was only there, bursting out of the fetid air and into the shiver of New Year's Eve, that I remembered. 'My dress!' I yelled. And, 'Oh, heavens.' I looked down at myself. 'Your uniform.'

'Never fret.' Charlie laughed. 'I've a spare and I can always run something up otherwise. Bring it back when... when you fetch your wages! And your dress.' Then she hugged me again, and disappeared back into the glimmering pit of the Pippin, leaving me stunned in the gutter with less than twenty minutes to get to the station.

On New Year's Eve.

In Soho.

*

Needless to say, I did not make it. Then it took an hour to find a taxi who would take me south of the river. At one point I did think of ringing Daddy, but then I'd have to confess to everything and ruin the whole carefully crafted plan.

I shouldn't have bothered trying. At least then I'd still have the half a crown, if not my dignity and freedom. Because, yes, I got home before midnight. But so, sadly, had Mummy and Daddy. And my absence, it seemed, was already legend.

I shan't recount the details as it is rather embarrassing, but if I say that a) Felicity, Trevor and Colin were, by some awful stroke of fate, also in attendance at the golf club cheese and port party, and b) Mummy made me take off my coat to air it as it smelled of 'sin' and caught my costume underneath, you will understand the level of Mummy's ire. Of course I told her the whole story (not including the penis thing, as in the end I only saw a glimpse of buttock, which doesn't count) and swore it was all the absolute truth, but she said that only made it all the more depressing, because it seems I am 'not just a deceiver but a fool to boot'. Daddy stayed silent throughout but I could see he was disappointed in me, which is almost worse than Mummy's anger.

So now I am half a crown down, Felicity hates me, and, what's more, I'm barred from the Pippin for life, which means I'll never see Charlie again. And oh! I do so want to see her, to be in her orbit. What a girl— no, a *woman*, she is! A walking, talking exclamation mark! I am not sure what that makes me. Something innocuous, like a comma, perhaps. At best, a semi-colon or rogue apostrophe. And yet, she seemed to like me despite it.

This was supposed to be a decade of 'yes'! Of new experiences and thrilling new people. Instead, I must suffer the first days of 1960 with my mother refusing me even oxtail soup for supper, and the only other company the wretched Mrs Dalloway after all.

On the bright side, it cannot get any worse.

TUESDAY 5 JANUARY

9 A.M.

I spoke too soon. After a weekend that would make a prison seem like Butlins (although Mummy would claim both are equally abhorrent), I am now back behind the reception desk at Arbuthnot and Bent (Mrs Peabody having tummy gip). Mummy says at least this way Daddy can keep an eye on me, but that I am not even to think I might get paid for this, and if I have any slumps in custom, I am not to be 'jotting down nonsense' in my 'notepad'. I said it wasn't a notepad and it wasn't nonsense, it was career preparation.

'What *career*?' demanded Mummy.

'A writer,' I announced, pouring myself orange juice (I am back on the good food, if only to fed my brain pre-exam). And it wasn't even a lie. I *would* like to become a writer, if only to get vengeance on Virginia.

Mummy said I could hardly become a writer if I didn't even get into university, to which I replied, 'Mark Twain managed it and anyway I can't write until I've *lived*, or how will I have anything to write *about*!'

'You *are* living!' insisted Mummy.

'Hardly,' I said, my voice one of practised gloom. 'What is there to write about here? Mrs Tredegar's root canal? Beverley Sanford's piles? Why Nigel Pickering (heir to Pickering's Greengrocer's, seven, once got a tuppence stuck up his nose) and the milkman both have ginger hair?' I sighed.

Mummy blanched. 'You're not supposed to know about things like that!'

'It's the only highlight in an otherwise interminable day,' I finished, and then sighed again for good measure.

The sighing didn't wash anyway. It is revision only for me from now on. Though I don't see why, when Mummy is 'jotting down nonsense' of her own, i.e. she is writing her annual round robin letter. She sends one every year – a hideous trumpeting of Arbuthnot achievements, which she types up on the Olympia Daddy gave her as a wedding present (when reception work beckoned gladly as an alternative to butchery), and then gets Mrs Peabody (or me now, I assume) to duplicate it. My 'escapade' will not be included, she has already warned me. In fact, I will be lucky to make it to paper at all, which only reinforces my conviction that I need to leave Surbiton, or how will I have a life that is novel-worthy?

THURSDAY
7 JANUARY

7 P.M.
My mention in the round robin was reduced to: 'Margaret is working hard towards her Cambridge entrance exam, with her eye on a place studying literature in the autumn.' Which is an outright lie. It's been a week since my 'escapade' and I know more than ever that I don't want to go to university. I don't want to sit in some stuffy lecture hall. I don't care about punts and dreaming spires. I want bright lights and bustle and London! Specifically, Soho. I want to see Charlie. I *need* to see Charlie, not least to give her back her 'uniform' and fetch back my dress, the absence of which Mummy has thankfully not yet noticed.

Except that's not really it. I don't care about clothes or even the half a crown. I just want to *be* with her. I feel that with Charlie, adventure is only ever seconds away. Instead I have Clarence Patterson's dodgy left molar and Chaucer. And what is the point of the latter, I ask you, when the best I can hope for is to end up as someone's secretary anyway? Probably right back here, knowing my luck.

FRIDAY
8 JANUARY

8 A.M.
Another day of unpaid labour awaits, listening to dentally compromised housewives complain about their teeth/feet/husbands, followed by an evening of unpaid labour babysitting the menace that is Julian. I don't know which is more tedious. Meanwhile, I suspect Soho is awash with glamour and intrigue. Charlie probably *has* been recruited to be a spy by now. It is so utterly unfair.

I hope Julian's bedtime is still six o'clock. At least that way I will have the drawing room to myself and access to Uncle Roy's library. According to John he has a copy of the *Kama Sutra* squirrelled away somewhere. Though the thought of Aunt Barbara in any sort of sexual repose is enough to put one off the whole thing completely. Not that I have any prospects where that is concerned. As Charlie says, one can't fall madly in love with someone called Colin.

10 P.M.

I do know which is more tedious. It is Julian.

His bedtime is now eight thirty (precisely, and not a second earlier, apparently) which means I had two long and boring hours of his unceasing factual monologues. I suppose on the bright side I now know:

1. How to spell out 'beef pie' in semaphore.
2. That the collective noun for flies is a 'business', which I contested on the grounds that flies are highly unbusinesslike, but he threatened to get out his junior encyclopaedia so I conceded swiftly.
3. That hours cannot be 'long'; they are all exactly sixty minutes, which is three thousand, six hundred seconds, and only boring people get bored. I asked if that was something Aunt Barbara had told him. He said no, it was his own deduction and judgement. I stopped asking any questions at that point.

Also I could not find the *Kama Sutra* anywhere. Though I did find a disturbing anatomy manual, which was rather more revealing than the dressing room at the Pippin, if only in pen and ink. How is one supposed to fit *that* in *there*? It is all quite alarming. Not that I shall have any reason to deal with that anyway (see above entry for evidence).

At least I am being ungrounded tomorrow.

SATURDAY
9 JANUARY

9 A.M.
Freedom! Or at least a day devoid of cavities and plaque. Not that there is anything in the vicinity to do unless you count a brisk walk across Hampton Wick in the drizzle. Felicity is still not speaking to me, and my other friends from school are off at university already (Hesters one and two), or have Saturday jobs (Marjory Leadbetter).

Perhaps I should get a Saturday job.

Or a job job. Once this wretched entrance is over I'll be swilling around until September getting in Mummy's way, or else consigned to Daddy's dental reception desk learning things I shouldn't, so Mummy can hardly complain about me being employed, can she?

9.15 A.M.
I take that back. Mummy has just taken me to task for eating the last of the cream crackers, meaning she had to have water biscuits with her Wensleydale yesterday evening, which are

substandard in her book (probably an actual book). Clearly she could complain about anything. I did not point out that the crackers were not my choice, as I have discovered to my detriment that it is unwise highlight these sort of things and I do not want to risk un-ungrounding. Especially as I now have a mission, i.e. find a job. I am going to check the local newspaper and the window of the Post Office where people sometimes pin up cards offering work. Also I am going to finish *Mrs Dalloway*, if only to tick it off my resolution list. Then, once I have a job I can get something done with my hair, and that will be two down. The 'LIVE!' one is harder of course, but I shall continue to say yes to opportunities and see where it leads me.

3 P.M.

The only jobs on offer for which I am even vaguely qualified are:

1. Cleaner at Surbiton Girls (no, thank you, and Mummy would argue that I am not actually qualified, given my inability to swill out the sink after I have brushed my teeth, although this is not actually about ability but because a spider once climbed out of the plug hole while I was doing so, and I am worried about it taking revenge).
2. Postal worker (again, no, thank you, as I know

from Mrs Weedon that one has to be up at five in the morning to sort the mail, and this is about as likely as me winning the pools (i.e. zero as Mummy says doing the pools is 'common')).
3. Receptionist at Dowling and Dowling, who are Daddy's biggest rivals, especially since Daddy's dental assistant Phyllis defected on the grounds they have better quality biscuits and white coats, so that is out.

I did, however, notice that there is a new temp agency above Pickering's (run by Mr Pickering – spits a lot, not ginger, married to Mrs Pickering of milkman fame). It was shut today, but I shall call in there on Monday.

MONDAY
11 JANUARY

10 A.M.
It is job-hunt morning! Or rather hour, as I am back filling in for Mrs Peabody, but will call in to the temp agency at lunchtime. I am feeling full of vim and conviction – surely today is the day opportunity will knock and I shall be able to seize it?

6 P.M.
It seems even in the world of temping, the opportunities that knock, or which I am qualified to seize, are limited. At least Mrs Pickering (for of course it is she running the agency, although alarmingly she has dyed her hair bright red, and one can only guess as to why) seemed to think so.

'What sort of job is you after?' she asked, her pink-sweatered breasts clashing alarmingly with her hair.

'Are,' I said, without thinking.

She frowned. 'Are what?'

'Nothing,' I said, quickly. 'Something with writing perhaps?'

'You mean typing, like?'

'Well, I suppose so.'

She looked unconvinced, as well she might. 'Words per minute?'

'I . . . Ten perhaps?'

At this point she sighed and lit up a cigarette, which seemed less than professional but I was at her mercy entirely so opted not to say anything.

'So what *can* you do?' she asked through a fug of Rothmans.

I tried to waft it inconspicuously as I pondered this. 'Well,' I began eventually, 'I can babysit a genius, and make a good cup of tea and I know an awful lot about gingivitis.'

'Ginger what?' she asked.

I blanched. 'Nothing,' I said, swiftly. 'Just gum problems.'

'Yes, well.' She stubbed the cigarette out in a saucer, an act that would make Mummy shudder. 'Not a lot that will get you round here.'

'Oh,' I said, my vim and conviction sinking like a plumbline. 'Well, perhaps you can telephone if anything suitable crops up? You have my number on file now.'

She thought for a moment. 'Don't suppose you'd be up for babysitting, would you? Only Ron's got his club tonight and I've . . . somewhere to be.'

I thought for a moment as well. 'A shame,' I said. 'But I have revision to be getting on with.'

And so now I am still jobless, and I still haven't finished with the wretched *Mrs Dalloway* and the exam is next Tuesday.

10 P.M.

I am still not done with the Woolf, but my guilt is assuaged because I remembered to swill out the sink and the spider failed to make a menacing appearance. Still, perhaps Mrs Pickering will call tomorrow. There is always hope, I find, if one looks hard enough.

TUESDAY
12 JANUARY

10 P.M.
Mrs Pickering has not called.

WEDNESDAY 13 JANUARY

10 P.M.

Mrs Pickering has not called.

THURSDAY
14 JANUARY

10 P.M.
Mrs Pickering has not called.

FRIDAY 15 JANUARY

10 P.M.
Mrs Pickering has not called and frankly, I am giving up. There is nothing to say yes to round here except for second helpings of flan, which I don't even like, and, worse, we don't have a dog to feed surreptitiously. I am so cross and disappointed that I have decided to have a weekend entirely devoted to pleasure, i.e. I shall reread *I Capture the Castle*, and go and talk to Felicity as an emergency measure. Admittedly the second is not particularly appealing, given the froideur since New Year, but it is that or Sunday lunch at Uncle Roy and Aunt Barbara's and so Felicity's frostiness is actually preferable.

SUNDAY
17 JANUARY

5 P.M.
Felicity is moving to Stebbing (where on earth is *that*?) because Trevor has got a job there (doing something unmemorable). So now not only am I jobless, I am friendless as well (Marjory Leadbetter is now courting Colin, and has been warned off me as a 'turncoat') – unless you count Charlie, which I do not, as:

1. She lives in actual London as opposed to the wretched edges.
2. I am forbidden to see her.
3. Even if I wasn't, she has probably forgotten me.

On the bright side, Mrs Peabody is back so I will be able to revise for the entire day tomorrow. Though I shall still probably fail my entrance and—

Oh! I cannot write any more!

Perhaps, in fact, I shall *literally* not write any more. As in ever. My life is clearly far too doomed to be worthy of a leather-bound journal and Indian ink, which is dear.

Farewell, then, dear diary. And farewell, resolutions. I tried, I did. But I am not cut out for ambition or glamour it seems. And despite sharing a life bereft of work, money and friends, I am not Cassandra Mortmain at all. I am not even poor dear Stephen Colley.

I am an unnamed character, who passes by in the background, leaving neither mark nor memory.

MONDAY 18 JANUARY

9.15 A.M.

I take it all back! Or at least some of it. Mrs Pickering has telephoned!

Thank heavens Mummy was in the scullery, and therefore out of range and earshot, or she would have had my guts for garters.

The upshot is, there is a job vacancy in Arding & Hobbs at Clapham Junction. It is on the make-up counter, of which I have almost zero experience, given Mummy's feelings on make-up (I am not '*that* sort of girl', apparently) but it is paid work, and in London to boot! How Mrs Pickering got wind of it I do not know, but I am not going to look a gift horse in the mouth, not even one in Clapham Junction, so of course I said yes!

The interview is at two, and – oh, larks! – I have worked out I will have time to get to Soho and back as well beforehand so I can fetch the black dress back from Charlie (which I shall wear to the interview as the blue has indelible egg on it and my old school uniform is hardly suitable), return her usherette costume, and tell her the good news, which is that by the end of the day I shall have enough money to come up to town on a weekly basis. I am not forbidden from seeing her, I realise, on closer examination of Mummy's exact words, just from entering the Pippin. On that point, I am going to leave a note saying I cannot study at home because of the noise from the vacuum, and that I will be home at five. It is not even a lie. Or at least, if it is, only a white one. And I shall take *Mrs Dalloway* to read on the train.

How ingenious I am! By the time I write again, I predict my life will be book-worthy after all. Plus, I will have secured the means to earn back the shillings I have had to borrow from the housekeeping jar to pay for the train.

5 P.M.

Like a meal involving tripe (shudder) and mashed potatoes (heaven), I shall start with the tripe to get it out of the way; that is to say: the interview.

Firstly, and in my defence, I should point out that Mrs Pickering had not warned me there would be a practical test, and, given that, as previously mentioned, make-up of any variety is frowned upon in this house, it is no wonder I made a ham-fist of the face of Gaynor (senior trainee, voice like a four-year-old, smelled of soup). How am I to know where eyebrows should be painted if one has plucked all trace of the originals away? Also, it is *not* innate knowledge that one must powder before applying lipstick to prevent colour bleeding. Although I agree, the resulting effect was of a terminally surprised clown. Still, Miss Clutton (head of cosmetics, complexion of a mandarin orange, ostentatious engagement ring) did admit that full training would be given on the job, and that it was more about my 'chairside manner'. Hopefully, she will overlook the sighing, and the time I snapped at Gaynor's eyelids for being 'slippery'. It didn't help, I think, that I only made it to the door of the shop with seconds to spare. But, do you know what? I don't think I would change that for the world. Not a second spent with Charlie and the rest – oh yes, there are more of them! – was a waste.

So, to Soho!

My heart was fast as a hare's as I made my way through the merry tangle of alleys and side streets that wends from Leicester Square up towards Beak Street. Then, as I reached the end of Bridle Lane and turned right, the sight of the Pippin itself sent the butterflies that had gathered scattering frantically, my whole insides suddenly awash with that volatile mix of panic and happiness.

'Let her be there,' I pleaded with myself.

Of course, she was not; it was far too early for curtain call. But Doris, the darling, sent me round to Lexington Street, and 'Pennington's'.

'Pennington's?' I repeated.

'Can't miss it,' said Doris, patting their starched hair. 'Looks like an explosion in a library.'

Doris was not exaggerating, for Pennington's was a bookshop, at least of sorts, but so far from Brown's in Surbiton as to be a completely different species. For this seemed to sell both new and second-hand books, but in no apparent order, and with still less effort, for the owner – Mr Pennington I assumed then, though he would soon be Rollo to me – was asleep at the counter face down on *The Times*.

'Hello?' I ventured. Then, when he failed to stir, jangled the door and its cowbell loudly, at which he shot upright, as if mortally harmed.

'Dear God!' the man – a wiry sort, I saw now, in his fifties perhaps, all cheekbones and wayward hair – exclaimed. 'Is someone dead? Am I dead? Is there a fire?'

'I . . . Oh, heavens,' I began, guilt sending my cheeks a vivid crimson. 'No, it's just . . . I just—'

'Are you quite all right?' He looked genuinely concerned. 'Did you want something . . . under the counter? Is that it? If so, we don't deal in those . . . publications. You'll have to go over to Bernie on Beak Street. Though, if you'll forgive me, you seem rather young to be mixed up in that.'

'No!' I blurted, despite not being entirely sure as to what he was insinuating, only that it was not the sort of thing of which Mummy would approve. 'I . . . that is to say . . .' What was wrong with me? This would not do. This was not Cassandra Mortmain behaviour at all! I snapped to. 'Doris sent me. I'm looking for Charlie.'

He softened, sighed. 'Of course you are. I'm so sorry. It's just we've had three today already. Soho is changing hands! And not for the better.' At which he went into some sort of reverie.

'Quite,' I agreed quietly, though again slightly unsure as to what he was getting at.

Then I waited.

And waited.

And waited. Then, mindful of the time, I coughed gently. No cowbells this time.

'Oh!' He was the one to snap to now. 'Charlie! Yes, yes. Back of the shop, up the stairs to the second floor.'

I frowned. 'Which door?' I asked, worried I might stumble into something . . . well, I didn't know what, but this was Soho and anything seemed possible.

He laughed. 'Oh, you can't miss it.'

He was right. Through a stockroom (though it was hard to tell it and the shop apart), past an unspeakable lavatory, then up two floors I went, my shoes clacking on a narrow staircase that tipped to the left, giving one the unnerving feeling of being on a listing ship. Thankful for the banister, grubby though it was, I arrived at the second floor, my heart back to a rabbit's. Charlie's room was marked by a scarf (Hermès) tied around the handle, and, as if that weren't enough, a hand-painted sketch of her face – watercolour, I think – tacked above.

'Charlie?' I knocked, gently, lest she was similarly asleep.

But no sooner had my hand dropped, the door flung open,

and there she was – that immaculate exclamation mark! Her hair a halo of gold, her endless legs clad in black tights of the sort one wore for modern dance, and over that a sliver of silver material that snagged every scrap of winter sun from the rattling sash window.

'Margaret!' she exclaimed. 'I knew you'd come. I was telling Ted only yesterday that you'd show up soon.'

'Ted,' I repeated. 'The man downstairs?'

She ushered me in to sit on her unmade bed – a swirl of mismatched sheets and paisley eiderdown. 'Heavens, no. That's Rollo, of course.' She plonked down next to me. 'Lovely but ancient. Ted's barely out of his teens. Dashed handsome but – alas! – not my sort.'

Bang! Bang! Bang! The information thwacked me in a barrage – a generous one, and I gathered it up hurriedly, saving it for later.

I on the other hand, managed only two words. 'Your uniform?' I offered it to her, or rather, the plain paper bag it was contained in.

'Oh, that thing?' She flapped a hand at what might have been a rug once, but was barely visible under a flurry of discarded outfits in every shade from midnight to vermillion. 'Drop it on the floordrobe.'

I hesitated, then did as asked. But there was something else of course. 'Could I have my dress? Only, I have this thing – an interview. In just over an hour, actually.'

'An interview!' She beamed. 'In Soho?'

'No.' I felt my already-skinny self shrink. 'Clapham, actually, but it's only twenty minutes on the train and then not far. And I hoped that if I get it . . . Well, you see, I—' My words, stubborn only a few seconds ago, flooded out all of a sudden. 'If I get it, I'd like—'

'To meet up? Oh, do say yes. I had a feeling. I told Ted I had a feeling! Shame the job's not on the doorstep but Clapham is better than . . . where did you say you lived? Sussex? Suffolk?'

'Surbiton.' The word was a stone in my throat. A lump of lamb gristle.

'Same thing. Anyway, enough of suburbs.' She flapped her hand at the floor again. 'The dress will be in there somewhere. We can rummage together.'

At that, she tipped herself onto the floor, while I knelt gingerly, afraid of what I might sink into, piecing through chiffon, silk, crepe de chine.

'Is this it?' A veritable Jack Horner, she held up a scrap of black fabric, which, I am sorry to say, was the dress in question.

I nodded. It was hardly a triumphant plum after all.

'Really? Oh dear.' Clearly in agreement, she frowned. 'I think we can do better than that.'

Suffice to say, in five minutes I had been hustled out of my pinafore and into a slip of charcoal something or other, that – Charlie was right – did bring out my eyes, even if it did need a belt to cinch it in and up (she has several inches on me in every direction). My hair was another matter – precious little can complement 'mouse' – but she managed to wrangle it into something resembling a chignon.

'Splendid.' She stood back to admire her work. 'You could model for Worth himself.'

I felt my insides slip and looked down at the dress. 'This is a Worth?'

She nodded. 'Second-hand, but good as new.'

'But . . . I can't,' I tried.

'You can and you must. I'll hear not another word about it. Here.' She handed me my black dress and the paper bag, into which I stuffed it quickly. 'Now promise you'll call me and let me know how it goes?'

'I . . . I promise?'

'Excellent. Soho 567. You won't be able to forget it.'

*

And I haven't. Not the number nor a single second of our thirty-six minutes together. Though thankfully the interview itself is becoming hazier by the second. Oh, gosh! I have never wanted a job more, nor expected to get one less. What is especially worrying is that I have done not a jot of revision for tomorrow. However, there are still several hours before bed, and all night, in fact, if I need it. And in my new-found spirit of optimism (Charlie is contagious) I will be positively bursting with *Mrs Dalloway* facts by the morning. Not even Virginia herself would have known more than I.

TUESDAY
19 JANUARY

8 A.M.

Virginia may yet triumph.

The fact is, I cannot concentrate. All I can think about is Charlie and Pennington's and Lexington Street. Oh, golly, please God, Allah and whoever else is up there, let me get the job! I am on tenterhooks awaiting a telephone call from Miss Clutton, or Mrs Pickering, or anyone in fact. Instead, the only caller this morning has been Aunt Barbara to remind me that Hull has some venerable alumni, and, being flat, is practically the Cambridge of the North. It is not, at least not from the pictures I have seen, but I dared not try to dissuade her. In any case, Daddy grabbed the phone off me to ask Roy if he wanted nine holes on Sunday as Angus Hammerton has dropped a tin of fishing weights on his foot and is out for the foreseeable, and I was left to my rising panic.

On the bright side, it will all be over in a few hours, my future decided, both shop-wise and university-wise. If I were being my previously negative self, I might say I am not at all sure I will succeed in either. But I am not that self. I am Miss

Optimistic still, and feel sure that my best will be good enough. And if it isn't, in the case of Cambridge, I shan't mind too much anyway.

6 P.M.

So, the exam.

I could not for the life of me decide whether the Wife of Bath or Mrs Dalloway have anything to say to contemporary women, and decided to go rogue and discuss the merits of Topaz Mortmain instead (she is a saint for suffering Mortmain himself, and who does *not* wish they knew an artist's model who wafts around the house in a silk dressing gown with hair like silver and a baritone voice?). Anyway, I feel it shows remarkable tenacity and original thinking, as well as the ability to turn the worst of situations to one's advantage, which must surely be an attribute? Plus it is all over now, and there is nothing to do but be patient and wait. Speaking of which, I popped into the temp agency on the way home but Mrs Pickering said she'd 'not heard a dicky bird' but that no news was probably bad news.

I am refusing to listen to her though, as I am still unstoppably optimistic. A state that even Mummy remarked upon, when I said 'oh, goody!' to mutton casserole, a meal I am wont to greet with a shudder.

'See,' she said, as I dug in to the stew. 'I knew university would appeal in the end.'

I merely nodded, thankful for the pearl onion that was occupying my mouth at that moment. If she knew the truth she might disown me.

WEDNESDAY 20 JANUARY

8 P.M.
There is still no news on the job. I have telephoned Charlie (from the dental surgery; Mrs Peabody has fleas. Or rather, her carpet does and she has to stay in for the fumigation man) to warn her, but she says she has a 'feeling' that it will all come good in the end. Also she said that Rollo asked after me.

'Really?' I checked.

'Yes. He said, "How is that young one from the suburbs? Did we put her off town?"'

'Oh, no!' I insisted. 'I wish I could come up now.'

'Why don't you?' she asked.

'Because I've four fillings and a gum boil to check in before five,' I explained.

'Grim,' said Charlie.

'Quite,' I agreed. At which point Mrs Fazackerly arrived with her Nigel (another one – they are everywhere here, like Hillman Minxes, or pigeons) and his rotten molar so I had to hang up.

THURSDAY 21 JANUARY

10 P.M.
Still no news.

FRIDAY 22 JANUARY

10 A.M.
There is news, but not of the optimistic kind. In short, I did not get the job.

The letter was hand-delivered by our postman Derek (fifty-six, arthritis, threatens to retire but never does), who has taken to knocking when he has something he suspects to be potentially notable, i.e. red bills (Daddy forgot to pay the telephone once. Only, he says it was Mummy's fault – but not to her face as he has more sense than that), billets doux (John was unfathomably popular at one point) and anything from Grandma Arbuthnot.

This, however, was a new addition.

'Arding and Hobbs,' he said, nodding at the vellum envelope. 'Looks official.'

'Not really,' I said, snatching it from him. 'I . . . bought a sofa.' Heaven knows why I said that as it was only delaying him further.

'Oh, a sofa, is it?' he went on. 'You moving out, then? Our Lavinia moved out once. Didn't stick.'

'No, I . . .' I tried to put the bovine Lavinia and her homing tendencies out of my head. 'It doesn't matter.' At which point I closed the door firmly in his face, just as Mummy showed up in the hall to see what the fuss was and whether it was Cambridge.

'No!' I insisted briskly, the envelope already stuffed up my jumper. 'It was something for next door.'

'That boy is hopeless.' Mummy frowned and stared at my midriff pointedly. 'Is there something the matter with your stomach?'

I shook my head, and tried to press less on the envelope, which had a sharp crackle to it. 'No,' I assured her. 'Just chilly. Brrrr.' I shivered dramatically.

'Well, if you will insist on not wearing a vest,' she said, 'what do you expect?' And she departed scullery-ward.

Who wants to wear a vest, I ask you? I'm eighteen, not eighty! I should be wearing silk lingerie, preferably French.

Not that there is any chance of that now. The letter, which I ripped open in the privacy of the bathroom (it has a lock, unlike my bedroom, which Mummy insists should be accessible by all at all times), was brief and to the point:

```
Dear Mrs Arbuthnot,
    I am sorry to let you know you have
been unsucessful in your application
for Cosmetics Asisstant.
```

```
We wish you lick in your next
endeavours.
    Sylvia Clutton (Miss)
```

I was tempted to write back and offer them my proofreading abilities, but I fear my typing might be worse even than hers.

I suppose I shall have to telephone Charlie and tell her I am stuck in the wretched provinces for the foreseeable future. Oh, woe! I shall become a Lavinia after all: living at home with my parents aged thirty-seven and thinking a turn around Hampton on a Saturday is akin to Paris. That or married to a sodding Colin after all.

11 A.M.

Charlie is not in. Or not up. No one is in or up on Lexington Street, it seems.

3 P.M.

There is still no one in or up.

5 P.M.

Charlie is up but departed five minutes ago for the Pippin. I have left a message: 'Tell her the job is off,' with a young man

(Ted?) who said she'll probably be back around two.

'A.m. or p.m.?' I asked.

'Who knows,' he replied, with a tinge of what sounded like regret. An emotion I suspect is common when it comes to Charlie.

I only hope it is two in the afternoon, as I shudder to think what Mummy will say if the telephone wakes her in the small hours.

SATURDAY 23 JANUARY

9 A.M.
Charlie has not rung.

10 A.M.
Charlie has not rung. I should never have left a message. Now the ball is in her court, and what if she never bats it back?

11 A.M.
Charlie has not rung and Mummy wants me to pick up a half pound of mince from Dewhurst's.

'Can't Daddy do it?' I begged.

'Even if he were available, which he is not – he is still at the club – I would not trust him not to come back with rump steak or a . . . a turbot.' She shuddered, and handed me a ten-shilling note.

12 P.M.

Charlie has (thankfully) not rung. Also Mummy is cross because I got lean mince by mistake.

'But I did get it in less than fifteen minutes,' I pointed out.

'Cooking is not a race,' she said.

If it were, she would win it.

2 P.M.

Charlie has still not rung.

Should I ring her, I wonder?

2.10 P.M.

Not yet. Perhaps she is still just stirring now.

2.20PM

Or yet.

2.30

Perhaps now. Yes, I shall go and— Oh! The phone!

Perhaps it's her.

Or perhaps it's Mrs Pickering saying it's all been a mistake?

Or Cambridge, offering me a place for my progressive question interpretation?

4 P.M.

It wasn't Cambridge or Mrs Pickering.

It *was* Charlie, after all! And – you won't believe this; I scarcely believe this. She has offered me a job! Or, rather, Rollo has. Or, rather, I think Rollo has been persuaded into it, but I am not going to think too hard about that; just the mere fact that there is a job vacancy at Pennington's and my name is on it.

Now, for the trickier thing. I have to sit down with Mummy and Daddy and persuade them of the sense of this. Though it is in a bookshop, meaning I will practically be being paid to read, so frankly I do not see how they can possibly say no!

5 P.M.

They did not say no.

However, they did not say yes, either.

Daddy said, 'Well done, Birdy.'

Mummy said, 'Are you mad?'

'Me?' said Daddy.

At that, she sighed. 'Both of you.' Then she turned to me, metaphorical sleeves rolled up. 'What on earth would you want with a job in London, anyway? How would you get there? How did you even hear of it? When did you interview? You're off to university in six months as it is. If you need pin money, then babysit your cousin.'

It was hard to know which to answer first, so I tried to combine it all in one succinct answer (I am not known for brevity, so this was quite the endeavour). 'It's someone I know from a while back' – it feels a while, anyway – 'whose uncle' – well, perhaps he is! – 'has a vacancy and she thought of me. Isn't that nice? And it's only an hour and eight minutes door to door. I've checked.'

'When did you check?'

At this, I floundered. 'Julian worked it out. With maps and ... and a timetable.' This was a downright lie, but apparently a believable one.

'I'll think about it,' she said eventually.

And that was her last word on the subject. I know this because I checked, and she said she would not be discussing it any further tonight as she had moussaka on her mind, and aubergines are terribly tricky things. I am waiting until tomorrow morning, when hopefully the aubergine conundrum will have been solved, and Mummy will be in a more favourable mood.

SUNDAY
24 JANUARY

11 A.M.
Mummy is still thinking. But on the bright side, the tricky aubergines have been wrangled. Although, I am under strict instructions not to mention their presence in the moussaka, and if John asks, it is a 'mince and vegetable layer'. He has always been petulant when it comes to food, preferring things bland and 'without bits'. It is one of Mummy's few disappointments in him.

3 P.M.
Mummy is still thinking, and I am also in trouble for revealing the true nature of the 'mince and vegetable layer'. Though if you ask me, it is John's fault for agreeing with Mummy that London was awfully far and Gloria's for saying there was a job in the post room at Gamages, if I was interested. Which I was not; I'd rather die, which I said. To which Gloria said I was ungrateful, and John called me 'The Accident' (which he does when he is cross – and because there are seven years between he and I, and

he says it is clear I was an afterthought, if a thought at all) and so I called him 'The First Pancake' (you know, the messy one that is usually binned) and so he kicked me under the table, which is when I shouted, 'It's moussaka! With aubergines!' and then Mummy erupted, because, on top of the John problem, Gloria is on a strict diet to avoid aggravating the 'downstairs issue' and she isn't sure 'foreign food' is advisable.

MONDAY
25 JANUARY

10 P.M.
Mummy is still thinking.

TUESDAY
26 JANUARY

10 P.M.
Mummy is still thinking.

WEDNESDAY 27 JANUARY

10 P.M.
Mummy is still thinking but has added a caveat, i.e. if I ask her one more time the answer will be an outright no. I have rung Charlie again, or rather, left a message with Ted (it *is* Ted; I checked this time) to say, 'Apologies for the delay. Outlook bleak.'

He said, 'It's not a telegram. You can say other stuff.'
I said, 'I would, but it pains me.'

THURSDAY 28 JANUARY

10 A.M.

Mummy is still thinking (I did not ask; she offered up the information before I even sat for breakfast).

I wish something magical would happen to intervene. It always does in books. Like a god or a genie or a fairy godmother. As it is, I am back at Daddy's practice (Mrs Peabody had a funny turn during *Dixon of Dock Green* last night), where the only appearances I am anticipating are a Mrs Hinge (chipped a molar on a florentine) and Mr Noakes (halitosis).

5 P.M.

Something magical *has* happened! Also something terrible, but this time I am skipping the tripe and going straight to pudding.

So, Mr Noakes had just been despatched with instructions to see Dr Ogle about his tonsils (riddled with pustules, according to Daddy), and I had snapped shut the appointments book, when the front door opened again. I was about to yell, 'Early closing on a Thursday! Come back tomorrow!' when a familiar voice said, 'There you are. I knew I'd find you.'

And when I looked up, it was Charlie!

'How did you know I'd be here?' I asked once we'd hugged (she is a wonderful hugger, unlike Mummy who is wont to go stiff, or Daddy, who is like a bear – unaware of his strength).

She pulled a face. 'How many dentists by the name of Arbuthnot do you think there are in this town?'

'One. In the country.' This was Daddy, who had emerged from the surgery and was already in his hat and overcoat ready for the walk home.

I felt myself redden. 'Daddy, this is Charlie,' I said. 'She's ... the one about the job?'

'Ah, the mysterious benefactor.' He held out a hand, which Charlie shook enthusiastically.

My insides, which had been roiling, calmed a little. Daddy is so good at this sort of thing. But of course, it wasn't Daddy who needed convincing.

And, if I thought it was a hard ask, by the time we got back to Magnolia Road (because of course she came with us, because Daddy can't help himself) the task had gone from large to gargantuan.

Mummy opened the door before Daddy had even slotted the key into the lock, a look on her face that suggested that her mother had turned up unannounced (this has happened twice; Mummy took to her bed for a week afterwards in both cases), which didn't bode well for Charlie. Though on the bright side, Mummy was so angry and distracted she quite forget to question Charlie's presence at all, merely marched us into the sitting room and pointed at the table.

There, on the polished mahogany, was not my maternal grandmother (which even for her, would have been odd, though not impossible) but a letter.

'It's from Cambridge,' she said, sharply.

I flinched. 'How do you know? Did Derek tell you?'

'He didn't need to. I opened it myself.'

'Sheila!' snapped Daddy.

I should have been cross as well, but I was trying too hard to swallow my panic. 'What . . . what does it say?' I asked.

'Read it,' she said.

I picked it up, my stomach lurching, my heart in my mouth, scanned it.

'I . . . I didn't get in,' I said.

'Oh, bad luck,' said Charlie.

Mummy swerved to her. 'Luck doesn't come into it. Idiocy is more like it.'

I sighed, handed Charlie the letter, who began to read aloud.

'"We're sorry to inform you that, despite the alluring picture you paint of Topaz Mortmain, we do not consider *I Capture the Castle* to be a worthy replacement for Chaucer, which was the text under question." What hogwash. I adored that book!' She touched my arm before continuing. '"You are invited to reapply in the next academic year, but we urge you to focus on set texts, and literature, not romantic or children's fiction."'

'Idiocy!' repeated my mother.

'Quite,' agreed Charlie. 'Though on their count, not our poor Margaret's.'

This time Mummy did turn on her. 'Who even are you?' she demanded.

'Charlie!' I blurted. 'From the ... the bookshop.'

'Well, the Pippin, really,' said Charlie before I could stop her. 'The bookshop's Rollo's baby. Being as he hasn't any of his own.'

I felt another lurch in me as Mummy's face, which had been puce, now paled to whey. 'So you're the one behind all this ... this nonsense.'

'Well, I don't think—' Charlie began.

But I couldn't let her fend here; this was my battle. 'It isn't nonsense!' I yelled. 'It's ... it's my dream!'

'Your dream?' Mummy was back to scarlet.

'Yes! To be in London. In Soho! To ... to live! Not to be stuck in some stuffy old college where they only want me to read books by dead people.'

'"Live"?' said Mummy. 'You keep saying that word, but you act as if "life" is no more than a party, an endless dance, and it isn't, it ... just isn't!' Her voice was wavering, as if she were the one suffering somehow, but I ignored that.

'I don't!' I snapped back, the salt of tears stinging my eyes now, half in anger, half in shame at Charlie having to witness this. 'I want to work. I want a career, just not . . . your idea of one.'

'A career? Shop work isn't a career!' insisted Mummy.

I said she should try telling that to Mr Pickering, or Mrs Booth from the haberdashery, or to lots of people in fact, and wasn't she from shop-girl stock?

She went terribly red at that and said, 'Yes, well you're not lots of people. You're not me. You're my . . . my only daughter, and I want you to do better than I.'

At which point Daddy put a hand on her shoulder and said, 'It will do for now, though, won't it, Sheila? Let her get it out of her system.'

I did not think Soho was something to be got out of the system, like dysentery, or a dicky egg, but I said nothing. Unlike my mother.

'What about . . . vice?' she cried, shaking off Daddy's hand. 'She could become a . . . a hostess! Or a gambler! Or heaven knows what else.'

'In a bookshop?' tried Charlie. 'Rollo may have a flutter on the gee-gees, but he's not running a crap shoot.'

Mummy gave her a piercing look. 'What about the commuting, then? Beryl Tredegar says her cousin Joyce got . . . *felt* on a Waterloo train.'

'I thought you didn't listen to gossip,' I said, without thinking.

'That is *not* the point,' replied my mother.

'She can stay,' said Charlie then.

'What?' said Mummy and I in unison.

'There's a spare room at Pennington's. Next to mine. Rent's ten shillings a week, though more often than not Rollo waives it, given the state of the place. Not that it's in disrepair!' she added quickly. 'Just that . . . we haven't got round to getting a cleaner yet.'

'Sheila?' Daddy tried.

'Mummy?' I added.

'I . . .' she began, but trailed off, as if summoning something and failing.

Charlie smiled then, and laid a hand on her arm. At first my mother stiffened, as did I. But when Charlie began to speak, something switched. 'My mother wasn't keen either,' she said. 'But here I am.' Charlie held up her hands. 'And tragedy hasn't befallen me yet, unless you count still working in wardrobe instead of opening the show.'

Mummy looked at her, then at me, then at Daddy.

'Please,' I said. 'I promise I'll be careful and . . . and wise. And I won't gamble or drink or . . . do anything you wouldn't do!' I realised this left precious little to actually do, but desperate times called for desperate measures. I had never wanted a 'yes' from my mother – the queen of 'I don't think so' – as much as I had at that moment.

And eventually it came. 'Very well then, yes,' she conceded, if weakly. 'But on your head be it when it all goes wrong.'

*

And so it has happened! Daddy is driving me up on Saturday and if he approves of the living conditions, and only if he approves, I will be allowed to stay. There are also a series of other strict measures that must be met:

1. I am to take a typing course and apply for a proper secretarial position at the earliest opportunity.
2. I am to attend a crammer come next January because I *will* be sitting Cambridge entrance again.
3. I am to come home once a month for Sunday lunch. She did demand once a week, so this is a hard-won compromise, again aided by Daddy who reminded her that she will be all hours at John's once the baby arrives (it is due in June).

I agreed, of course, to all, so high was I on how the day had played out, and all thanks to Charlie.

It seems I do have a fairy godmother after all. Which would make me Cinderella, I suppose. Not that Mummy is a wicked anything. But there is something enchanting about it all, isn't there? And I wouldn't say no to a handsome prince either. But even if I lose a shoe, and he still doesn't appear, I shan't be too disappointed. How could I be, when I'll be living with Charlie, and in the very centre of the world!

SATURDAY 30 JANUARY

10 A.M.

It is D-Day, i.e. Departure Day according to me, and Damnation Day, according to Mummy, who is still convinced I am to fall prey to any number of unsavoury men, women or vices in general. In addition to the list above, I have had to swear on Daddy's life (she wouldn't let me use Gloria's) that I won't get pregnant, go without a bra, or eat mussels (*they* eat excrement, apparently).

I pointed out that:

1. My budget shan't run to mussels,
2. At an A cup, there is little to ruin, and,
3. The last thing I want, having witnessed Gloria's wincing, is to get pregnant. Besides which, I would need a man for that, and a willing one, and aside from Colin, who wasn't all that willing in the first place, there is no such handsome prince on the horizon (I was still in Cinderella mode).

She said, 'Promise me anyway,' so I did. And now she is shut in the bedroom having a lie down for her nerves. Honestly, anyone would think I were heading to Timbuctoo, or even Birmingham. As it is, I am a perpetual disappointment to her so I am surprised she is not glad to see the back of me.

Which she will in less than ten minutes. Eek! The next time I write, I will (Daddy's clean bill of health to Pennington's pending) be a citizen of Soho!

11 P.M.

There is so much to report, but only one thing really necessary to say: I am here. And by here, I mean the first bedroom to the left on the second floor of Pennington's, on Lexington Street, in Soho.

Down below me the city is in full swing: Charlie is still at the Pippin; Rollo is at somewhere called the French, playing chess. Ted remains elusive for now, shut up in his attic, gramophone music – jazz – filtering down through the floorboards, but Charlie promised me I would meet him 'at some point' and that he was an 'absolute darling'.

Mummy emerged from the bedroom in time to say goodbye. She didn't cry, but she did manage, 'Well, I don't know *what* I'm going to say on my round robin now.'

'That's a whole year away, Mummy,' I placated. 'I might be—'
'Pregnant!' she interrupted. 'Dead!'

'I was going to say "a writer", actually.'

'A secretary,' corrected John, who had come to provide moral support (to Mummy, not to me).

'Well, that,' I conceded, my fingers quickly crossing behind my back.

But perhaps I might be a writer. Or . . . well, anything! The possibilities feel endless now I am here, in this room lit by streetlamps and neon; in which even the dust seems bewitching.

Daddy slipped me ten pounds before he left. 'Your wages from the practice,' he said. Then added, 'Don't tell your mother. It can be our little secret.'

Ten pounds is far too much and I said so, but he closed my hand around the note, and then hugged me. And then he was gone, back in the Wolseley and heading south west back to the suburbs and Mummy.

Leaving me here, a seed sown in Soho. Ripe as the place itself. Readied. For Soho is, more than anything, a waiting room for the wondrous, the air hung with expectancy, as if everyone and everything were on the brink of something wonderful.

As if *I* am on the brink of something wonderful. And I am, aren't I? Because I have a whole year. A year of 'yes!' Of . . . living dangerously!

Or just living, in the truest sense of the word.

FEBRUARY 1960

MONDAY
1 FEBRUARY

9.30 A.M.
It is as if I've been asleep for years and only now woken up, and what's more, in a foreign country or a never-never-land. As if someone has cut a slice of the gateau that is Paris and airdropped it east of Mayfair. Or perhaps it is a fiefdom, a state of its own; it seems to operate on singular time and with its own set of rules. And best of all, everyone is welcome – Turks and Greeks up on Dean Street, Italians on Frith, men and women of colour in the clubs and bars, and homosexuals, well, everywhere. All those 'scourges' of Surbiton have washed up here and, oh! How glorious it all is! It's hard to know where to start. Perhaps . . . by describing a day. Yes, in Cassandra Mortmain fashion, I will capture that!

The morning starts at six, perhaps earlier, with the clatter of barrow boys heading for Berwick Street market, their deep-voiced calls punctuating the morning, along with the chatter and stamp of schoolchildren – for yes, there is a school here! – walking, crocodile-style, along Wardour Street. Then, this vast cast – the respectable day players – packs up at five and scatters like ants, and the scene switches to another sort of hustle and hum; people spilling in and out of clubs, the gutter filling with dropped bottles and lost earrings and cigarette ends, but all of it rainbowed with spilled gasoline, casting a patina of promise on even the wretched. Then the sounds fade around two in the morning before it all cranks up again at six. And not just the sounds, but the smells as well: of smoke, of foreign food – at least, foreign to the majority of Surbiton. Garlic wafting across from the French pub on Dean Street, hot buttery croissants and pastries from Maison Bertaux on Greek, then across Shaftesbury Avenue and into Chinatown with its red Peking ducks glistening on spits in the window – as far from the anaemic chickens in Goddard's on the Kingston Road as a goose from a monkey.

Mummy calls it a square mile of vice; regards it, I know, as if it were no better than a leper colony. But here, in this tawdry and glorious grid between Charing Cross Road and Regent Street, Oxford Circus and Leicester Square, is the very epitome of Life. The rest of London, compared to it, is a staid old maid, while Soho? Soho is an adolescent; even the dilapidated bits seem teen-aged somehow, brimming with possibility. Or, what was it Charlie called it? Oh, yes! A 'racy aunt'.

'One who lifts her skirt and shows you her knickers,' she said with relish at breakfast.

'If she's even wearing any,' added Rollo from behind *The Times* (he is quite like Daddy in some ways, though in others it is geese and monkeys again).

Anyway, the point is, Surbiton is nothing but a dormitory: asleep and not even dreaming. Whereas Soho is teeming. And at the very heart of it is this, Pennington's! I would try to capture it now, but I'm due to open up in a moment, so it will have to be at lunch or during a lull, the latter of which is unlikely as, though Rollo seems not to sell many books, he has an awful lot of 'customers' who come not to buy but to idle time.

1 P.M.

Lunch (i.e. a hastily fashioned hard-cheese sandwich, though the bread is fresh and French, so it's not all terrible), and so to capturing Pennington's:

27 Lexington Street is wedged between a launderette and a pet shop, the canary calls of which I can hear through the wall if ever there's a quiet moment, though these, predictably, are rare. So far today the following have dropped in: Doris from the Pippin, to discuss something about Valentine's absence last week; an odd, gobliny sort of man whom Rollo referred to as 'Eggs' when he walked in the door, but whom I later discovered is a famous painter by the name of Francis Bacon – though having been shown one of his 'portraits' (it hangs on the landing), I find this hard to believe; two Roberts, an hour apart, both wanting to complain about the other; and a rather darling-looking woman by the improbable name of 'Panth' also wanting to discuss Valentine, who, by the tone of her,

Doris's and Rollo's voices, is somewhat of a lost cause.

What else? I've already mentioned the three floors, the stairs at their dizzying angle, making one permanently tipsy. Then, well, books. Books are everything and everywhere. They seem to breed, and not just on the shop floor. They sit in little piles up the staircase to the flat we inhabit, and even there they colonise every surface: the floor space, the hallway, the bathroom as well. Not just books, but newspapers too: *The Stage*, *Racing Times*, the actual *Times*, discarded haphazardly and left until they're yellowed and fraying and someone needs one to wrap up broken glass or a dead pigeon (you would be surprised how frequent an occurrence both have already been) before dropping it into the kitchen bin—

Oh, the kitchen! The kitchen is recklessly messy. There are pans and pots in no sort of order, hung from the ceiling along with a string of onions and, once a week, Charlie's underwear (she says it is because it is the warmest room, although it sends Ted red and fleeing back to his attic). The refrigerator, well . . . on a good day one might open it and find half a desiccated lemon and a bottle of vodka. On a bad one, half a pint of milk so gone-off it's become yoghurt. Elsewhere, nothing is where it should be. Every drawer bursts with an eclectic mess. In one alone I have found six forks, the wishbone from a chicken, a prescription for morphine, three ten-shilling notes, a sock, and four conkers. It wouldn't surprise me if I turned up a skeleton next time, which I said to Rollo. At this, he looked sheepish.

'No!' I yelled. 'Where?'

'Ted's bedroom,' he explained. 'A medical student boarded here during the war.'

'Didn't he take it with him when he graduated?' I asked.

Charlie put a hand on my arm. 'He never graduated,' she said. 'Doodlebug somewhere near St Mary's.'

'His mother didn't want it,' Rollo went on, before my shudder turned to something worse. 'And it felt wrong to throw her out.'

'Naturally,' I agreed, then clocked something. 'Her?'

'She's called Muriel,' said Charlie, matter of fact. 'She's a darling. And Ted says she's useful, though God knows what for.'

Quite, as I am sure he isn't a doctor, or ghoul. Although I shall at least recount what I do know about him later, when I move on to capturing the people. For now, it's time to get back to work, so I shall merely add: the floorboards creak, the pipes rattle and clang, the kitchen taps drip and the bathroom ones groan when they do work, but, goodness, I love it!

TUESDAY 2 FEBRUARY

1 P.M.

I had no time last night in the end – there was an emergency with a leaking pipe; the first I knew of it was when something dripped from the ceiling onto the copy of *The Three Musketeers* I was engrossed in. When I rushed upstairs to the kitchen, there was Ted, naked from the waist up, and wrestling with one of the aforementioned taps. So perhaps I shall start with him.

Undressed, he is surprisingly statuesque – all muscle and sinew; quite the David, in fact. Clothed, he is as inconspicuous as his accent and habits. All I know is that by day he works as a handyman, cash in hand, for Rollo's many acquaintances, and by evening and at the weekend he is up to something in his room. I don't know what, as the door to the attic is locked whether he is in or out (believe me, I have checked), but I intend to find out.

Hopefully it will be something thrilling, like an inventor or a poet. That would be quite the turn for the story, as so far his life has been terribly difficult (according to Doris, who popped in again to see if Rollo wanted to head to the French for a 'snifter'). His mother was Rollo's live-in housekeeper but she died just after the war and so, with no father to speak of, and nowhere else to go, Ted stayed on here, a sort of surrogate son to Rollo.

What with me, Ted and Charlie, Rollo is quite the benefactor. And while he is far from Magwitchian, he is as eccentric as Pennington's itself. He rarely gets up before twelve; he dines out in style once a week courtesy of the *Herald* (he is their restaurant critic), the rest of the time eating only dry toast and hard-boiled eggs; and his list of dislikes is inexplicable though not unfamiliar, as my mother has one too of course. But while hers centres on anything that could possibly be deemed 'common', his is more like the kitchen drawer, i.e. so wide-ranging and cluttered as to include: the colour turquoise, Panama hats, gorillas, the name 'Gervaise', soup, all dogs bar whippets, talcum powder, eggs (unless hard-boiled), doctors, overly large horses, luncheon meat. There are no doubt more, but these are the ones that have been revealed in heated conversation so far. Though most are, in Soho anyway, avoidable. Perhaps it is this finickiness that has ensured he has never married and has no children of his own. Instead he surrounds himself with friends, the very best being Valentine – erstwhile owner of the Pippin, cousin of some aunt of Charlie, and lamentably absent according to both Doris and that Panth lady.

Like Rollo, chaos seems to trail Valentine like a ragged

dog. He is frequently penniless, apparently, and reliant on the comfort of friends and occasionally strangers. Though his generosity is endless as well; what little he does have, and has not frittered on drink, clearly ends up in his darling Charlie's pocket. I suspect her continued employment is down to this benevolent affection, because it is surely not thanks to her manner or talent. She is late to work often, slapdash with the actors and dismissive of the audience a lot of the time. But he seems to forgive her every slip-up or slight. And it's hard not to see why. I've already described her on these pages, so I shan't go on too much more, but what is worth recounting is what she makes of me. I'm not used to it – to being so . . . wanted. Mummy always said I was a 'bit much', and so with the girls at school – even with Felicity – I felt myself shrink, or at least try to – as if pushing a pound of sausage meat into an eight-ounce tin. But Charlie doesn't seem to want that at all. Rather, I do believe she'd take as much of me as I could muster, in an infinite sheep's stomach, which rather makes up for any of her own shortcomings, of which Rollo has listed fickleness and self-indulgence, but I shall make my own judgement.

Also, I am aware the sheep stomach metaphor is stretching a little thin, as well as making me queasy, but, still, it is a thing worth noting. Everyone here is notable. There's Doris of course, on the stage door at the Pippin when they aren't in here bothering Rollo. The flyman, Spanish Stan, who isn't a speck of continental, but once went somewhere called Benidorm and won't shut up about it. An arthritic pianist called Carmine who takes the coveted corner seat in the French, and is dressed perpetually in black. 'Who are they mourning?' I asked Rollo. 'Dior, of course,' he replied. Then there are: Polish Nell, whose poodle wears the same shade of nail polish; the two Roberts – one capriciously tall, the other defiantly squat – who share an artists' studio somewhere in Hammersmith and a bed above the deli on Berwick Street; Sinjon Smith, who is barely five foot, has a strawberry nose and a foul temper – a sort of malevolent elf: charismatic and repulsive all at once. At least two of them have been tenants of Rollo's at one time or another, and judging by the pile of post that we receive daily – for a Dr Hugo Bloomington, a Mr Lewis McGee, a Miss Charity Pakenham (Honourable, at that!) – there have been several more of them as well. And every one of them seems to have a story – lives that have staggered from the gutter to The Ritz and back again.

In contrast, of course, I am quite the plain Jane, and yet, as soon as I had stepped over the threshold of Pennington's, I knew I belonged. Here, in this pocket of promise, class, inheritance, wealth seem not to exist, or rather, not to matter – as long as you are different and interesting, or at the very least, *interested*, then you are one of them: a Sohovian.

And I am a Sohovian. Oh, how I am!

SATURDAY 13 FEBRUARY

1 P.M.

I am quite used to newness, am au fait now with revelations and surprises (Muriel the skeleton notwithstanding; I have yet to meet her) but yesterday's is by far the greatest yet: The Honourable Miss Charity Pakenham is Charlie!

I know this because another letter arrived – this one embossed vellum, heavy, carrying the weight of an invitation (wedding, I assumed) inside. I was just about to bin the thing when Rollo snatched it from my hand (saving it from a fate of congealed bean juice) and put it aside. 'It's about time she dealt with it,' he told me, 'I'll let her know,' before heading out the pub.

Well, who is 'she'? I thought, assuming another of our many regulars or his past tenants. And to that end, kept an eye on the thing lest someone who still had a key should nip in to fetch it. But of course there was no one until Charlie slunk in from the Pippin near midnight (there is a new show due in now that *Measure for Measure* has finished, so she is flat out with wardrobe) while I was filling a hot water bottle, upon which, she picked up the letter and was about to bin it herself when I stopped her.

'Apparently Charity is fetching it later,' I said. 'Only who Charity is, is a mystery!'

I had given this line my best air of drama, but Charlie merely sighed, raised one of her neat brows, and said 'mystery no more' before opening it with an ivory knife she found in the dried goods cupboard, scanning its contents, and saying, 'as I thought' before binning it after all.

'Explain!' I bade her.

'A christening,' she said. 'For one of my myriad nephews and nieces. Four siblings,' she added. 'I'm the youngest and the black sheep, quite obviously. Though given two are married to vicars, what hope? Anyway, I shan't be going. Babies are all the same.'

'Not *that*!' I blurted. 'You're . . . *you're* Charity? You're an *honourable*? You're . . . oh my heavens.' Something clicked in me. 'That's why Rollo sometimes calls you "Deb". Not Deborah; *a* deb, he means.'

'Yes, except of course I wasn't. That's why Mummy and I aren't speaking.'

'What do you mean?' I patted one of the rickety chairs at the worn oak table at which we might dine, were we so inclined, but which was mostly a book repository.

'I, well . . .' – she plonked down with a sigh – 'I ran away.'

Then she explained the whole sorry state of affairs (or rather, the abridged version, as she said we'd need a day for the detail): that her grandfather was Lord Balfour, her own father somewhere in line to the throne, and so of course, like her sisters, she'd been destined to be a debutante – one of the last, in fact, given 'coming out' is no longer a thing. But she had baulked at it, having never wanted that life, and had come to Soho instead to find her fortune, much to her mother's disgust. So I am not alone in that respect, albeit if from rather a different start point, both geographically and financially.

'I tried Sheba for a bit,' she went on, 'as a name. You know, after Bathsheba from the Bible? But it didn't stick. I kept forgetting and never answered when anyone said it. At least Charlie has some of the same letters in it.'

'Charity, though?' I pressed her. 'That's your real name?'

'Charity Evangeline Pakenham.' She curtseyed, dramatically. 'So named because I was Daddy's last act of charity before he left for the war.'

'Charity' seemed a poor reflection on her parents' relationship, and for such a glittering child, but I said nothing on that. 'Is that how he . . . died?' I asked instead (I knew he was no longer alive, at least, from Rollo). 'In the war?'

'No. Although he might as well have. He came back a different man, by all accounts. Hollowed out somehow. He tried very hard, but . . . he couldn't face life after a while.'

'Oh!' I exclaimed. 'I'm so very sorry.'

She shrugged. 'I barely knew him. Though Mummy went to a health farm for a whole month to recover.'

'After the funeral?'

'Oh. No, I meant after I left. So, you see, I can't really show up to a christening now, can I?'

I nodded. 'I suppose.'

She stood then. 'Right, I'm off to bed.'

And for once she didn't even mix herself a gin, so I knew the whole thing had got to her. And this morning, she was up by eleven and off to the Pippin, without a word on the subject at all. She is a strange fish. But an honourable one!

Oh, how riven with envy I am. To think – I am living with a deb! Perhaps now I shall capture a castle one day after all.

MONDAY
15 FEBRUARY

10 P.M.

I am as far from castles as one could possibly get, and wondering if perhaps that is a good thing.

To explain: tonight was my inaugural typing class, which in itself might have been fine, had it been in Soho, or somewhere closer, but the course Mummy had found was at the Morley College in Waterloo. Again, in itself not an especially problematic location (though Waterloo does symbolise the dreary gate to suburbia, i.e. purgatory), except for the presence of a particularly militant newspaper seller, who seemed hellbent on being a fly in an already annoying ointment.

He accosted me on the steps of the station, thrusting a copy of *The Worker* under my nose as if it were a truncheon and he the thought police. 'Read all about it,' he said. 'Government's latest play against the unions!'

If I was surprised, it wasn't only at the suddenness of it, but at how young he was – not much more than I, I decided – and, while lacking a tie or a hat, his clothing still had an air of refinement. The oddest thing, though, was his voice, which was not at all like the hawkers of the *Evening Standard* who can match the barrow boys for their foghorn calls, but, rather, refined – if somewhat aggressive.

'We take *The Times*,' I said, firmly, 'but thank you.' And tried to move past.

He was having none of it, however, replacing the paper with himself. 'Propaganda,' he said. 'Pure and simple. How do expect to change anything if you're swallowing what the authorities feed you?'

I felt myself bristle. 'Well, if it helps, I sometimes flick through the *Mirror* in the Lorelei.'

'The coffee bar on Frith Street?' He frowned, as if unable to picture me in there.

I bristled again. 'Where else? Now, if you don't mind, I'm late for typing class.'

He was not swayed. Instead, he snorted. 'And what are you going to learn in typing class? How to be an obedient little secretary, I suppose.'

Bristling turned to raised hackles. 'What if . . . what if I was going to write *Das Kapital* . . . the sequel?' I asked.

He raised an eyebrow. 'Are you?'

'Probably not,' I admitted, 'but that's not the point. The point is I'm going to be late, and you should be encouraging me, not – not getting in my way. I am one of the masses, after all, about to be educated!'

'Masses?' He laughed, his wide mouth revealing a gap

between his front teeth that at any other time I might have found endearing. 'Where did you go to school?' he demanded. 'Roedean? Benenden?'

'Hardly!' I replied.

'So where?'

I felt myself flush. 'Surbiton Girls.'

'Same thing. Still middle class.'

'Class is dead, haven't you heard?' I told him. 'Macmillan said so.'

'Macmillan's an idiot.'

I couldn't argue with that; even Daddy is inclined to agree and he voted for him. Instead I snapped, 'And so are you!' and pushed past his arm and on down Westminster Bridge Road.

The whole thing was ridiculous – he was hardly Marx, himself – and yet it continued to needle me throughout the evening class. No wonder Miss Beveridge (steel hair, steel stare) lamented my finger co-ordination.

'This is awfully dull, isn't it,' I said to the girl next to me at one point – a sweet thing, though painfully gaunt and a little haunted around the eyes. 'And tricky. I wish I hadn't come.'

She frowned. 'Oh, no. I'm lucky,' she said, her accent more of what I'd expected from the newspaper man. 'At this rate I'll be out and away in six months.'

'From your parents'?' I asked, eagerly, sensing a kindred spirit after all.

She pulled a face. 'Cripes, no. I meant my husband.'

I took her in then, saw a different fate for myself, had I been born even a few roads over from my own. Saw the opportunities I had and she hadn't. Saw, as well, the pink ring of scar tissue on the back of her hand, the exact size, I realised, of a cigarette end. How naïve I was. How unthinking.

'I'm sorry,' I told her. 'I should . . . get on, shouldn't I?' And I left her to her words per minute, which, at forty, were already more than double mine.

On the way home, I still felt puffed up, like a cat put out for the night against its will. Both my typing companion and that haranguing man had got under my skin a little in their own ways: he slapping me with my privilege as if it were a cane, she merely highlighting its existence by the absence of her own.

I am lucky, and I shall have to remind myself of that. Soho is my castle, after all, isn't it? This life I have managed to find – the life I have come from, even – is a gift horse in itself, and I shall not look it in the mouth again.

SUNDAY 28 FEBRUARY

10 A.M.
It is more than a month since I moved out, which means today I must face up to the horror of having to go back to Magnolia Road. And yes, gift horses and all that, but, really, Surbiton is a form of torture, albeit one with expensive pelmets and brass doorknobs and roast beef on a Sunday.

7 P.M.
Magnolia Road was as predictable as it was ridiculous.

'All right, Accident?' said John the moment I walked in.

'I wish you wouldn't call her that,' my father said, before I could get in a retort.

'Thank you, Daddy,' I said instead, just as Mummy stalked past with her rubber gloves on and a determined expression.

'Gerry. Sink!' she commanded (it gets blocked on a regular basis, though she can no longer blame me for tipping un-sinkable things down it, at least).

Daddy sighed, put down *The Sunday Times*, and plodded

after her, a disconsolate dog. John rolled his eyes. He has a point about the accident thing. My mother organises everything meticulously, so not to have planned me would seem an oversight so gargantuan as to be unthinkable.

'Maybe it's because you're so annoying that she waited so long to have me,' I retorted finally.

'Probably wishes she hadn't bothered now,' he batted back.

And on it went until Daddy returned from the kitchen, his sweater damp and his face flecked with sweat (our plunger is stubborn). 'Stop it, the both of you,' he snapped.

'Sorry, Pa,' I said quickly, not wanting to get on anyone's wrong side, at least not this early.

Luckily Mummy emerged with the roast (not beef – pork loin; she is on an economy drive) at that point anyway, so all talk of accidents was moot while she gave me a sort of vocal round robin rundown on who has died (Derek Letchworth, Number 11, stroke), who has got new and unsuitable net curtains (Aunt Barbara, tendency to the 'common'), and who has developed swollen ankles like an elephant (Gloria, to add to the piles). For someone who claims to eschew gossip, she is remarkably well-informed, which I said, which was obviously a mistake. Thankfully Daddy stepped in quickly to ask how typing was going, and I was able to tell him I was now able to manage nineteen words a minute accurately, and twenty-seven less so.

'And have you met anyone *interesting*?' asked my mother.

This said in a tone that indicated what she meant by 'interesting' was 'eligible' and by 'eligible', 'male'.

I feigned ignorance. 'Well, there's June, who works at a fishmonger's on the Walworth Road, and Mo who's at the jam factory, and Betty with the awful husband. She's gained her first Pittman certificate of merit! One more to go and she might be able to leave him!' (Though the next is in shorthand, which is literal gobbledegook, so I am not hedging bets yet. I will be sad to see her leave this class in any case. She was at least tolerant of my truncated hammering, while everyone else eyes me with a mixture of pity and belligerence. I can't say I blame them: I do take up a lot of Miss Beveridge's time and ire, thence she is short with everyone.)

'I didn't mean . . . women,' said Mummy, confirming my fears.

'Well there's the communist fellow who sells *The Worker*; he's quite *interesting*.' Which he is, in one sense. Or at least, he's persistent. This week he was lying in wait but I had worked out a scheme: I used a shilling I'd found in the bathroom cabinet and bought one of his silly papers. He was so stunned I was away before he had time to close his gaping mouth. 'Not that he's on the course,' I added. 'Secretarial work is too middle class, apparently, and props up the patriarchy.'

'Leap Year day tomorrow though,' said Daddy.

'If you're highlighting this because women can propose, then I don't see how it's progression, given that marriage is also a form of modern slavery. Look at Mummy and all the cleaning!' I wasn't sure where that came from, and frankly wish it had stayed in there, but it was too late.

'I suppose all the women *you* meet are . . . are *progressive*!' Mummy exclaimed. 'I suppose they *drink* and do . . . do *drugs* and . . . and leave their husbands!'

I smiled and speared a piece of pork, dipped it in redcurrant jelly. 'Oh, Soho is the drug, Mother.' Which, even if I say it myself, is quite the line!

Mummy did not think so, and flounced into the kitchen to fetch a J-cloth because John had spilled gravy on the second-best tablecloth, which sort of proves my point, but *that* I managed to keep to myself. The rest of the meal passed in stilted conversation about hydrangeas, and I was back on the platform for the four ten train heading back to this den of iniquity/blissful mile of vice.

The whole proposal thing is nonsense, though, and I stick by it. Even I were minded, to whom would I betroth myself? Ted? Rollo? Doris?

See? Preposterous.

10.10 P.M.

I mean, that man who sells the paper is rather good-looking under the bluff and swagger, but I wouldn't give him the satisfaction of letting him know even that.

10.11 P.M.
Would I?

10.15 P.M.
No, I wouldn't.

MONDAY
29 FEBRUARY

10 P.M.
I have proposed to no one. The Worker (I don't know what else to call him) wasn't even there. I was almost disappointed.
　　Almost.

MARCH 1960

MARCH 1960

WEDNESDAY 2 MARCH

2 P.M.

It is my afternoon off and I am, unbelievably, at a loose end. I offered to work through if Rollo wasn't feeling up to flying solo (his tummy is a bit dicky some days. He blames the water; I blame the wine.) But he said I was entitled to a half day and I should jolly well take it. I could have pointed out I was also entitled to living conditions that did not involve woodlice infestations and a dead mouse in the water tank, but given I am getting free bed and board, it seemed a little churlish. Instead, I suggested I might see a film, but his retort to that was, 'Darling, Soho *is* a film.' So now I am somewhat stuck, and in persistently Arctic conditions.

The thing is, I know I said I adored it, but the longer I am here, the longer I realise that the set-up is far from five-star. The boiler for the hot water and radiators is temperamental; a recalcitrant cat that needs coaxing into co-operation. And as for any other heating – well, there are coal fires in the kitchen and sitting room and elsewhere we have hot water bottles and as many layers as we can fit on in one go. Mortmain said cold was inspiring of course, but all it inspires in me is a prickly mood and a greed for cake. Charlie says there were rumours of a bar heater at one point, but no one has ever unearthed it, though she also says this is probably a good thing as the last time she used one, while reading a book back at Balfour Hall, she managed to set herself aflame. 'Mummy was appalled,' she told me.

'Well, of course. You might have died.'

'Oh, no. More that it was my best sweater. Also the book was The Sheikh, which she said was not at all improving.'

All of which brings me to my next point: the chaos. It seemed bohemian at first – the mess. Glamorous. A sort of anti-Magnolia Road. But now I think I understand my mother a little. It's not that it's an eyesore – although it is; a veritable rubbish dump some mornings – more the danger of it. I am tired of stubbing my toes on volumes of de Beauvoir, or risking my life when I make a cup of tea because the milk practically heaves with bacteria. My mother would struggle and so, it seems, do I. It's like brown eyes or red hair, only in this case I've inherited a snub nose, freckles, and a penchant for cleanliness.

There was a cleaner, Charlie says: Ted's mother. But, well, I've explained all that. And a 'Mrs C' did for a few months, but left after a spat over where eggs should be kept and since then everyone has been left to their own devices, which are, apparently, 'someone else will do it'.

2.10 P.M.

I've had an idea. What if that someone were me? I have an excellent record of good deeds and fixing things, e.g. two months in the Brownies (before I got barred over an argument about the existence of 'piskies'), and the time Felicity spilled custard down her blazer on the day of the school photograph and I offered up mine (given I had already been banished to the back row for 'incongruous socks').

2.15 P.M.

Yes, it *shall* be me! I shall be the golden girl, the invisible angel of kindness, and am rolling up my sleeves (literally) and tackling the worst of it. At the very least it will keep me warm and occupied. Rollo is at the French, so heaven knows when he'll be back; Ted is locked in his attic doing whatever Ted does up there; and Charlie has gone off to work in a vile mood because there was a cougher in one of the boxes last night and she took him up a lozenge and then got castigated as if she were the one ruining everyone's evening. She is quite put out. Well, this will cheer her up, I am sure, and Rollo, who must be heartily tired of never being able to find his spectacles (they are usually on his head, the toilet cistern, or – inexplicably – the fridge).

8 P.M.

I am done and dusted (also literally!). Plus, I have stocked the pantry and fridge with basic necessities (eggs, milk, cheese that isn't impenetrable or so green as to be a new life form) and replenished the lavatory paper, as we were all sick of using *The Times*, appropriate though Charlie claimed that to be. Now all that is left is for Ted to come down and Rollo and Charlie to come home. What a surprise it will be!

11 P.M.

A 'surprise' is perhaps not quite the word.

Rollo said nothing, merely wandered around like a displaced cat – is still doing it now, by the sound of tramping coming from next door. I should probably butter his paws to stop him fleeing back to the French. Ted just muttered 'Blimey' when he emerged to fetch a slice of bread and butter. Though I note he did not have to spend ten minutes trying to find either ingredient or a clean knife, which is quite usual here. Charlie, at least, was far more vocal.

'Well, you can take the girl out of Surbiton . . .' she said, hands on her hips, surveying the kitchen as if it were a new home entirely.

I flinched and my skin pinked. 'It's not about that,' I snapped. 'It's about kindness and . . . and standards,' I said. 'You're . . . you're spoilt, the lot of you. Do you know there were two dead mice in the cutlery drawer? Two!'

Charlie shrank a little. 'Well . . .' She seemed to fight for an answer. 'You'd better not have touched my room, that's all I can say.'

I felt my throat tighten as Charlie clattered up the stairs, two at a time, and I scuttled behind her, a mouse myself.

'Damn you,' came the yell as she burst into her room. 'Nothing is where I left it!'

'Yes, but—' I began.

'Where is my red cape? Where are all my silver mules?'

Now this I could answer plainly. 'On the shoe stand. Well, two and half pairs are anyway. How many does one need?'

'Well, three pairs, clearly. But I lost one in the Gargoyle after some do of Lucian's. I still miss it,' she added, wistfully. 'Anyway, that's not the point. Where is everything else?'

'Where it should be,' I said, my hands on my hips, emboldened now.

'The pink cashmere cardigan? The one with the moth hole in the awkward place.'

'Darned and aired and put away in the bottom drawer of the wardrobe.'

'Oh. Well . . . what about that darling red belt with the gold buckle?'

'In a bag on the back of the door, along with thirty-seven belts that all look the same.'

'Touché,' I heard her mutter. 'Right, I could use a drink.'

At that she stomped back out and back to the kitchen, where she proceeded to open and shut every cupboard, seemingly in a bid to catch me out.

'Gin?' she demanded.

'Drinks cabinet.'

'Soda?'

'Sideboard.'

'For heaven's sake. God, you're sensible. Lemon?'

'Refrigerator.'

She opened it, cut herself a slice, and then spied something else. 'Bitters! Who knew we had bitters?' And at that, she grinned, and kissed me on the cheek.

I allowed myself a smug smile at that, though I turned down the offer of gin, despite my 'yes' promise – drink being on Mummy's forbidden list. Instead, I had a celebratory cup of tea, with fresh milk, and the knowledge I will sleep the sleep of the just, in clean sheets and a dust-free room for once.

THURSDAY
3 MARCH

8 P.M.
There has been quite the revelation at Lexington Street! Or at least, it was news to me. It is that Ted is not an inventor, nor some sort of spook or ghoul; he is an artist! More, he is a painter of naked ladies, and more specifically, one naked lady, with whom I am familiar. Although not as familiar, it seems, as he.

I found this out by accident, not design. Or rather, when I asked Charlie what Ted was up to, she said, 'Stuff. Ask Ted.' Only, when I asked Ted directly, he just said, 'Stuff,' and disappeared back up to the attic, so I took that as a cue not to enquire further. Instead, I have taken every chance to try to peek into his bedroom, which has hitherto proven impossible as the only key to the attic seems to be about his person. This afternoon, however, he was called out to a blocked drain on Poland Street, and in his rush to fetch some specific spanner from the attic, he forgot to lock the door behind him. Well, I am not one to look opportunity in the eye and say, 'Not today, thank you', so I slipped in with a promise to myself to only take the briefest of peeks and then leave the room entirely unruffled.

That was the intention, but, heavens! The moment I entered, I was rendered cement. Because there, amongst the cluttered eaves, dust motes dancing in vast shafts of winter sun licking down from skylights, were a hundred Charlies, rendered in aggressive and meaty sweeps of paint, and all in various states of undress.

My mouth must have gaped frog-like as I took it all in – Charlie, on the moth-eaten chaise longue with a copy of something in her hand, the arc of her breasts quite visible either side of the book's spine. Charlie leaning at the window of her own room, her front to the world, her buttocks to the painter – to Ted! Charlie in the bath, suds covering her nether regions but two nipples quite visible among the bubbles. There was more Charlie than anyone but her mother or a lover must have seen, although she had denied Ted this of course, so what else was I to believe but that he was a peeping Tom?

Enraged, I lay in wait until he returned, half an hour later, his size-ten steps thundering past the first floor, the second floor, then into the room, his face red, his eyes wild.

'What the hell?' he demanded.

I steeled myself, though he is quite imposing when he needs to be. 'I might ask the same of you,' I said, in measured tones. 'Quite the dark horse, aren't we?'

'None of your bloody business,' he retorted.

'It is my business if you're painting filthy pictures of my friend,' I said, cleverly (or so I thought). 'How do you think she'd feel if she knew you'd been ogling her?'

'I haven't been . . . ogling, for God's sake.'

'No? How else, then? And don't say "imagination" because it's too . . . too *Charlie* to be invented.'

He sighed, and stuck his hands in his pockets then. 'What if I said she let me?'

I frowned. 'Pardon?'

'You heard me.'

I was agape again. The thought of Charlie lying there, starkers, letting a strange man paint her, seemed impossible. Foolish. Or . . . was it? Was it I who was the foolish one? Green? 'An absolute beginner' Rollo had called me once, when I flushed at someone who asked for a copy of the Marquis de Sade. Hadn't Topaz Mortmain herself been painted naked – an artist's model, after all?

'You mean . . . she sits for you?' I asked.

He nodded.

I was still frowning. 'Then . . . why so cloak and dagger about it? If she doesn't care?'

He looked to the floor then. 'Because I care.'

'I don't understand.'

He met my eye, defiant again. 'Because look at them. They're . . . they're amateur. I haven't had lessons, have I? Haven't been to art school or whatnot. Haven't even got proper equipment. I use what's left of household emulsion and the dregs of a set Charlie got me last Christmas. I've got cardboard instead of canvas, for God's sake.'

'But still,' I said, 'they're ... they're extraordinary.'

And they were – they are! They're not realistic by any means, but they're real, visceral, the flesh so very ... fleshy. Nothing covered up or flattered. Sort of Bacon-esque, but far, far more beautiful.

'Still, you can't say anything.'

'But what will you do?' I asked, exasperated.

He shrugged. 'Practise? Get better? I'm saving up for lessons, but ... there's always something round here that needs fixing and food doesn't buy itself – not even dry toast and hard-boiled eggs.'

'You're subsidising Rollo,' I realised.

'We all are,' he said. 'The house is a money pit and his coffers were gone a long time ago. Every so often he threatens to sell up, and then something will appear from somewhere.'

'Valentine,' I surmised, who had been in twice in the last few days, once with a Robert, once without.

He nodded. 'Probably. But he's hardly minted.'

I sighed. 'I'm sorry I snuck in,' I said. 'But ... you have talent. I don't know much about art, but I do know that.'

He smiled thinly. 'Talent isn't everything. Opportunity needs to knock and all.'

It was my turn to nod, and, as I beat a quick retreat, I made a promise to myself to listen for opportunity as hard as he, in case he missed it.

SATURDAY
5 MARCH

10 P.M.

It seems it isn't just Ted who's the dark horse round here. Rather, Charlie has even more of a story than I thought. No wonder her mother is rattled!

So, we went for a quick bite between the shows in our regular, the Lorelei (yes, I have a regular coffee bar! Isn't it thrilling? It is tiny and dark and smells of hot fat, and is exactly the sort of place Mummy would put on the proscribed list for being 'common' – hence I adore it) and there was a couple in there – you know the sort. She: a neat chignon, impeccable make-up, Astrakhan coat; a deb, by all measures. He: a banker, perhaps, or civil servant; a real John sort, only several Grades higher judging by the cut of his suit. But both fish out of water on Frith Street.

'How green they seem,' I said, as I expertly squeezed ketchup from the perpetually stopped-up bottle. 'Did I look that bad when I arrived?' I asked.

Charlie glanced up and immediately paled, her already porcelain skin vampirish now. 'Oh,' she managed. A single sound.

Then, before I knew what was going on, I was being hauled out onto the pavement, my eggs quite abandoned.

'What on earth?' I said once we'd stumbled across Wardour onto Meard Street. 'I'm famished.'

'That ... that was my ex,' she stammered.

'I ... Really?' Surprised was an understatement. 'The one your mother was so exercised about?'

'Yes.'

'But he looks ... benign.'

There was a pause. 'Not he,' she said. '*She.*'

It took a second for it to sink in. Several for me to take possession of my faculties again.

'Promise you won't say a word?' she begged.

'I ... Of course.' I'd not mentioned Ted to anyone, had I? And only would, if it was a clear opportunity for him. 'So ... who is she?'

Charlie leaned back against a lamppost. 'Lady Caroline Fitzpatrick. Fitz. She was my first love.' This with a wistful air about it.

'And she ended it?' I prompted.

Charlie nodded. 'A week before the whole deb ceremony. Said it was time to ... grow up. That's what she called it. As if it were all a childish parlour game, like cribbage or whist. She was engaged in days. To him, I assume.'

He was evidently eligible. 'And there hasn't been anyone else?'

She shook her head. 'A couple of crushes. Nothing tangible.

Not like her. I could lose myself in her eyes. In the way she laughed. And her body—' She stopped herself.

I felt myself redden. 'And you don't want to . . . you know, with a man, I mean?'

'Sometimes,' she admitted. 'Though not as much, I think. Or rather, no one has ever made me feel like she did. It's . . . hard to explain.'

'And Ted?' I suggested, thinking of the way he blushed at her underwear, and yet painted her naked with such obvious love.

She shook her head. 'Like a brother.'

Poor boy, I thought. 'Does your mother . . .' I began, then changed tack – of course she knew. 'Is this part of why she's livid?'

She nodded, sighed, then patted her sides, evidently looking for a cigarette. 'Oh, heavens, my coat!' she exclaimed. 'I left it on my chair. But . . . I can't possibly go back.'

'I'll fetch it,' I said. 'Wait there.'

She shook her head. 'I can't. Not with her so . . . close. I'll go on to work. It's five minutes away, so I shan't freeze. And Doris has ciggies.'

'Fine. Try not to think about it.' I grasped her arm. 'And I'll see you after, yes?'

'Yes. We can . . . we can go out and drink gin and obliterate everything!'

I laughed. 'Maybe.'

But she was already gone, and so I plodded back across the

road to the Lorelei, and clanged open the door, just as someone else hurried out.

I'd expected it to be Lady Caroline or her betrothed, but, 'You!' I exclaimed.

'And *you*,' said the Communist. 'Slumming it, are we?'

I puffed myself up. 'It's my regular, actually. I just... I forgot my coat.'

He looked me up and down, at the sensible duffel I had on, and which I now cursed for myriad reasons.

'Well, a friend forgot hers,' I admitted. 'There was a . . . a to-do with an ex, or there could have been, and we had to leave in a rush.'

He looked behind him. 'Your ex is in here?'

'Not mine,' I said, quickly. 'Hers. But . . . could you just let me pass. You have a terrible habit of road blocking.'

At that, he laughed. 'You're right. I'm, sorry, my lady.' And he stood aside with a flourish.

'Why, thank you, my liege,' I said graciously as I passed him, then added, 'I'm not really a lady.' But when I turned to see if he was still smiling, he had already gone.

Actual-Lady Caroline and the man had disappeared as well, meaning I couldn't get another glance to capture her properly. Though I've been thinking of her since, or rather, of that feeling Charlie talked about. Of losing yourself – in someone's eyes or breath or whatever. I only ever get that when I'm writing. Mummy says love is about sensible choices and romance is for novels and morons (with sex, I suspect, being about hygiene and efficiency) but I do hope she's wrong.

I also hope Charlie has forgotten about the gin and obliteration as I'm actually rather tired. Soho time is rather unlike Surbiton's – everything starts so much later, and yet there is still work to be got up for. How she manages it I do not know. I am reminded of that poem by Edna St. Vincent Millay, about the beauty of a candle burning at both ends. I think it sums up Charlie. She does burn so terribly brightly, without once guttering – at least not until today.

I just hope she can rekindle her flame, and has enough wick left to get through this.

SUNDAY
6 MARCH

9 A.M.
Oh.

11 A.M.
Oh dear. I have what I believe is referred to as a hangover. Or, as Rollo put it when I stumbled into the kitchen for aspirin, tea, sympathy: I have cashed a cheque my liver cannot pay.

Why on earth do people do it? Drink, I mean? This is quite the vilest feeling I have ever experienced, bar the one time Mummy relented and let me have an ice-cream cone from a van in Aberystwyth and I was sick eleven times, including once on my own shoes and once on a lady's in the chemist's.

On the bright side, I can remember almost nothing about last night, other than we were somewhere called the Colony. Also, there is nothing to do today so I am free to lie in bed, feel sorry for myself and drink copious coffee, which is what Rollo prescribed (along with a raw egg, but I am ignoring that bit).

11.10 A.M.

And possibly work out why I didn't think to get undressed or brush my teeth, but I did manage to put a bucket next to the bed.

3 P.M.

Oh, dear God.

On the back of six espressos and a bacon sandwich (Rollo is surprisingly fatherly in this respect, although not, I realise, much like my own father, who would have been barred from such ministries by Mummy) I have remembered some things about last night.

I'll start with the good things. To wit: the Colony Room Club itself, which is a private members' bar on Dean Street.

'But I'm not a member,' I recall saying.

'Not a problem,' said Charlie. 'Just look interesting and be interesting and she'll let you in.'

I wasn't sure I did or was, but I followed her lead.

'Walk in with confidence,' she said.

'But—'

'Do it, or she'll slaughter you.' She being the owner – a magnificent pug of a woman whom Charlie says created the place from scratch. 'She was forced to leave home, being Sapphic herself,' she continued. 'Or at the very least, *versatile*. So she created her own.'

'Her own colony!' I said, getting it.

'Exactly,' said Charlie, to my delight.

And it was delight, at least at first: dark as an underground burrow, to the point that I knew when we left I would emerge blinking into the light like a mole on a June morning. But that was later; right then I was drinking gin slings in the centre of something sweaty and electric; its filthy ceiling ricocheting the clink of glasses; its walls thumping, catching barked laughter, secrets stage-whispered into cupped ears, the rise and fall of a soprano demonstrating an aria from a show at the ENO, whence she'd just jumped off stage. And elsewhere there were artists, actors, gangsters even – all levelled, somehow, by the wonder that is Soho, and the Colony.

'That's Lucian,' said Charlie, pointing out a dark-haired, slightly cadaverous chap with a piercing stare and an arresting girlfriend. 'And next to him is Francis Bacon.'

'Eggs!' I said. 'Rollo has a portrait of his on the landing, and a sketch in the downstairs lav. The woman with a hole in her head? Says it'll be worth a fortune one day.'

Charlie nodded. 'Hard to believe, isn't it— Oh!' she exclaimed suddenly. 'Come with me!'

And at that she grabbed my hand and dragged me through a crowd that parted as if it were the red sea and she Moses (there is a distinct advantage in being lofty and gorgeous) before coming to a halt a few feet away from a man one could only describe as Gatsby-esque. By which I mean, he looked like an advertisement: all flopping hair and open shirt and T. J. Eckleburg eyes.

'Alan Barrow,' she informed me. 'Actor, philanthropist and definitely N. S. I. T.'

'N. S. I. T.?' I repeated.

'Not Safe In Taxis,' she explained, and then immediately draped herself around him.

I flinched, but within minutes he had bought us both more gins, and after that, I am sorry to say, it is all reduced to flashes:

Someone dancing on a table, before being told to get down or have their bottom spanked, and Francis offering to do it.

Someone else dancing with a dog.

Valentine spying us and begging Alan to star in his next production of *Hamlet*.

Alan offering to show Charlie his apartment on Archer Street.

Valentine protesting but Charlie insisting she was a big girl, and demanding to prove it by arm wrestling (declined).

A gallant Valentine delivering me to the door, Rollo somehow managing to get me up to my room and into my bed, thankfully not undressing me, but leaving a glass of water and the bucket.

So: mystery solved. Although God knows if Charlie is even home yet. She wasn't when I had to go to the bathroom to reacquaint the bacon sandwich with the outside world; her bed is unslept in, so I can only assume she stayed at Alan's. About which I feel horribly guilty. If he is not safe in taxis, what is he like in his own flat? I wish I hadn't drunk the gins. I wish I'd insisted she'd come home with me. I wish—

Oh! There go the stairs. Perhaps that is her now? Please let it be so!

3.05 P.M.

It was not her. It was Ted, with another coffee and a tall glass of water, as he'd heard me being sick and thought I might need it. He is being terribly kind since the whole Charlie naked debacle. I must find a way to repay him somehow.

Oh. I hear the stairs again. I suspect Rollo with more bacon. Or perhaps a steamed pudding with syrup, like Mummy sometimes made on a Sunday.

Or is that wishful thinking?

3.10 P.M.

It was wishful thinking. There is no bacon or steamed pudding. There is, however – and thankfully – Charlie, whose opening greeting was, 'Get the bloody hell up, Arbuthnot, darling.'

'Why?' I protested, pulling the eiderdown tighter. 'And more importantly, where have you been?'

'Doesn't matter,' she said. 'Come on, up. I have to be at Aster's for high tea at half-four, and the way my head feels, I'll need back-up.'

'Aster?' I asked, as I hauled myself upright (there is no arguing with Charlie I have realised, even if I weren't in a 'yes' mode).

'Mother's ex-best friend. Long story. Called her "Aunt" since I was small.' (She tends to scatter-gun when she is in a hurry.)

I looked down at last night's dress – presentable when I left yesterday, now irreparably creased, stinking of cigarettes and with a smear of something unidentifiable across the chest. 'I've nothing to wear,' I said.

She put her hands on her hips; quite the mother when she wanted to be. 'Come with me,' she instructed.

I did, and in seconds was face to face with a glorious off-white Givenchy.

'It's the only thing I have from before,' she explained. 'Everything else I've scavenged or blagged, or made myself.'

'Why keep this one?' I asked, as I held it up against myself.

'Oh, well, I was wearing it. When I bolted from the deb hoo-hah. Well, this and a mink coat, but I had to sell that to pay for the last time the boiler died. Hideous, isn't it?'

'It's beautiful. But, not very . . .' Practical? 'You.'

She laughed. 'The worst thing was, everyone looked the same. All fourteen hundred and forty-two of us. Well, fourteen hundred and forty-one in the end, I suppose, once I'd bolted.'

I jinked at the bigness of it. 'And where were you running *to*?' I asked, cautiously.

'I had no idea,' she admitted. 'Luckily, I bumped into Aunt Panth—'

'Panth!' I exclaimed. 'I've met her. In Pennington's.'

'Well, she's one of Aster's sisters – there are three. And Val's cousin. Panth's not her real name of course. Anyway, not the point.' She was scatter-gunning again. 'She picked me up – literally, I'd fallen in a heap on the floor – and took me straight to Aster's until it all calmed down. Which it didn't; it made Mummy worse. But then Valentine came up with this place. Luckily. I think Cal and I would have killed each other.'

'Cal? Is that Aster's son?'

She snorted. 'God, no. Cal is Panth's boy. Adopted. Also a long story. Now, chop-chop.' She snatched away the dress. 'On second thoughts, it's not at all "high tea at Aster's". Here.' She handed me a navy shift – chic and mini on her; knee-length on me, but do-able. 'Keep it,' she added. 'I'll alter it when I have the time.'

'Do you regret the deb thing?' I asked as she pinned my hair up expertly.

'Not in the least – God, this could do with a chop as well. We should have done that last night. Again, another time.' She paused. 'Although I did miss out on the most glorious Sacher Torte. I haven't tasted proper chocolate gateau in years.' This accompanied by quite the most pitiful sigh. 'Right, you're done. And very well, if I say so myself. Now, give me ten minutes to sort myself out, then Marchmont Street, here we come!'

And it's been about fifteen, but I shall forgive her, as actually, in the absence of syrup pudding, I'm rather looking forward to fish paste sandwiches and heavy cake – Mummy's hallmarks of a good high tea.

10 P.M.

There are times I cannot quite believe how far I have come in such little time. Nor quite how fascinating the people by whom I am now surrounded:

1. Aster is *the* Aster Mannering, dress designer to Princess Margaret and portrait painter to anyone who's anyone.
2. Aster and Daphne – Charlie's mother – had some sort of falling-out before the war and haven't spoken since.

I hissed, 'About what?' when Aster left the room to answer the door.

'Aster refuses to say,' Charlie hissed back, 'and Mummy won't even have her name mentioned, so your guess is as good as mine.'

'Perhaps she rather fancied your father herself?' I tried.

Charlie snorted. 'I doubt it. For a start, I am told he was a dear but terribly cheese-faced. For a second start, let's just say Aster understands my predicament with Fitz. Such a horrible shame about Topaz.' She petered off at this point and I didn't dare question her further, but a little digging later (I grilled Rollo) unearthed that this was bright young thing Topaz Attlesey, possible spy, definite icon, now sadly deceased.

3. Aster's three sisters are all as fascinating as she. Panth, of course, is also *the* Panther Mannering (though I suppose it would hard to find another Panther anywhere), the MP who once wrote a novel (a racy one at that, according to Aster); Marigold runs a farm in Essex with someone called Hugo; and Dinah is on a yacht sailing around the world. They are all very derring-do – saying yes to things, having adventures – and as such I am determined to meet all of them. Only, this may be compromised by my next point.
4. When Aster came back from the door she was accompanied by the Communist!

'You!' I said, reddening for some inexplicable reason.

'You!' he repeated, equally indignant though markedly less scarlet.

'You know Cal?' asked Charlie.

I composed myself. 'Yes— well, no. I know a tiresome communist who is always getting in my way. But I rather thought he lived in the East End, or somewhere.'

At this, Charlie snorted.

Aster sighed. 'I do wish you'd stop that nonsense,' she said, clipping him with her copy of the *Guardian*. 'Pretending to be destitute.'

'I wasn't pretending anything,' he snapped. 'She never asked.'

'I didn't think I needed to,' I retorted.

'Children, children,' chastised Aster. 'At least save the fighting for the French or wherever it is you youngsters cavort these days.'

'Oh, he won't go in,' said Charlie. 'A protest against the fact they serve wine not beer.'

'There's a surprise,' said Aster. She turned to her nephew. 'What *don't* you protest, darling boy?'

He ignored her obvious affection. 'At least someone's trying to change things,' he said, and at that, slumped on a sleek settee, which somehow matched Aster – all angles and elegance.

> 5. High tea in Charlie's circles is quite unlike Surbiton's version. There is no heavy cake. There is no heavy anything, still less fish paste from a jar, which, when I asked about its whereabouts, Aster actually patted my arm and called me a 'darling'. And usually I would have minded the tone, which was quite Aunt Barbara-ish, but Aster somehow makes 'brusque' seem appealing. Possibly also aided by the actual components of high tea, which were sticky-sweet baklava from the Greek bakery on Poland Street, rose-scented

madeleines from Maison Bertaux, and
a bottle of sherry, which I had thought
to refuse, given last night's debacle,
but she said would be 'hair of the dog'
and Charlie seemed quite revived by hers
and then there's the whole 'yes' thing, so I
tried it, and it worked almost as well as the
coffee and bacon. So revived was I, in fact,
that I decided then and there that Aster
must become Ted's benefactor, or at
least his art teacher, and told her so.

'You know about Ted?' demanded Charlie.

'I do,' I said. 'I have seen it all!' This accompanied by much knowing glancing at her chest area.

'Well, it all had to come out at some point, I suppose,' she said. 'No pun intended. But don't blame me if he gets upset.'

'Why should he be upset?' asked Aster.

'He's embarrassed, I think,' I said. 'Doesn't want help or handouts.'

'Unlike some.' Charlie stared pointedly at Cal.

Cal scowled. Aster ignored them both. 'You really are a "fixer", aren't you?' she said to me. 'Oh – I've heard about the cleaning,' she added, when I went to protest. 'Well, perhaps I shall come round and see if he's all that.'

I am choosing to see the 'fixer' thing as a compliment,

because it is precisely what I intended, isn't it? In any case, I shan't tell Ted; Charlie says it will only panic him. She also said I should go easy on the coffee, and possibly the sherry as well, as apparently I am far more lightweight than she had anticipated.

Given the queasiness that besets me again, I suspect she is right.

SUNDAY 27 MARCH

10 A.M.
Sunday, and lunch at Magnolia Road looms large and menacing, not aided by the fact that there has been little sign of Charlie for two weeks. If I were to guess, I would say she is spending her nights at Alan Barrow's apartment, but it *is* only a guess as, on the rare occasions I have spotted her, she is in too much of a rush – fetching clean knickers, throwing out her post – to get any sense out of her. As long as she's turning up for work, I suppose it's okay. Although I must say, I miss her, even in somewhere as bustling as Soho. Rollo is company in the day, yes – and the most marvellous company at that. He is funny, kind, and quite the raconteur. But he does have a tendency to dash off at any and all invitations and spends most evenings with Val in any case. And Ted is too busy with his nudes to play backgammon or Scrabble, plus I have a terrible suspicion spelling isn't his strong point; Rollo says he barely went to school.

Perhaps she'll be back by the time I return. Today is her day off, after all, and she surely can't spend all that time doing whatever it is they are doing – being 'versatile', as she put it, I assume. A term that only serves to remind me how unschooled I am in love, or at least 'relations', despite being a Londoner for nearly two months now. At least that will please Mummy, if nothing else does.

7 P.M.

The news from Surbiton:

1. Mrs Peabody has had a radical haircut and it does not do anything for her face, which Mummy says is too porcine for a permanent wave.
2. Julian has passed his eleven plus with flying colours. This is in no way a surprise, though I suspect whichever grammar he is headed to will regret not having some kind of personality test as well.
3. In stark contrast, Nigel Pickering has been in hospital with a nostril-related incident again, this time with a tin soldier. John said perhaps they should seal the things up, but Mummy said she had already suggested this and been given quite the look. And Daddy said did I remember when I thought buttocks were called nostrils? Which I said I didn't

(I did) and changed the subject to the merits of bread sauce (if there is one thing I miss about Surbiton, it is Mummy's cooking).

Also, Gloria wants to name the baby 'Tallulah' if it's a girl, a fact that has Mummy enraged, as she says it is far too American. I said she'd already dismissed 'Sharon' as being 'common' and 'Clementine' as having 'notions', i.e. ideas above its station, so where did America fit in? And she said America is *both* common and has 'notions'. I asked what she did consider a good name for a girl in that case. She said, 'Margaret.' I said they were hardly going to call the baby after me, and John said, 'What, Accident Arbuthnot?' and then the usual row ensued, with kicking.

I did not avail them of my news, other than I can now type at thirty words per minute, which Daddy says is 'impressive', though I know he is being kind, as Mummy pointed out that even Mrs Peabody can do sixty, and she is compromised by gout in her left hand and the new haircut (how bad can it be?).

Worse, when I got back, Charlie was still nowhere to be seen. I suggested an advance party to Archer Street but Rollo insisted she'll be back when she's bored. 'They all get bored in the end,' he said, wistfully.

I didn't enquire further, as it felt too much of an intrusion. Though I do wonder at his story – he's obviously quite posh: went to Harrow, which is where he met Val, and yet verges on bankruptcy from what I can make out of the accounts. Perhaps it's the gambling. Mummy would be livid; there is nothing she detests more than squandered opportunity, and I am quite minded to agree.

Not that I am entirely like Mummy. If nothing else, today's naming debacle proved that. I rather like both 'Clementine' *and* 'Tallulah' and frankly, I wouldn't mind being American.

Though 'Sohovian' will do for now.

APRIL 1960

FRIDAY
1 APRIL

10 A.M.
Pinch, punch, first day of the month!

I would do it on Charlie, but she is still missing, presumed smitten; Ted is over at the French fixing a dicky urinal; and Rollo is feeling a bit peaky and didn't look at all pinchable, so I have sent him back to bed until he feels well enough to consume the soup I made last night (one of Mummy's creations – only chicken, but delicious with a hot roll. I had to ring to ask for the recipe, and then felt terrible when she seemed put out I merely wanted her for soup, so I asked what news, and immediately regretted it. Suffice to say it involved Gloria and her digestion).

I shall save my pinch-punching for whoever walks through the door of the shop first. There have been days of late when this might have taken hours, but the sun is already warming my new window display (it had not been updated since 1957, according to Ted, and even that was only because someone called Fish Stegley fell into it) and I feel that only good things can happen from now on. Adventures, yes. That is what I predict for spring!

11 P.M.

I am never making predictions again.

On the bright side, Charlie is back. On the other, well, let's just say I didn't expect to be pinch-punching minor aristocracy, nor arguing with Cal Mannering (if that is his name) over which hospital was closest – Univ or Guy's.

It was gone lunch (a delicious pastry from the Turkish cafe near Ham Yard) before the door of 27 Lexington Street began to jangle. I stood, primed then delighted as the door opened and a limb manifested before me, clad in a fitted wool jacket in a shade of light sage Mummy would describe as impractical but which I describe as 'to die for'.

'Pinch, punch, first day of the month!' I yelled in triumph as I grasped then batted the jacketed arm.

'What the devil?' demanded the owner of said arm.

I felt my face – quite heated with the excitement – chill and my stomach drop, as I realised the owner of the voice was Aster Mannering, all willowy five foot nine of her, who, once she'd shaken me off with some force, proceeded to glide into the dim fust of the shop (no vacuum cleaner has been manufactured that can handle Rollo's accumulated filth; he says after a few years it just cannot get any worse) like an angel into the bowels of hell.

'One can't pinch-punch after noon,' she said with precision. 'Did no one teach you that?'

'I—' I began, but was stoppered up as I felt my own arm being pinched and then the toe of a boot aimed at my shin.

'A pinch and a kick for being so quick,' said Cal, who had followed Aster into the shop, quite the stray dog with his matted hair and battered Macintosh.

'Ow!' I complained, trying not to limp as I shut the door firmly behind them. 'One can't pinch-punch after noon!' I added. 'Did no one teach you that?'

Cal smiled – a wry thing that revealed a dimple in his right cheek I'd not seen before. I caught myself staring and had to force myself to focus on Aster, who was casting a critical eye over the latest paperbacks with the intensity of Mummy at Pickering's when the tomatoes are past their prime.

'I suppose Charlie is still in bed?' she said, picking up a Colin MacInnes and reading the blurb.

'I . . .' I snatched at an answer. 'Well, she might be?'

At that, Aster's eyes met mine finally. 'Is she or isn't she?'

'Honestly, I don't know,' I found myself saying. 'She went to visit Alan Barrow's flat weeks ago and has barely been seen since.'

Aster's expression at this was unreadable. Her feelings were not. 'That girl is a magnet for disaster,' she declared. 'And this is the latest. Very well, this Ted fellow. Is he in?'

'In the attic,' I said, quickly. 'I heard someone come in the back way an hour ago, so it's either him or a burglar. Rollo's in bed. Dicky tummy, I think.'

'Self-inflicted, no doubt,' said Aster, then sighed. 'So, I'll go up and see if this chap is worth anything, shall I?'

'I... Hadn't I better warn him?' I tried.

'Oh, no,' said Aster. 'I find surprise quite the best way to deal with these things.' And at this, she winked, and I found my embarrassment at the pinching dissipate a little.

The next thing I knew, Cal and I were alone in the shop, the air fat with static and the throaty sound of Nina Simone coming from Rollo's gramophone in the corner.

'Nice pipes,' he said. 'Though I'm more of a Pete Seeger man, myself.'

His lexicon seemed to veer from Bow to Chelsea in a single sentence. He is quite the mystery. Though in Soho, that is nothing unusual.

'You like jazz?' he said as he flicked through the collection of records.

'Oh, God, no.' I found my voice. 'It's either frantic and rackety or meandering and inexplicable.'

He laughed, and I felt as if an invisible hand had patted me on the back.

'Anyway, jazz is dead,' I continued. 'Elvis is King now, isn't he?'

He shrugged, and the hand snapped back. 'If that's your bag. But I suppose it would be, wouldn't it? Where are you from again? Surbiton?'

I bristled. 'What's that got to do with anything?'

He ignored me. 'What is all this?' he asked then, gesturing around him.

'What do you mean?' My voice was hard then, flinty.

'Why are you *here*, is what I mean. Lodging above a shop, playing at poverty—'

'I'm not playing at anything.'

'You could go home if you wanted, at any time.'

I steeled myself. 'And so could you.'

I could tell he was about to say something else sharp and smart when a terrific thump interrupted us – something leaden falling on the floor above.

'What the hell?' we both said, and looked at each other. Then, without even bothering to lock the door, we ran pell-mell up the stairs, scanning the kitchen, sitting room, then, finally finding the cause of the 'whomp' lying on the floor of his bedroom: Rollo, white as a sheet and clutching his stomach.

Aster and a red-faced Ted appeared just seconds later.

'This isn't drink,' said Aster, ashen herself. 'Nor something funny he's eaten. Call the hospital, will you?' This, to Ted.

But Rollo yelled. 'No hospital!'

'Rowland, I—'

'No!' he managed to insist. 'Val. Just . . . get Val.'

Aster, unbelievably, conceded. 'You two run to the Pippin; Ted and I will get him back into bed.'

We burst onto Lexington Street like pigeon peas from a shooting straw. 'He won't be at the Pippin,' I said, grabbing Cal as he made to turn left. 'Not yet.'

'Where, then?' Cal looked at distraught as I felt, and I warmed to him slightly again.

I checked my watch – just gone two. 'The French,' I said.

I was right as well. He was arguing at the bar with a man with one eye.

'Val?' I said. (Cal had stayed outside; not even dire illness can sway him from his boycott apparently.)

He turned, saw my face, and said, 'Rollo?'

Was this a frequent occurrence? I wondered. And if so, what would happen if none of us had been there? I didn't get a chance to ask either question, as Val grabbed his coat, left his drink on the counter, where it was eagerly seized by the one-eyed man, and dashed back to Pennington's, Cal and I silent in pursuit.

By the time we got back, Rollo was propped up in bed with a flannel on his forehead, Ted trying to feed him tea, and Val holding his hand.

'I wish you wouldn't keep scaring us,' said Val.

'I'm sorry,' replied Rollo, his voice weak and reedy – not Rollo-like at all.

'Are you . . .' I turned to Val. 'Is he all right?'

'I *can* speak for myself,' Rollo said. 'I'm fine. It's nothing. A bit of old gip, that's all.'

It wasn't nothing – *isn't* nothing. Gloria said the same when she was sick on the hydrangeas on Bonfire Night and then a month later announced she was pregnant. And while *that* is obviously impossible in this case, something untoward is up. But what, exactly, was clearly not going to come out today. Not least because that was the moment Aster, who had been absent from the bedside scene, arrived, hauling a disconsolate Charlie with her.

'Rollo!' Charlie sobbed, and flung herself across him, spilling tea in the process, and dislodging the flannel, which slipped down his face so as to gag him entirely.

'Oh, for heaven's sake,' said Aster, snatching the thing away. 'Stop the histrionics and do something useful.'

Charlie hauled herself up, her face a smear of mascara and lipstick, but apparently blank of ideas as to what this might be.

'Kettle,' I prompted. 'I'll help.'

'Where have you been?' I asked as I tipped Bath Olivers onto a chipped plate.

'Where do you think?'

I went to open my mouth but Charlie shook her head. 'Please don't start.' She opened the refrigerator, sniffed the milk out of habit, and tipped it into a Ravilious jug. 'I know this is some sort of punishment on me for . . . well, everything.'

I frowned. 'I don't think that's how it works,' I said. 'It's just . . . rotten luck.'

Charlie looked at me, her face bleak and pleading. 'He will be all right, won't he?'

I paused. 'Of course.' Then I hugged her, swift and tight. 'It's good to see you,' I said.

That, at least, wasn't a lie.

'And you,' she said back. 'And you.'

*

Cal and Aster scattered not long after, and Ted went back to the attic, though not without berating me for saying anything about his paintings in the first place.

'But isn't she going to help you?' I asked.

'Yes, but—'

'Then, frankly, I don't see the problem.'

Normally I would have apologised, would have felt sorry for him and myself, but I was too discombobulated by Rollo, by Charlie, and by Cal as well. I can't work out if he likes me or loathes me, and in either case, why.

And, more to the point, I can't tell if I like or loathe him. I just know I feel his presence in a way that's almost electric. But then I felt like that about Deborah Petticoat, who was president of chess club and first violin in the school orchestra, and that turned out to be mostly fear, so who knows what this might be? Not I. And I am too tired to fathom it now.

What a day. I pray tomorrow is at the very least less adventurous.

SATURDAY
2 APRIL

3 P.M.

If I felt discombobulated yesterday, then today it is as if I have been spun too fast on a child's roundabout and am staggering across the playground trying to right myself.

This time, it is Charlie and the bath. Or rather Charlie in the bath. Or, to be exact about it, Charlie and I in the bath. And yes, at the same time. And the strangest thing of all is that, to Charlie, at least, this wasn't in the least bit strange. I am going to capture it now to see if, on reading, it is perhaps less incredible than it felt at the time.

To wit: after the events of yesterday, I awoke in a state of soreness and exhaustion – my very bones seemed to ache, for no reason other than the shock of it all, I suppose. So, Ted having fixed the hot water boiler only two days ago, and Rollo insisting I have a day off to recover, I decided to indulge in a long, morning bath – the kind with bubbles, and lavender-scented salts (and a telling-off from Mummy afterwards when I leave a violet-stained ring around the enamel). I had only been in there minutes, had only closed my eyes seconds ago, when I heard the door to the bathroom open and the words, 'Room for a little one?' (Clearly Ted hadn't yet fixed the lock.)

I opened my eyes wide and sloshed upright (only making a difficult situation worse), to see Charlie about to unbelt her paisley robe.

I clamped my hands over my breasts. 'What are you doing?'

'Well, you've clearly had all the hot water, and I need a soak.' Her robe was unbelted and lying in a heap on the floor by now. I had as full and frank a view of Charlie as Ted must have done, and I can certainly see why he'd want to paint her. 'Budge up, won't you?'

'I... But...'

She smiled. 'Don't be such a prude.' By this point she was already one leg in. 'And if you're worried I might jump you, I can assure you – you're not my type.'

She sat down, the tips of her toes touching mine, her ample breasts floating on the surface like unleashed blancmange, and the water threatening to slop over the edges with every ripple. I pulled my feet up to my buttocks and prayed the bubbles would hide the worst of me.

'Anyway,' she continued, oblivious to my discomfort. 'I'm done with schoolgirl crushes, aren't you?'

'I... well,' I began. Though in truth, I've never had one: another strand of life I seem to have failed at. Though I did have a thing for our vicar, Reverend Elsom, aged about ten (enthusiastic about everything from poetry to pigeons; entirely unobtainable, only adding to the romance) and he had a substantial moustache, which would have rendered him a menace in Mummy's eyes, quite aside from being two decades older. 'I suppose so,' I managed in the end. Though I didn't think he was quite on the same scale of parental unacceptability (moustache notwithstanding), nor did I believe for a second that Fitz had been nothing more than a crush.

'Pass me the sponge, would you?' she asked.

I did so, and wondered how Charlie manages to be so unembarrassed by, well, flesh. Perhaps it is growing up with so many siblings. Or communal baths at boarding school. In any case, I felt awkward. Tawdry, or, worse, childlike by comparison to her brilliance, her womanliness.

As if on cue, she announced, 'Lucian once said I had the best tits in London.'

I jinked. 'How did he even see them?'

'Fancy dress party of Rollo's. I came as Venus de Milo, got a little tipsy and stripped. Everyone did. It wasn't sexual in the slightest. Just . . . free.'

I had never felt further from Surbiton. Imagine Aunt Barbara doing this at the golf club! 'He's probably right,' I said, trying not to stare, though this was difficult, given their size and proximity.

'Oh, you are a darling.' I must have subconsciously covered my own at that point as she added, 'Yours are lovely.'

'Really?' I said, and glanced down. 'I rather hate them.

They're awfully small, and one is crooked.'

'Everyone's are crooked. Mine included. And I've never met a man – or woman – who minded.'

I smiled, beginning to settle into this proximity. 'Do you think men worry?' I asked then. 'About their ... you know.'

'All the time,' she said, matter of fact. 'Apparently Fitzgerald got Hemingway to check his in the lav at Les Deux Magots.'

'Oh. And ...?'

She frowned. 'Hemingway was not at all reassuring. Cigarette?' She reached over the side of the tub for her packet of slims and lighter.

'No, thanks,' I said.

'You are sensible. It's a terrible expense.'

'Also bad for your teeth,' I said, remembering Daddy's lectures. 'It causes gum disease, halitosis; they can fall out even.'

Charlie put down the packet. 'Thanks for that. I feel quite revolting.'

'Sorry,' I said.

She smiled and shook her head. 'No, you're right. It's a bad habit, Cal is always telling me so.'

I found myself pinking at the mention of him, blustered to cover it. 'He's an odd fellow, isn't he?'

'Cal? I suppose so. An Angry Young Man in the Osborne mould. Railing against the very existence of the upper classes, when he's one of them.'

'Not originally,' I said, quickly.

'Well, no. But adoptively, so as good as. And he still thinks he's Jimmy Porter, when really he's closer to the Duke of Kent now.'

I didn't think it was the same at all – being born into the aristocracy compared to finding oneself in it – but didn't correct her. Instead I said, 'I don't know the Duke of Kent.'

'Really?' asked Charlie. 'I thought everyone did. Anyway, he fights the good fight – Cal, I mean. Or tries to. Got injured in the Notting Hill riots. Stood on myriad picket lines. But he sleeps at Aster's when it suits him and still takes Panth's handouts. So he's quite the hypocrite if you ask me.'

I changed the subject. 'Thank heaven Aster found you yesterday.'

'Well, quite. Poor Rollo, he does suffer with his tummy.'

I frowned. 'This has happened before?'

'Not as bad as this, but he's had gripe since I moved in two years ago. It's all that rich food the papers pays him to eat, I suppose. He thinks it's cheaper to live like that, eating like a church mouse in between, but it's hardly cheap if you end up off work. Not that he pays himself, anyway.'

'He doesn't pay himself?' I was aghast.

'Well, if he does, it's hard to tell where it comes from or goes. This place' – she looked up at the cracked coving, the patchy plaster – 'is a wreck. Aster has offered to sub him, but he won't take her money.'

'Aster seems so . . . kind,' I went on, 'and sensible. I don't understand how she and your mother can have fallen out so badly.'

Charlie shrugged, sending another slosh of water slopping onto the floor. 'My mother can hold a grudge for decades, it seems. I'm not sure who she hates more, in fact – me or Aster. Anyway, it's not uncommon. Rollo still isn't speaking to some chap after a row in 1925 over a plate of beans.'

'I don't think this is over a plate of beans,' I said.

'Well, no.' She went quiet at that, sort of far-awayish.

I segued again. 'So, are you going to stay at Alan's again soon?'

She snapped back. 'Alan? Oh, no. He's gone off to Hollywood.' She mustered, smiled. 'Says he's going to get me into films! I think I'll have more chance in films than theatre. You can do all sorts of things with camera angles to make people look smaller.'

I wasn't sure you could do anything with cameras to correct her terrible pronunciation or the fact she barely managed to remember a page of lines (I had been running them with her for weeks before the Alan shenanigans) but said nothing.

'Did you . . . sleep with him?' I asked.

She looked at me then. 'Would you think terribly of me if I said yes?'

I shook my head.

'Yes, then.'

'And was it . . . all right?' I knew the mechanics but had

no idea, still, what it might feel like. Physically and in the emotional sense.

She frowned. 'The run up's all right. The kissing, I mean – although it's so very scratchy with a man. And he knew what he was doing down there with his hands, I suppose. Just . . .' She trailed off.

'Does it hurt?' I pressed.

'A little bit. Mostly it just feels very . . . full. And so terribly energetic – like a games lesson. I kept expecting Miss Spiggot to pipe up, "Catch the ball, Pakenham!" Then there was a sort of victory cheer and he rolled off leaving me a bit, well, messy.'

'Didn't he use a . . .' God, what was the right word for it? 'Sheath?'

She shook her head. 'Oh, no. Alan says they're uncomfortable and anyway, I'd only just had my monthly so it would be impossible to get pregnant.'

I didn't think it worked like that, but didn't dare say so. I'm sure she'll be fine anyway, given it was just the once.

If it was just the once.

'Heavens, I am quite the prune.' Charlie inspected raisined fingers, then stood in a whoosh, obvious to the water cascading everywhere. 'Come on. Coffee at the Lorelei. My treat.'

I tried not to stare at, well, that, whilst assembling an air of nonchalance (this was a feat beyond me right now, but I suppose I shall perfect it, like everything else. And truthfully, I had quite liked the sisterly feeling of it all). 'I'll be out in a moment,' I promised.

She grinned, snatched up her damp towel from the floor, then departed, leaving me to muse on how beautiful she is, even wet from the bath— no, *especially* wet from the bath; I must perfect that as well, rather than the bedraggled dog I tend to resemble.

I confess I tried to think of it then – doing *you know what* with a woman. Not the mechanics of it (heaven knows how that works) as much as a general impression. I was almost disappointed to feel nothing. Though when I tried it with Cal in my head the effect was much the same.

Perhaps I am just not a sexual being. How disappointing that would be. Although possibly not for Mummy, who seems to regard it as being fraught with as much peril as fire-eating or taming tigers. Oh! I have remembered a line from *I Capture the Castle* – that one about tigers, all tamed and shabby. It's from a poem originally, I think. That is what Surbiton is to me – a sad little circus of tamed and shabby animals. Whereas this – with its shared baths, and naked painting and, and, and everything – is the Greatest Show on Earth! And here I am, privileged with a ringside seat, when I could be up on the trapeze myself, if only I remembered those excellent 'yes'es. Well, I shall hold on to that, and embrace whatever Soho has to offer me, including my own body, however un-Charlie-like it is.

And sex?

Well, perhaps I shall embrace that as well.

3.05 P.M.
Although probably best to start with a kiss.

MONDAY
11 APRIL

10 A.M.
There has been no kissing as yet, but I am doing well on embracing my body, quite literally (though I am not going to detail *that* in here), and metaphorically, i.e. I am going to do something with my hair, finally. I asked after a reputable salon but Charlie says she is quite au fait with scissors – she does both Rollo and Ted – and will see to me later this week, saving me a good twelve bob for the kitty. Oh, yes, I forgot to document that I have started an anonymous kitty for milk, bread, tea and suchlike; currently it is mostly me paying in, and doing the shopping, but I have high hopes for the others once they realise the sense of it. And in their own way, they are all turning over new leaves for spring:

> – Rollo is being tougher on money, i.e. making sure customers pay their bills (preferably on time but at all would be good), and not taking in any blaggers. This after some poet called George Viceroy knocked on the door after

closing and Rollo hid behind The Victorians, forbidding me to let him in.

'Last time he dropped by he stayed for six months,' he admitted.

'Did he pay rent?' I asked.

At this, Rollo looked sheepish, and I told him he must smarten up his attitude to money, hence the above.

> – Ted has started his lessons with Aster, which seem to be going well. She has taken him to the Royal Academy today, apparently aghast that the only art he has been exposed to this far is Rollo's eclectic collection, or on the walls of the pubs and clubs that he does odd jobs for.

'One cannot learn from hideous prints of dogs playing billiards,' she declared as she marched him off down Lexington Street not ten minutes ago.

> – Charlie has an audition for somewhere other than the Pippin. 'Just until Alan gets in touch,' she says, though it has been two weeks and she's heard not a dicky bird. This job – as Eliza Doolittle – isn't a given either. When she plays herself, she is mesmerising, but when she tries

to be anyone else she is stilted and difficult, and her cockney accent is unbearable.

'Teach me!' she begged when I suggested she sounded more American than Bow Bells.

'How common do you think I am?' I asked.

'Ted then.' She turned to him, but he looked suitably bruised too.

'How about Cal?' I said then. 'Wasn't he born in Aldgate?'

Which is why he is now ensconced in Charlie's bedroom, both of them sounding out 'How now, brown cow?' endlessly and appallingly. I predict this will not end well for either of them.

7 P.M.

I was right. Within the hour, Cal had been ejected and came clattering downstairs sounding off about 'toffs' and 'copycats'.

'At least she's looking for work,' I pointed out.

'What's that supposed to mean?' snapped Cal, harder than I expected at the time. Though on reflection I deserved it.

'I just mean . . . well . . .' I was flustered and it showed. 'I don't suppose you get paid much for selling the whatsit news—'

'*The Worker*,' he corrected.

'Exactly,' I said, the irony not lost on me. 'And as you're so keen to defend workers' rights, wouldn't it be good to have some of your own to defend?' I was quite proud of that.

Cal, though, looked as sheepish as Rollo had been. 'Doing what?' he asked.

'I don't know. Look in the cabinet outside Armitage's. Don't they post jobs?'

He snorted. 'Not for the kind I'm not willing to do.'

Rollo guffawed at that. 'Sweet child,' he said.

I ignored him, and my pinking cheeks. 'Can you play an instrument?' I suggested. 'There are queues of men outside the Musicians Union on Archer Street every morning.'

'Not a note,' admitted Cal. 'Honestly, I'm good at one thing: protesting.'

'You'll be going on the march, then?' said Rollo.

'What march?' We both turned to him.

'Aldermaston. Against nuclear weapons?'

'CND?' He pulled a face. 'Not likely. They're all weirdies and beardies. Privileged. Bourgeois.' The latter spat out like tricky pips from a tangerine.

Rollo sighed. 'Well, someone has to do something. There won't be a world to fight for if they don't.' At that he swept off – to the French, no doubt – leaving Cal and I to man (or woman) the tills.

'He has a point,' I said. 'About nuclear weapons.'

Cal sighed. 'Panther would agree.'

'Your mother?' I said without thinking.

'No,' he snapped, then steadied himself, adding quietly, 'my mum's dead, isn't she.'

'I'm sorry,' I said. 'I don't know what I was thinking.'

He sighed. 'It's fine. Panther and Freddy, well, they adopted us, didn't they. I mean – we were evacuated there first, me and my brother, Jack, and my mum. Only, she never made it, so when the war was over and nobody come for us . . . Well, Panther asked if we wanted to stay. And, being, what? All of four? Five? We said yes. And they're great, don't get me wrong, but . . .' He trailed off then.

'What about your father?' I said, carefully.

Cal stared at me, and for a second I thought he might lash out again, but in the end he just shrugged. 'No idea. Don't even know his name.'

My heart clenched for him. 'You've not asked Panther?'

He shook his head. 'Jack says we're better off without. Says he must be a nobody, so what's the gain?'

'And you?'

He shrugged again. 'I don't know, do I. Maybe he is nobody.'

'Or maybe he's *somebody*.' The words came out before I could stop them.

Cal stared again. 'Maybe,' he said.

And for a second, just for a second, the air was electric again. Then Charlie stamped in and, giving Cal a hard stare, demanded I come up at once for my haircut. I said perhaps now wasn't the time, given the shop (and her mood; I didn't say that bit) but she said Cal could just as easily mind the till as I, given the lack of customers, and it was now or never, so I took now.

Reader (i.e. future me), I regret it. My hair is shorn short as a boy's – shorter than Cal's even, which he pointed out with relish. I said, trying to be polite, that it was rather 'unexpected'. Charlie said hardly, and that I'd asked for Jean Seberg and so Jean Seberg I had got.

'Simmons!' I yelled. 'Jean Simmons, not Jean Seberg!'

'Oh,' said Charlie. 'Not from *Bonjour Tristesse*, then.'

'No!' I wailed. 'From *Great Expectations* and . . . and *Guys and Dolls*!'

Cal was crying with laughter by now, but Charlie blanched, which is quite unlike her.

'Never mind,' I said quickly, touching the fuzzy nape of my neck – soft as the stubble on a velveteen rabbit. 'I'm sure I'll get used to it.'

'I'm sure *I* won't,' said Cal.

'Well, good job no one asked you, then,' snapped Charlie, then turned back to me. 'It does suit you. You're terribly Cécile. Gamine as anything. Not like clodhopping me.'

I forced a smile – if you try long enough it becomes real; Daddy taught me that. And Rollo agrees with him. 'We're all smoke and mirrors, darling,' he tells me at frequent intervals.

'You're right,' I said. 'It's darling and I'm grateful.'

Anyway, I shall get used to it. I shall.

7.15 P.M.
And if not, there are hats.

TUESDAY 12 APRIL

11 A.M.
I *shall* get used it. Though this morning I awoke and thought a strange man was in our bathroom, and Rollo, having stayed out until heaven knows when last night, actually screamed when he saw me. Ted, however, seems unperturbed. So unperturbed that he has asked if he can paint me.

'With clothes?' I asked, hopefully.

Ted said nothing.

'But you've got Charlie for that,' I protested.

This time he managed to mumble something.

'Pardon?' I asked.

'I . . . well . . . Aster says she's . . . she's too good-looking.' He grimaced.

I bristled. 'Oh, well, then, yes! How could I refuse an offer like that?' If you had cut me, I would have bled sarcasm.

Ted reddened further, though it seemed impossible. 'I didn't mean . . . just that, with your hair, and . . . You . . . you're lovely,' he tried. 'Just not . . .'

I sighed. 'Not Charlie,' I finished for him.

He nodded, an air of sorrow to it that somehow infected me. I thought of the 'yes'es as well; this was an opportunity to be seized, wasn't it? To be a Topaz Mortmain, and, better, to help Ted, only ... something was stopping me.

'I'll think about it,' I offered. 'That's as much as I can give right now.'

He took it.

And I am thinking about it.

WEDNESDAY
13 APRIL

10 P.M.
I'm still thinking about it.

THURSDAY 14 APRIL

10 P.M.
I'm still thinking about it.

FRIDAY 15 APRIL

11 A.M.
I'm still thinking about it. Although Charlie says I *must* do it, as it means I'll be a) immortalised and b) worth a fortune one day. 'Look at Aster's portraits of my mother,' she said. 'Going for a mint in Christie's.'

I was about to raise again the spectre of Daphne and Aster but at that point the door went and she stamped off to answer it. (I have instigated a doorbell rota on top of the house kitty and it is her week. Ted is unamused as he has farthest to go, so I said I would trade him two days' washing up if he liked. He demurred.)

2 P.M.
It was Cal, who had been to see a man about a job off Oxford Street. It sounded hopeful when he described it – assistant to a literary agent (some friend of Aster's) but then he discovered that they handle Macmillan and several other leading Tories (or 'capitalist pigs' as he described them) and he

stormed out in protest.

'You really are rather good at that, at least,' Charlie pointed out as she headed off to her own audition.

'Good luck!' I called after her, but too late – she was already halfway down the stairs declaiming 'the rain in Spain' loudly and appallingly. I turned to Cal – lying on the moth-eaten chaise with his hands behind his head and his eyes ceiling-ward. 'She's right; you're born to it.'

He shifted so that he could look at me, cross-legged on the rug. 'I don't know what I'm born to, though, do I.'

A few days ago I might have jinked at this, but something – my haircut perhaps, in a reverse Samson-act – was giving me fresh confidence. 'So find out.'

'What?'

'Not "what", "pardon",' I said, automatically. 'And find out what you're born to. There are ways. Birth certificates and all that.' I recalled demanding mine for verification in a fit of indignation at not being an orphan or adopted – the very best heroines in children's books all seem to be.

'I . . . maybe.' He fixated again on the ceiling. 'I'm going on the march though.'

'Aldermaston?' I asked.

He nodded. 'Want to come?'

This time I did jink. 'I . . .'

'Oh, come on. What else are you going to do? Rearrange the larder?'

'Oh, ha ha,' I replied, tired of this particular witticism, which had been trolled out by Rollo several times of late. Tired of the implications as well – that I'm nothing but a suburban housewife in waiting. Well, that did it. 'I'm busy,' I said then. 'So the answer is no.'

'Busy doing what?' he demanded.

I jutted my chin. 'If you must know, Ted is painting me. Naked,' I added for effect.

'What— I mean, pardon— I mean, what?'

'You heard me. I'm *modelling* for Ted.' That word emphasised to give it heft beyond the 'sitting around getting chilly' I imagine it to be.

'I don't believe it. Naked? And you're just . . . going to let him?'

'Charlie does it,' I said.

He was upright by now, his hands jigging in the lap of his battered corduroys. 'Yes, but . . . you're not Charlie.'

Those words again. But did I care? 'That's exactly the point,' I snapped. 'And anyway, you . . . you can't stop me!'

He looked bemused, as well he might. 'I wasn't going to. Just . . .'

'Just what?' I challenged him.

'Nothing.' He shook his head. 'Good luck, then.'

'Where are you going?' I asked as he stood.

'Aldermaston,' he said.

Touché, I thought, as he departed without another word.

Only now, I regret letting him go, and to make matters worse, I shall have to be painted naked after all, if only to save face.

SUNDAY 17 APRIL

12 P.M.

Charlie, unsurprisingly, did not get the role of Eliza Doolittle. She said the director said she was 'too tall', but I suspect other factors at play.

'Perhaps you should stop claiming to be five foot eight on your curriculum vitae,' I suggested.

'If I do that,' she snapped, 'I won't even be allowed to cattle calls.'

Anyway, she is understudying Juliet for Val again. Romeo is a good six inches shorter than her, and thirty-seven, so God knows what the play will be like, but it's keeping her happy enough. She has gone to Aster's for Easter lunch as Cal is otherwise engaged with his marching, and Rollo has gone to the Colony for a more liquid meal. Thankfully I am excused Surbiton, as everyone has decamped to Gloria's parents in Wimbledon. Mummy will be beside herself – they have net curtains and a crocheted lavatory roll cover. Though she would be more outraged if she knew what I was about to get up to, i.e. modelling.

I am trying to be blithe about it, as if it is almost too boring to consider, which is how Charlie informed me I must look at it. Then I imagine telling Mummy and her having an immediate conniption fit and it all goes to pot. What passes for mundane in Soho is really quite astonishing.

Still, perhaps I shall feel pre-Raphaelite and Topaz-like once I get down to it. Plus, the quicker I get on, the quicker I can tick 'LIVE!' off my resolutions list, because if this isn't living, I don't know what is.

8 P.M.

Well, I might not know what living is, but I know it isn't sitting stark staring naked on a rickety chair, getting chilly bits while Ted complains my angles are 'tricky'. Charlie was right – it is almost too boring to consider. Instead of feeling pre-Raphaelite and Topaz-like I had the distinct air of being a cow being sized up for market and found wanting. Worse, I have to do it all again tomorrow. Honestly, I do not know how anyone stands it. But, as Ted points out, I have nothing better to do as the shop is shut for the bank holiday and there are only so many times I can rearrange the larder.

MONDAY
18 APRIL

8 P.M.

On the downside, when I left – more of this in a second – my portrait looked worryingly like the boy in *The Prince and the Pauper*. On the bright side, oh! What a day! And to think I nearly said no!

So, I had been sitting for what felt like an entire week, although Ted informs me was an hour and forty-three minutes, and still barely two in the afternoon, when I invented a sudden need for the lav as an excuse to move, but Ted was not forthcoming.

'Ten more minutes,' he said.

'I might have had an accident by then,' I threatened.

Ted remained unmoved, and so I deliberately fidgeted.

'Now it's another ten,' he said, 'because I've got to redo your armpit.'

'For heaven's sake,' I complained, 'who even wants to see my armpit?'

Ted ignored me entirely this time and I went back to counting cracks in the plaster when, as if summoned by my silent pleas, I heard the bell of the shop clang loudly.

'I'll go!' I jumped up.

'We're not even open!' Ted protested.

'What if it's a millionaire with a library to fill?' I suggested, wrapping myself in Charlie's voluminous bathrobe.

'It'll be Rollo forgetting his keys again,' muttered Ted. 'Just . . . hurry up.'

Well, I did hurry, and it wasn't Rollo (or a millionaire) – it was Cal, red-faced and breathless, and grinning.

'The march is over, then?' I said, leaning as casually as one can against a doorframe when one is wearing bedwear on a Sunday in Soho.

'That's just it!' he said. 'It's still going. We've filled Trafalgar Square; it's really something.' At this, he grasped my hand. 'You have to come!'

I stared at my hand, as did he and dropped it immediately. But the sensation remained, seemed to glow almost. I folded my arms in case he could see. 'I'm hardly dressed for it.'

He glanced me up and down. 'How long will it take to put on something . . . else?'

'Two minutes, ten seconds,' I said, confidently (Julian timed me once, in case of a fire).

'You are strange, Margaret Arbuthnot,' he said. 'Go. And shoes!' he added. 'Don't forget shoes.'

And, somehow, I did. I pulled on a sweater and my best capri pants, the penny loafers I once wore to school, and then suddenly my hand was in Cal's again and I was being pulled through Easter-quiet streets down to Shaftesbury Avenue, through Chinatown – the hubbub rising above the rooftops now – and then bursting out into a clamouring Trafalgar Square, packed so tight it might have been a million sardines in a vast tin. Everywhere were placards and posters and people, people, people! All trying to change the world; to save it, even.

Cal waved at a man on the platform who was holding a megaphone, ready to speak. To my astonishment, the man waved back.

'Who's that?' I asked.

'Frank Cousins,' he said. 'Labour chap. I met him somewhere between Bracknell and Staines; he told me it's gaining traction in the party. Gaitskell's against it but Cousins reckons it'll pass at party conference.'

'What will?' I asked, greenly.

'Unilateral disarmament!' He had to shout to be heard above the crowd and as he did, earned pats on the backs from our neighbours.

'Charlie was right.' It dawned on me there and then. 'This *is* what you're good at. And what you love.'

He shrugged. 'What job will give me that? And don't say MP because I'm not sucking up to Panther and trying to fill her shoes. They're far too big.'

I shook my head, smiled. It seemed so obvious that I couldn't believe I hadn't thought of it before. 'Journalist,' I said.

'What?'

I didn't correct him this time. 'You write about it,' I clarified. 'You take all this . . . this passion and . . . and facts – you quote Cousins even, and others – and you turn it into an article. Papers will pay for it, if it's good enough.'

'But . . . I can't type,' he said. 'I'm not even sure I can write.'

I smiled again. 'I can, though. Well, the latter. My typing's still barely forty words a minute but it's getting there.'

He frowned. 'Are you offering to help?'

Was I? I thought. Yes, yes I was. I nodded. 'You dictate, or write long-hand, and I'll type and edit. Between us we can muster something.'

There was a pause, then, 'Little Miss Fixer,' he said.

I shrank. 'Well, if that's—'

'No!' He blurted. 'No. I just . . . *Yes*,' he said then. 'Yes, please.'

So that's what we're going to do. And who knows if it will be worth the paper it's typed on, but – today? It felt exactly like Living with that capital 'L' and I want to keep hold of it. Do more of it. And this is a way to do that. And, well, so I have to spend more time with Cal. But . . . the thing is . . . I think I want to.

SUNDAY 24 APRIL

5 P.M.
Today's monthly lunch in the suburbs (beef casserole and dumplings) was even more strained than usual. This is partly due to my haircut, which has not gone down at all well on Magnolia Road. Mummy says I look like a criminal, and that even Julian has a more flattering style (he does not; Aunt Barbara uses the sick bowl to cut around. If anyone looks menacing, it is him). Daddy did not say a single word, not even to rescue me, which is damnation itself. The main act though was my apparent dissidence with the whole Aldermaston article. Mummy accused me of having 'switched sides' and potentially ruining my reputation by 'penning lies' for the 'commie' press. I said:

1. The *Guardian* is hardly a communist paper; it is barely left of *The Times* on occasion (thanks to Cal for that fact) and they should be glad it wasn't the *Mirror* or the *Morning Star*.

2. It's not lies, it's facts and opinion gathered by both Cal and I at the rally. On top of Cousins (establishment) we spoke to three women from Maidenhead (the middle England opinion) and a young actress called Glenda Jackson whom I am convinced is going places, though this may be based on the fact that she had admired my haircut and asked after my stylist.
3. It's not my reputation at stake as my name isn't on the article. It's not even Cal's name; he refused to use Mannering as he didn't want to be accused of nepotism, so the only reputation at stake is that of one 'Cal Bannister', and that's if it even gets published, because:
4. It's only been submitted for consideration. As yet, we haven't heard anything back.

After that, the conversation reverted to whether or not Daddy's practice partner, Mr Bent (tall, hairy ears), is likely to retire this year or next, and when it happens, whom he should look to recruit. At this, much lamentation ensued that John has not followed in the 'family business' and usually I would have complained that no one ever lamented my lack of dental ambition but my head was too full of the *Guardian* and Cal. The thing is, I loved every second as much as he – the research, the working out a structure – as intricate yet obvious as the arc of a fairy tale – the using clever sentences to get a point across; I fear we may have both caught the bug. But the greatest surprise was Cal. He works hard when he lets go of the damaged man act, forgets himself and is all for the story. It was really quite inspiring. *He* is quite inspiring. *And* he likes Elvis after all; I put Charlie's copy of 'Love Me Tender' on the gramophone and he actually sang along – not realising what he was doing until we both got to the end of the song and I harmonised (not brilliantly, admittedly; there is a reason I was barred from choir).

When I came to, Mummy and Daddy were arguing over whether or not Surbiton might cope with a French dentist as there is a young man called Gaston something or other who is quite the dab hand with a root canal apparently. I could sense discord descending – and a possible pudding embargo – and decided to throw myself to the wolves as a distraction. 'Ted painted me naked,' I said.

Needless to say, Gaston something or other was swiftly forgotten.

Mummy said I was a 'Jezebel' again and 'performing in porn'.

'What will the neighbours think?' she wailed. 'This is just like the time you took all your clothes off at the Tredegars' garden party.'

'I was four!' I protested. 'And John had been deliberately sick on me!' But neither washed with Mummy.

Daddy was rather less accusatory, instead worrying I might be hard up for money and offering me ten shillings (only earning himself another shouting). I said I was neither broke (well, not quite) nor a Jezebel, and it was art and had the Aster Mannering seal of approval (at least, she has told Ted it shows real promise but that I need to sit again as my arms are currently so disproportionately long as to make me look gibbonish) and if they were that concerned they could see the thing itself before it goes on display and veto it if necessary.

I don't know why I said that, as it's as unlikely as it is horrifying, but it placated Mummy temporarily and treacle tart was forthcoming, leaving me to wonder at what a month this has been – the bath with Charlie, naked painting with Ted, the article with Cal. All landmarks for me; all Life with a capital L, if not every letter; all banishing the spectre of Charlie's disappearance and Rollo's 'turn' with a double helping of cream.

MAY 1960

MONDAY 2 MAY

7 P.M.

May, and what should be another month of new shoots and blooms – of spring sunshine – is wrapped in a metaphorical fog to rival any February pea-souper. It is because Cal's article has been sent back by the *Guardian*, with a letter from the political editor explaining that if and when Cal becomes 'someone of relevance' then his journalism may throw around opinions willy-nilly, but, until then, he'd be better off as a cub reporter at a local rag, and sticking to the facts.

'I don't know why I bothered,' he snapped, flinging the pages at me across the shop.

I said nothing at first, just gathered them up and read the cover sheet carefully. 'At least he calls it "journalism",' I tried. 'That's something.'

'Cold comfort,' Cal replied.

'Perhaps you should have used your own name after all? At least everyone's heard of the Mannerings.'

'No!' he snapped. 'Whatever I do, I want to do it on my own merit. Besides, it isn't my name, is it?'

This again. 'Well, it could be. I mean, if I had any vague connection to a . . . a' – I scrabbled to think of a literary heroine – 'Brontë, then I would capitalise on it. As it is, the only Arbuthnot to make it into the national press is Daddy's Great Uncle Sid and that was for winning a pig show.' I saw a smile tease the corners of his lips. 'Although Daddy once wrote about a particularly tricky underbite for *Teeth Today*.'

The smile quirked one cheek, sinking his dimple. 'That's an actual magazine?'

'Sells quite well. Or at least, there's a copy in every surgery I've ever visited. Daddy used to make John and I check out the competition for ideas,' I added as explanation.

'John's your brother?'

I nodded. 'Yonks older and a bore. But well-meaning. Yours?' I had only heard Jack's name mentioned a couple of times and only in passing. Cal seemed to prefer not to acknowledge his existence.

Any vestige of a grin disappeared. 'Year older, also a bore. Not even well-meaning. Acts as if to the manner born, like he isn't some . . . some slum kid.'

I flinched. 'Perhaps that's easier.'

'Of course it is, only . . .'

'Only?'

'I don't know. It just feels . . . fake.'

'Can't we all be different people though?' I wondered. 'To the ones we were born to be, I mean? The ones our parents plan out? The world would be a depressing place if not. I'd be stuck as a dental receptionist in Surbiton for one thing. Better to decide for ourselves who we're going to be, surely?'

'But I don't *know* who I'm going to be,' he said then. 'How can I, when I don't even know where I come from?'

Heavens, he looked dejected, so I locked up and took him for coffee at the Lorelei. It was going to be on me but the owner, Stav, said it was on the house as we both looked 'like death warmed up'. I was quite grateful really, given that Rollo hasn't paid me for last week yet. I would ask but he keeps disappearing with the regulars whenever they pop in, and when he is here, he's locked in the downstairs lav (his tummy is playing up again. I do hope it isn't catching).

Anyway, my mission for this month is to cheer up the lot of them: Cal and Rollo, and Charlie as well, who is as preoccupied as Rollo with something or other. It's probably *Romeo and Juliet* – it opens next week and she still only knows half the lines. It's a good job she's only the understudy, and the costumes are mostly strategically draped sheets due to budget constraints.

TUESDAY
10 MAY

1 P.M.
I have found a solution to both Cal and Rollo's woes! Or rather, a solution has presented itself rather conveniently: Rollo's tummy is too dicky to do his latest restaurant review (it is Sheekey's, i.e. shellfish-heavy) so I have offered to go in his place with Cal. Cal and I can write it up together and hand it in under Rollo's name and no one will be any the wiser, except that we shall know we are published! I mean, it isn't a novel exactly, nor serious journalism even, but it is writing, and that is all that counts.

Charlie is fuming as she has rehearsals to attend, plus she has given up whichever diet she was on and food seems to be all the rage with her again. 'I am craving mussels like nobody's business,' she declared in the bathroom this morning.

'Oh, I shan't be eating mussels,' I said. 'Mummy says they eat excrement.'

'Well, you must try the oysters then,' she carried on. 'They're to die for.'

I made a non-committal noise, and a note to check with

Cal what oysters eat before I try any. I had telephoned him at once and he is coming, but 'reluctantly' he says, and it is mainly because Aster is away and the refrigerator is bare, so he's been hungry since Saturday. I said he could have come over for toast but he said he didn't want to bore me. I said he never bored me. And then Charlie marched past giving me *quite* the look so I hung up. Anyway, the reservation is at seven in the name of the newspaper and Rollo has given us instructions to 'go mad' as the paper is paying. I shall not, obviously, as I do not want to be locked in the downstairs lav myself and the upstairs one, as you know from the bath incident, has no lock at all.

WEDNESDAY 11 MAY

11 A.M.
Heavens, Sheekey's was a treat! Or rather, the room itself was – all dark panelling, and glimmering crystal and waiters dressed for a wedding. Even the toilets were opulence itself; I wish I'd had a camera just to take a photograph of the taps. The food, though, was less salubrious. I mean, gosh, oysters are fiddly things, and not worth it when you do manage to swallow one. Like eating fishy snot, which I said to Cal at the table.

'My dining partner, new to oysters, described them as "fishy snot",' he declaimed.

I grinned. 'Well, they are. Why not be honest about it?'

'I'm not sure the *Herald* wants honesty, more, "colour" and wit.'

'I thought that *was* quite witty,' I said. 'Anyway, write it down. And "chewy mucus" while you're at it. I like the assonance of that one.'

And he did, and my comment that the mash was more cold poultice than potato, and that my mother would have something to say about the broccoli, which was a tad on the claggy side.

All of which made for a strange but rather wonderful dinner – getting to think and write while eating – and stranger still to leave without paying. I felt quite the criminal! Still, I suppose we made up for it with the work after – we stayed up until one in the morning getting the wording right, and now I have until three to type it all up – which I'm doing between customers (so mostly I am only typing) – and then Rollo will run it over to Fleet Street himself. He has vetoed only one sentence, at which I was surprised and relieved.

'About time someone stirred things up at the *Herald*,' he said. 'And I'm glad it's me, if only in name.'

I rang Cal to see if he wanted to come and check it through but Aster is still away and he's not answering. He didn't leave until three in the end; Rollo offered him the sofa but he said he'd better get back to check on the cats – Aster has adopted two of her sister's Marigold's latest batch. They are called Norman and General Eisenhower (Marigold's youngest named them and there is no changing it, apparently) and mostly claw the soft furnishings and throw up. This is why we have never had pets at Magnolia Road; Mummy can't be bothered with the mopping.

Anyway, I must get back to the typing. I still have several paragraphs to go and my words per minute aren't yet 'professional', according to Miss Beveridge. She can't even bring herself to comment on my shorthand, just screws her face up as she passes, whereas Betty has already graduated and moved to

Lewes. (She sent me a postcard last week – she's secretary to a solicitor's in Eastbourne and has filed for divorce. I sent her back a 'congratulations' card, which I suspect Mummy would declare 'tasteless', but if one can't be congratulated for leaving a brute, then when?)

FRIDAY 13 MAY

5 P.M.

Unlucky for some, but not Cal and I, as the latest 'Round Town with Rollo' column is published today!

They have taken out some of the harsher comments, and amended 'fishy snot' to 'something bodily', but the note about Mummy and the broccoli is still in.

'It feels rather good, doesn't it?' I said to him as we pored over it in the Lorelei on my lunch break. 'Seeing one's words in print. Even with someone else's name on it.'

Cal frowned. 'It really does.'

'So, what next?' I folded up the paper and put it in my bag to show Rollo later.

'What do you mean?' he asked.

'What's the next big protest?' I added sugar to my cappuccino (quite the most delicious thing invented). 'There must be something.'

He shrugged. 'It's the homosexuality debate next month. That could be something.'

I thought of Charlie, of Aster as well. 'Great idea,' I said.

'You could . . . interview some famous homosexuals.'

'Like who? Aster? Rollo?'

'Rollo is homosexual?' I blurted.

'Oh, Little Bird.' He smiled.

I started. 'Why did you call me that? Daddy calls me that. Well, "Birdy". But still . . .'

He shrugged again. 'I don't know. I suppose because you are a bit bird-like. A fledgling, emerging from the nest at last.'

'And failing to fly with the grown-ups?' I snapped sarcastically.

'Did I say that?'

I sighed. 'Shame I can't sing.'

'Nor can crows,' he replied, 'and they do all right.'

'A crow? You never said I had to be a crow.' I was joking now, and it showed.

'A pigeon, then?' He joined in. 'Or a . . . a parrot?'

'I like to think I'm more of a sparrow, actually.' I grinned. 'Industrious, inconspicuous, but actually quite delightful if you take the time to watch.'

'Then, *Birdy* Arbuthnot, a sparrow you shall be.'

And I admit I have been trying out the name all day, both aloud and written. It does rather suit me and is better in any case than Margaret. Birdy Arbuthnot. Birdy Arbuthnot. See?

Birdy Mannering.

Oh! No, no. I must stop that. That is quite absurd. And thank heaven Charlie has just walked in. Though she is wearing an air of doom not seen since the Eliza Doolittle debacle. I am going to find out what is wrong (and also am abandoning any 'Mannering' ideas right now).

7 P.M.

The curse of Friday the thirteenth has certainly struck someone.

There is no witty or pretty way to say it: Charlie is pregnant.

'Are you sure?' I asked, trying hard to rearrange my face into something less obviously shocked. '*Sure* sure?'

'I've not had my monthly since March and I'm craving liver. *Liver*! I hate the stuff.'

'Oh,' I managed. 'Well, is it Alan's?'

'Obviously,' she snapped, before falling to self-pity. 'Oh, God. What a fool I am—'

'No, no!' I insisted. 'This isn't your fault. Well, not entirely. Two to tango and all that.' I was not helping. 'Does he know?' I tried instead.

She shook her head. 'And he can't. Or he won't help me get to Hollywood, will he? No one wants a brood mare on set.'

'I don't think—'

'Well, I do. I *know*.'

'I meant . . . what if he wanted to' – I scrabbled for the right words; I had never been in this situation before and my lexicon was consequently lacking – 'do right by you?' (I know. Terrible. But it was the best I could muster under the circumstance.)

If there is a bright side, it is only that Rollo stuck his head around the door at this moment to congratulate me on a 'splendid effort'. 'We'll make a Michelin of you yet,' he added, before espying Charlie and pulling a face. 'Girls' talk?' he asked.

I nodded and flapped a hand to send him away; he duly and predictably obliged. In this, as well as other ways, he and Daddy are peas in a pod.

'You mustn't say a word,' Charlie begged me then. 'Not to Rollo, not to Alan, not to . . . to Val. Oh, God. Val! If he finds out, then Aster will find out and then . . .' She wailed again.

'I promise,' I told her. 'Of course I do. But . . . won't it become obvious?'

To which she replied, 'There are ways,' – a phrase I have been pondering ever since. Can she mean adaptable clothing? Or something more . . . permanent? I suppose I shall find out soon enough. She has gone out again for now – I assume rehearsal. In any case she has taken an emergency bag with her as, on top of the liver cravings, she has morning sickness, which, to her annoyance is not confined to a particular time of day at all but can strike at any moment.

Heavens. A baby.

The worst of it, selfishly, is that it will inevitably change her, won't it? Render her sensible. Take her away from her dreams. Or at least that seems to be the case for Mummy, whom I know for a fact once harboured an ambition to trek across America on a pony.

'What happened?' I asked her once.

'I grew up,' she said, as if it were obvious; as if I were the fool for asking.

I am all for being grown up, but it's such a shame we have to leave *all* the childish things behind.

SATURDAY 14 MAY

11 A.M.
I am not sure gin and cigarettes count as childish, but they certainly count as foolish when pregnant. However, Charlie is, apparently, leaving nothing behind. She didn't come in until two this morning – I heard her curse as she tried to unlock the sticky door, then the clatter of her staggering about in the kitchen doing something with bread (there are slices of it willy-nilly on the table, countertop and floor). She failed to even make it to bed, instead falling asleep on the sofa, still fully dressed, where she languishes now. I suppose we should be grateful for that, at least.

Ted is frying bacon in an effort to revive her, while Rollo has gone for more coffee, as Cal had the last when he showed up on the doorstep half an hour ago announcing that he wants to help out in the shop on a voluntary basis, just until Rollo is fighting fit again.

'I am fit,' argued Rollo. 'Just . . . under the weather.'

I ignored this, turning instead to Cal. 'Are you mad?' I asked. 'There are barely any actual customers as it is. Just Eggs and the two Roberts, who never buy a single book between them. Habitual malingerers.'

'Well, Birdy,' Cal replied, putting down his espresso cup, 'I thought you might teach me to type in between.'

'Oh, you did, did you?' I asked, faux-horrified. 'On your head be it. It will be the inept leading the thoroughly incompetent.'

'"Birdy".' Rollo nodded, pulling on his Macintosh (despite the fact that the weather is positively balmy). 'It rather suits you. But are you a jay or a jackdaw?'

'A sparrow!' I shouted to his departing back, then swung round to see if my outburst had roused Charlie.

It had not.

'I'll fetch the typewriter down, shall I?' offered Cal.

I sighed. 'Very well. Perhaps our ham-fisted attempts will wake her.'

And so he is fetching it, while I eat a bacon sandwich and wonder what on earth I'm to do with my friend, and why I feel so oddly, embarrassingly happy, while she is evidently desperate.

8 P.M.

The bright side, if there is one, is that Cal is, irritatingly, a willing pupil and far better learner than I, and is already up to thirty words a minute. The downside is that Charlie, having finally woken at two this afternoon, been sick a perfunctory once and then thoroughly washed (by me) in the bath, is deaf to my pleas for her to amend her ways and stay in this evening. Instead, she is off to the Colony with Doris.

'It's my last weekend off before the play opens,' she announced, 'and I mean to use it wisely.'

I tried to reason, but Cal stayed me. 'Let her,' he said, as she disappeared in a cloud of Chanel No 5 and abandon. 'She's young; she's—'

'Pregnant!' I blurted. 'She's pregnant, Cal.' I slapped my hand on my mouth. 'Oh, God. I wasn't to say anything. You mustn't tell anyone. Promise me you won't tell!'

Cal grasped my arms. 'Birdy, calm down. I won't say a word. But . . . really? She's up the junction?'

I bristled at the slang. 'Don't,' I said. 'It's bad enough without that.'

'You're right. I'm sorry.' He hung his head, then raised it to meet my eyes. 'Just . . . How could she be so . . . ?'

'Stupid? That's what you were going to say, wasn't it?' I shook him off, folded my arms.

'I—'

'It takes two to tango.' I repeated the words I'd thrown at Charlie only yesterday. 'And the man usually leads.'

He left not long after, which at the time I was relieved about. But now I wish I'd asked him to stay, to come with me and keep an eye on Charlie at the Colony, or even to wait in for her inevitable messy return.

If this is what it's like, being a mother – worrying what your child might have got up to when out; worrying when they'll come in (*if* they'll come in) – then I'm not surprised Charlie wants nothing of it. Frankly, I'm not sure why anyone would.

SATURDAY 21 MAY

9 A.M.

It has been a week since and not a thing has improved. Charlie is either out heaven knows where, or, when she is in, is refusing to discuss the subject to the point where I am having to ignore the fact that most conversations are punctuated by her having to leave the room to dry heave.

Worse, I can't even ask for help as she has forbidden me to discuss it. It would be easier, I think, if she were on speaking terms with her mother. Although, when I think about it, perhaps not. I am not sure mine would offer anything other than an 'I told you so' and a basin. Wouldn't most mothers?

9.30 A.M.

Most mothers, perhaps. But not all women. Isn't this exactly the sort of situation when wise aunts come in handy? And isn't Aster the wisest of aunts? Or almost-aunts, at least?

I know Charlie told me not to breathe a word, but she only actually specified Rollo and Alan and Val. And, yes, I've already blabbed to Cal, but he's kept it to himself, so there's no reason to think Aster won't be equally discreet.

Yes! This is the answer. (Or at least the only answer I can come up with without locking her in her room and feeding her crackers through the gap until she faces up to the debacle.) I shall run it by Cal when he arrives at ten and between us I believe we can muster something before she drags herself out of bed (at least she made it there this time) and starts the whole sorry process again.

11 A.M.

Cal is in agreement! Well, mostly. He did question several times exactly how livid Charlie would be but I said we would cross that bridge when we come to it.

He said, 'As long as it's more of a humpback one than the Humber crossing.' Which was quite clever but I wasn't in the mood to tell him so; instead I just bade him telephone Aster and summon her to the house on a Ted pretext.

'Saying what?'

'I don't know,' I said. 'Say he's having a crisis of confidence! Say he's made my breasts into ice cream cones!'

He stared at my chest.

'Not really!' I yanked my cardigan around myself. 'Actually, he's done quite well, given the . . . lack of subject matter.'

Cal said nothing to this, I note, but dutifully went to the

telephone. Thankfully, Aster apparently has nothing better to do, and is livid with Norman, who has disgraced himself on her bed, so now we are anticipating her arrival with all the trepidation and desperation of a dental patient awaiting the pulling of a rotten tooth.

3 P.M.

Well, that didn't exactly go to plan. I am not sure how to explain it in reference to my previous metaphor, other than the dentist and patient are livid with each other and any teeth are still very much attached. In literal terms:

Aster told Charlie she knows a 'sympathetic' doctor who can 'rectify' the situation, i.e. someone called Egg, who is a friend of Freddy, i.e. Cal's adoptive father, and *very* highly trained – as opposed to Eggs, she added, who is in no way medical, and must never be allowed to minister medicine, nor even a sticking plaster, to anyone.

1. Charlie said she wasn't letting Eggs nor Egg near her, especially not her nether regions.
2. At which point, Ted walked in and demanded to know why anyone was going near Charlie's nether regions.
3. This caused quite the rumpus, which awoke Rollo from his afternoon nap (a recent habit)

>   so that the entire occupants of 27 Lexington
>   Street now know about Charlie's condition.
> 4. As a result of which, Charlie is now not
>   speaking to anyone, in particular, me.
>   And I cannot rectify this as she's gone out
>   and is not to be found at either the Pippin
>   or the Colony (Cal has checked).

I suppose at least Val doesn't know. It's two days before press night and the last thing he needs is a pregnant and hysterical wardrobe mistress, let alone potential leading lady.

4 P.M.

Val is now here, and in a terrible state, having bumped into Cal grilling Doris on the door. Aster has made tea and sent Cal out for cannoli from Lina Stores for sustenance while we keep vigil. He has been instructed to speak to no one but Francesco for fear the entirety of Soho gets involved.

5 P.M.

Charlie is not back.

7 P.M.
Charlie is not back.

10 P.M.
Charlie is not back.

1 A.M.
Charlie is not back and I am going to have to give up and go to bed as I have to drag myself to Surbiton tomorrow for lunch and there is no getting out of this one as it's Daddy's birthday and he is going to be fifty, i.e. officially elderly. I suppose at least she will be home by the time I wake, which is something, even if I am still in Coventry.

SUNDAY 22 MAY

11 A.M.
Charlie is still not back and if I don't depart to catch my train within the next ten minutes Mummy won't be speaking to me either. I am leaving instructions with Cal (previously on the sofa, now on a search party) that he is make sure she knows how sorry I am. He said I can tell her myself later, as he's sure she will understand once she's seen reason. Also, perhaps we should instigate a protest about single parenthood and/or abortion law? I said a) I wish I had his faith, and b) now is *not* the time.

I do wish I had his faith. As it is, I fear my return to Surbiton may be somewhat more permanent than luncheon.

10 P.M.
I am back in Soho. By the skin of my teeth, but still, it is to the sound of drunken hoots and pigeon coos that I shall fall asleep tonight, rather than Mummy's vigil of checking the Teasmade is on, the sockets are off, and the back door is double-locked.

The scene at Magnolia Road unfolded in predictable fashion. Daddy acted thrilled with his birthday presents: a new Ian Fleming novel (me), golf balls (John and Gloria) novelty socks (Aunt Barbara and Uncle Roy) and sock socks (Mummy, who does not approve of novelty anything, especially clothing-wise); everyone acted thrilled with roast chicken even though it is weeks since they had beef (ongoing economy drive); and I acted thrilled with my new life, even though it had been thrown into utter turmoil – albeit not entirely without my assistance.

Daddy broached it, once pudding (stewed rhubarb; Daddy's and my favourite) was done and the others had returned home on the pretexts of early nights (John and Gloria)/a programme on television about the Panama Canal (Julian, therefore Aunt Barbara and Uncle Roy).

'Going to tell us what's up, Birdy?' he asked.

At the name, I winced. I'd just begun to embrace it from Cal; now I might never hear it again on his lips. 'Nothing,' I said, sullenly.

'Nonsense,' he said. 'You've looked like a wet weekend in Bridlington since the minute you walked in and you barely touched your rhubarb and I know it's your favourite.'

This was true. 'It's . . .' I couldn't tell him, though. Not after everything Charlie had said.

Except, how much worse could it get? She might never speak to me again as it was, and who else might console me? And I didn't have to spill everything, after all.

'I . . . Charlie's not talking to me,' I admitted.

'Why on earth not?' demanded Mummy. 'What have you done this time?'

'It's not me!' I insisted.

But Mummy was undeterred and I knew from experience there was no backing out now. 'Out with it,' she said.

I took a deep breath. 'Because she's pregnant,' I said, 'and I blabbed it to Aster.'

'Who's Aster?' asked Daddy.

'Aster Mannering,' Mummy snapped back. 'You know this, Gerry! She's pregnant?' At this she turned to me again.

I nodded disconsolately.

'And . . . what is she going to do?'

'I . . . I don't know,' I admitted. 'She hasn't decided.'

'But she can't be thinking . . .' But Mummy couldn't finish the sentence and we all knew why.

Any attempt I made at conversation after that was ignored or swatted away, like a bothersome moth.

'I think I should go,' I said eventually.

My mother said nothing. My father, for his part, walked me to the station. 'Look after Charlie,' he said, 'won't you?'

'Of course!' I replied, as if anything else were impossible. 'And, well, look after Mummy, I suppose,' I added, somewhat reluctantly.

'She means well,' he said. 'It's just . . . she worries.'

I shrugged. 'Me too,' I said. 'Me too.'

*

When I walked in, I could hear quite the cacophony going on upstairs and practically heaved with relief. She was back, then. But in what mood?

I stampeded through the shop and up the back stairs, but even I, in my wildest imagination (and it is quite wild, as you know) could not have predicted the scene that would await on the landing. For there was Charlie, pale as whey yet still acutely beautiful; in front of her, Ted, down on one knee, proffering a ring that looked as if it had come from a cracker (because in fact it had, it emerged later); and behind them an audience including Rollo, Cal, Aster, Val, Doris and several people I'd never even set eyes on before. But my eyes snapped back to Charlie.

'For heaven's sake, Ted,' she was saying. 'You don't need—'

'But . . . but I love you,' he insisted.

'I know,' she said. 'And I love you, but not in the same way. You deserve much more than me.'

'Is it because I'm not rich . . . or . . . or famous?'

'No,' she said, firmly. 'It's because . . . well' – she glanced at Aster – 'because I don't really like men at all. Not in bed, anyway. No offence, boys.' She grimaced at the assembled.

'But, Alan—' The words left my mouth before I could stop them.

'Was a desperate mistake.' She met my eye. 'For which I am now paying.'

At this, her hand rested on her belly for a second. And I

saw it, seized it – a 'yes', but this time not for me; for Charlie, for all of us. And I admit I rather wanted to 'fix' things again, and perhaps I also rather liked the drama of it, but more than anything, I just wanted to show Charlie she was capable.

'If you want to keep it, keep it,' I said, defiantly. 'Prove to your mother you're not useless.'

I saw her wince. 'She wouldn't care.'

I was undeterred. 'Then prove to yourself,' I said. 'We can help,' I added, taken with it. 'We'll raise it together, all of us, won't we?' I glared at Cal et al., who stood as if struck by a basilisk's gaze. 'Won't we?' I repeated.

'I... Of course,' said Val.

'It will be a Soho baby!' I continued. 'Think of it. Rollo will be a grandfather.' At this, he nodded. 'And Aster—'

'Another aunt,' she interjected. 'Don't saddle me with grandparenthood yet.'

'An aunt,' I echoed, 'as shall I be, and Cal and Val shall be uncles. Doris and...'

'Letty,' said one of the bystanders.

'Nerys,' another.

'Doris and Letty and Nerys will be... cousins or something.' I had taken it too far but my point remained. 'We'll be your family. We'll do this together.'

Charlie was staring at me, her hand still in place. And then it came, her answer, tentative, but an answer all the same. 'We will?' she said.

I nodded. 'We will.'

*

Once everyone had been ushered out, I took Charlie up to her room, where she let me undress her and put her to bed. I didn't ask where she'd been, but I knew she wouldn't go there again, at least for a while – seven months, I made it.

And, yes, it feels immense, and it's not even my burden to carry, but also, somehow do-able, because there's all of us – a family, albeit a higgledy one. But one whom I understand and who understands me and Charlie. And more, perhaps, than either of ours.

JUNE 1960

WEDNESDAY
1 JUNE

11 A.M.
June, and it is all change at 27 Lexington Street!

Charlie is quite transformed; she has already made herself two new dresses (using a pair of curtains from a box in the stockroom) to accommodate her anticipated expansion, and has replaced drinking and smoking with eating, to which I have been gallantly catering. Thankfully she has moved on from liver and it is all about cheese now – in sandwiches, in flans, in these dear little pastries from Maison Bertaux; I haven't yet mustered myself enough to attempt a soufflé, but I shall telephone Mummy later for a recipe. The only gloomy side is that Rollo cannot eat any of it (his tummy is worse than ever) but even that has a bonus in that he has begged Cal and I to carry on with his column for the moment. He is paying us fifty per cent of the fee, my half of which will go straight into the kitty jar and Cal's to Aster (minus his Socialist Party subs). In addition, Cal is still doing shifts at the shop in return for typing lessons. I realise, of course, that it is effectively me paying his salary, but neither of us dare mention it to Rollo for fear of aggravating his pain. Besides, it is an arrangement that suits us both as I have company, even if it is accompanied by a constant clackety-clack. We are working our way through the poems of Coleridge currently. Partly as they are usefully long, and partly because Rollo has ten editions he is trying to shift and we are hoping any customers might be moved by my declaiming.

Even Ted is affected by Charlie's new state, and in the most surprising way. Aster woman-handled him to a private view on Cork Street yesterday. He had to borrow a jacket of Cal's and even then complained he would stand out like a sore thumb. Though if he did, it must have been in a good way as he came home with an 'overnight guest'! Not only that, but when she crept into the kitchen to fetch a glass of water, Charlie exclaimed, 'Minty?' and Minty (rosebud lips, cheekbones like geometry, eyes as large as a cow), exclaimed, 'Cha-Cha?' And there was brief squealing and hugging, before a mutual agreement not to let each other's mothers have even an inkling they had clapped eyes on each other, as this Minty Brigham was supposed to be staying in Chelsea with someone called Pandora Fox-Cotton (again I am reminded that Margaret Arbuthnot is not a terribly glamorous moniker, although 'Birdy' seems to have stuck with one and all now, and that is, I suppose, something). I rather think Ted was disappointed that Charlie wasn't in the least bit jealous; on the contrary, she congratulated him, as Minty is heiress to a biscuit baron and can also do the box splits (this said with more awe than the biscuit thing).

6 P.M.

Mummy is still not speaking to me. I telephoned for the soufflé recipe and before I could ask about flouring ramekins she handed the receiver to Daddy. He claimed she was busy with the lupins, but I could sense a definite lingering froideur. In the end I didn't manage to get the recipe (Daddy regards cookery books as I might maps of Antarctica, or dental records) but I did find out that:

1. Mrs Peabody has handed in her notice and Daddy has placed an advertisement with Mrs Pickering for a new receptionist. He has high hopes for someone who is confident and jolly, or at least less prone to illness/tittle-tattle. I did not bother to dissuade him; I am sure Mummy is doing that for me.
2. Gloria has already had two false alarms as regards labour. The first was doughnut related (she has eaten for at least three in the last trimester); the second something called Braxton Hicks, which are sort of practise contractions, which seem mad to me. Why practise excruciating pain? Surely it is better to just do it the once? How Mummy endured it twice over is frightening, though I am not mentioning my qualms to Charlie, for obvious reasons.

3. Julian got his head stuck in the railings again yesterday, this time at Surbiton Boys'. He says it was a physics experiment, but Aunt Barbara says betting is all the rage at the moment and she suspects he is an easy target for some of the swarthier brutes. I note Aunt Barbara did not go through it more than once, but then if Julian was the result, who would?

WEDNESDAY 8 JUNE

3 P.M.
Rollo has managed to rouse himself from bed long enough to inform Cal and me that tonight's dinner reservation is not at Wheeler's, as previously stated, but at The Ritz.

Yes, you read that correctly: The Ritz!

Cal was, thankfully, quick to object. 'Are you off your rocker? The Ritz?'

'Well...' tried Rollo.

'And I can't, I just... can't,' I added. 'I have nothing to wear, for a start.'

'Forget the dress code, it's the social code,' Cal snapped. 'I'd rather chew tinfoil than sit down with that bunch of—'

'I'll go,' said Charlie. 'Their cheese board is glorious.'

'Fine by me,' I said, eyeing Cal.

'Haven't you already got a job?' asked Rollo.

Charlie frowned, a slice of melted Cheddar on granary poised halfway to her lips. 'Oh, heavens, yes!' She checked the kitchen clock, and dropped the toast. 'Half an hour until the half! Well, at least let me find you something to wear.'

'But, I—'

'Please?' Rollo said, with an air of desperation I hadn't caught in his voice before. 'I really need you to do this.'

I looked at Cal – one of my hardest stares.

'Fine.' He held up his hands. 'But on your head be it if I get kicked out for calling a prig a prig when I see one.'

At that, Charlie grasped my hand and we scarpered upstairs before he could change his mind.

'The Ritz!' I exclaimed as she flung open the door to her wardrobe. 'What does one wear to The Ritz, for heaven's sake?'

But Charlie knew exactly what one wore. 'This,' she said.

I gasped. It was the debutante dress – that glimmering, off-white Givenchy. 'But . . . it's too much,' I insisted. 'For dinner, for . . . for anything.' *For me*, I meant.

'Nonsense,' she replied. 'It will need a tweak or two to fit you, but I can do that between costume changes, now chip-chop and slip it on.'

There was no brooking argument, so I did as I was told and stood stock still as she pinned this and that and here and there. I shan't know the end result until she is back at six after the matinee, but oh, heaven, the feel of it! And The Ritz! I can't stop thinking about it. Will Princess Margaret be there? What if there is unidentifiable cutlery? Shall I make a fool of myself and find my face or name in *Tatler* or *The Sketch*?

10 P.M.

Princess Margaret wasn't there, but nor was there unidentifiable cutlery and I did not make a fool of myself, not even to Cal. And the dress? The dress was ... everything.

'Are you sure?' I checked as Charlie fastened the last of the covered buttons.

'Sure as sure can be,' she said, neat as a pin. 'I won't fit into it soon and anyway, the debs are dead. None of that matters any more. Class and all that.'

Cal scoffed. 'It will always matter.'

'Why fight, then?' I asked.

'I ...'

'Just because something is impossible, doesn't mean you can't try,' said Rollo from the corner (he has taken to sitting in the green wingback chair in the kitchen when he isn't in bed). 'Chip away at it, I say.'

'Precisely,' said Charlie. Then turned me so I could see myself in the chrome of the refrigerator. 'There. All done, darling.'

If I had hoped she would render me the sort of siren who might stop the traffic on Piccadilly I was slightly disappointed. If anything, I was convinced I resembled nothing more than a toddler playing dress up and said so.

'Don't be absurd,' she retorted. 'You look the epitome of chic, especially with your hair.'

'I do?' I wasn't playing fey; this was genuine doubt.

'You do.' She turned to Cal. 'She looks marvellous, doesn't she?'

Cal said nothing but nodded slowly, which was something, I supposed.

I smoothed the fitted skirt, looked at it dubiously. 'What if I spill sauce?'

'You won't,' Charlie assured me. 'You'll order the chateaubriand and have a splendid time, and then you'll come home and write something brilliant and witty again.' She winked at Cal, who reddened.

And the thing is, we did.

*

Oh, it was heaven! I shall start with the Arlington bar, which was like walking into a jewellery box, or, as we chose to put it, 'as if every deb in London had spilled their emeralds at the afterparty of class'. We had a single cocktail each – I had argued for none but Rollo had insisted 'some of us' should enjoy ourselves. Something maternal seemed to burgeon in me at that, or rather, he seemed so very paternal, and I vowed to do him justice and ordered a Brandy Alexander, which is quite the most delicious thing – all cream and chocolate – although Cal said it was a bit outré these days.

'Then outré I shall be,' I insisted, sipping it without lifting, so scared was I of spillage.

He laughed at the sight of it, and I smiled, happy to indulge him, though the stares were something to be reckoned with.

'Here,' he said, as we stood for supper itself, and made a diamond of his arm.

I slipped my own through, steadied myself as the brandy went to my legs briefly, then, emboldened, channelling Charlie herself, walked past the gawpers with something approaching hauteur.

'How the other half live,' Cal stage-whispered to me as we tucked into our chateaubriand – a shared tenderloin steak, it turns out. Quite the most delicious thing I've eaten in my life, though I shan't tell Mummy that (when and if she is ever speaking to me again).

'You *are* the other half,' I pointed out, blithely.

At this, he bristled. 'I'm not, though.' He took in the room again – the chandeliers, the panelling, the carpet thick enough to stand a match in and barely see the head. 'Not even Panther would come here.'

I changed the subject, sensing my mistake. 'She sounds rather marvellous.'

'She is, she is. It's just...'

I had made another clanger and my heart sank (though my stomach was happy enough to keep eating, I noted). I attempted to rescue the situation. 'Why not try to find him?' I suggested. 'Your real father, I mean.'

Cal flushed again. 'Keep it down!' he snapped.

I glanced around. 'No one's looking any more,' I told him. 'And you have to. Otherwise, it'll bother you quietly but constantly. Like a niggling toothache or a . . . a conviction that life might be brighter outside Surbiton.' Two things with which I was intimately acquainted. 'I'll come with you, if you like?'

He shrugged. 'Perhaps.'

The rest of supper – a heavenly pêche Melba, and (Charlie was right) quite the most glorious cheeseboard – passed in silence, which I chose to see as a) amiable and b) reverence for the food. But as we got back, and I typed out his rough words, I felt eyes on me and looked up.

He was staring at me. 'You're quite a picture, you know.'

I fidgeted, pictured Charlie when she tries to diminish herself – I've seen her do it: pull her cardigan tight and let her hair hang badly. 'If I can be Charlie on a bad day, I'll be happy,' I said.

He shook his head, that smile teasing the left side of his lips again. 'You're not Charlie, not even on a bad day.'

'Oh.' My insides slumped, my vanity (rightly) shattered.

'I mean you're *you*,' he said quickly.

'And that's a good thing?' I asked.

He nodded. 'Very much.' Suddenly, he stood. 'I should go,' he said, and nodded at the copy piled by the typewriter.

'Of course.' I handed him the sheaf of papers to drop off at Fleet Street.

Part of me wanted to suggest we went together, but something had switched, tilted, so that the air between us almost rattled.

'So, see you tomorrow,' I said.

'Yes, tomorrow,' he replied, his mind clearly elsewhere already. And then he was gone.

And he is nothing to me but a colleague, a sort-of cousin of my flatmate with a chip on his shoulder the size of a log. So why, as I sit on my bed, listening to the sound of almost-midsummer trickling in, do I feel as bereft as Cinderella when the clock has struck midnight, the coach has turned back to a pumpkin and her fairy godmother is nowhere to be seen?

FRIDAY 10 JUNE

11 A.M.
There is no sign of Cal as yet. What is the point of volunteering to work and then shirking it? I expect he will claim it is Aster and the cats – Norman may not be quite as male as anyone thought, as he appears to be pregnant, and more worryingly, by his own brother— sorry, *her* own brother. Though Charlie says it is quite common to fall for people, only to find out they are estranged relatives. I am not sure it *is* entirely common, though now I shall be alert to any Arbuthnot traits in potential suitors. Not that there is any sign on the horizon, not even if I raise a periscope. Perhaps I should have invested thoughts into finding Ted attractive before he coupled up with Minty? Although, I am thinking about it now and it is like lesbianism all over again – nothing. Besides, he is very definitely 'otherwise engaged' – I went to seek unbuttoning help last night after Cal left, lest I be forced to sleep in the Givenchy I had hitherto managed to keep pristine, and there were all sorts of noises coming from the attic, none of them paint-related. In the end, I had to wait for Charlie to get back to do the deed, only she then decided it was

time for a midnight feast so we sat up eating cheese and pickle sandwiches until gone one. So now I am bloated, exhausted, and entirely discombobulated by a dream about bees.

On the bright side, 'Round Town with Rollo' is out and it is a hoot! What is more, there has been a 'letter to the editor' about the last one, praising our description of the bread pudding as 'leaden' and 'potentially weapons-grade' and congratulating Rollo on 'bucking up' his ideas after several months of 'subpar scribing'.

I do hope he hasn't seen it. I am going to clip the column out (perhaps I shall start a scrapbook!) and use the rest of the newspaper for cleaning the shop windows (a tip from Mummy, from the days when she couldn't wait to tell me things, even if they were exasperated exhortations to tidy my room or eat more peas).

SATURDAY 11 JUNE

7 P.M.

Cal is back. It wasn't Norman (although she is very definitely pregnant, though possibly – and very much thankfully – not by incest as apparently the Mortimers next door have a Persian called Boris who is very 'free and easy' with his affections). It was all this business with his background – he says he went to the Somerset House indexes to request his birth certificate on a whim, only now he is absolutely rattled and doesn't think he can go back to fetch it.

'I'll come with you, then!' I said, my enthusiasm, in retrospect, a little too vivid.

'I . . . well, thank you, but I'm not sure I want to—'

'Nonsense,' I interrupted. 'This is the only way you will have . . . what do the Americans call it? Closure? And perhaps an opening. Perhaps he will turn out to be someone famous? An actor or . . . or a politician?'

At this, he sighed. 'You've read far too many books.'

At least he is pleased as punch at the column and the letter to the editor (which I kept behind for him, in my pocket, on the grounds that if Rollo somehow found it I would eat it then and there).

'Perhaps he's a writer,' I said then. 'Your father, I mean. Perhaps even Hemingway! Or F. Scott Fitzgerald!'

'And how would Hemingway meet an East End char?' he asked. 'He'll be a Dave or a Bob or a John, most likely.'

'Nothing wrong with that,' I added, thinking of my own John – boring but respectable anyway.

He shook his head. 'Exactly. Nothing wrong at all.' And yet, his words seemed to throb with displeasure, or fear, perhaps.

In any case, we've agreed to go on Wednesday afternoon, when Rollo often shuts up for 'early closing' (i.e. the French). I for one am vicariously thrilled. By Wednesday we shall know the name of Cal's dad. And while I do expect it is a John or a Bob – average, manageable – there is a small part of me (the untrammelled hope) that prays it will say 'F. Scott' after all!

8 P.M.

Rollo says it will not say 'F. Scott', because even if he is (which he isn't) he wouldn't allow his name to appear on the birth certificate. He would have persuaded her to put 'John Smith' in any case.

'You can do that?' I asked, as we made a pot of tea for Ted and Charlie, who were playing cards loudly at the table (it was a miracle to all be in the same room, and so I was drawing it out as long as possible).

'You can do what you like, within reason,' he said. 'I mean, I suppose they'd have to actually exist. You couldn't put down "Father Christmas" – or "Jay Gatsby", for that matter.'

Something hit me then. 'Did you ever want children?' I asked.

He frowned, as if completely bemused. 'Look around you,' he said.

I did – took in Ted, paint-flecked and dog-tired, hollows around his eyes from his early mornings odd-jobbing and late nights with his canvas or with Minty; Charlie with one hand ever on her belly these days; me, even – not entirely a waif, but a stray anyway, whom he's taken in, cared about (if not cared *for*; it's us looking after him these days).

'See,' he finished. 'I've got them.'

WEDNESDAY 15 JUNE

9 A.M.
It is another D-Day, i.e. Dad-Day, for Cal, although I shall not call it that in front of him, as I have already made that mistake with Charlie and she has (rightly) chided me for being blasé and insensitive.

'What if it's someone awful?' she pointed out. 'Stalin, or... Hitler, or that cad of an American, what was his name? Buck something.'

'Buchanan,' I finished for her. All girls knew of the infamous Buck, who had impregnated half of London in the 1920s, then started in on New York when he was exiled in disgrace.

'Exactly. Him.'

'Why would Buck be in East London in war time?' I asked. 'Or Hitler, for that matter. You'd think someone would have spotted him, with that awful moustache.'

'Well, as likely him as F. Scott,' she retorted crossly, then sighed. 'It'll be a nobody, you'll see. If he was worth a jot, he'd have come for Cal himself already.'

It wasn't a question so I didn't offer an answer, but I knew she was right, and felt a pang for Cal and what we were about to uncover.

'Do you miss yours?' I asked then.

She paused in her generous buttering of crackers, but didn't look up. 'I . . . don't remember him,' she said. 'Not really. So, nothing to miss.'

I knew this wasn't the truth or, if it was, barely. Even if she only missed the idea of him, there was a lack there – had to be. Same for Ted. I thought of my own dear Daddy then, and made a mental note to appreciate him all the more. And another mental note not to get Cal's hopes up too much.

Charlie's right: it might not be Hitler, or Buck, but it's likely to be someone pretty damn caddish all the same. Hasn't his brother Jack already said the same thing?

9.10 A.M.

Unless, what if the man doesn't actually know that Cal – and Jack, of course – even exist? What if he's a war hero, or a reclusive writer like Mortmain, or some sort of spy, even? Yes, better to think positively – even ambitiously – and commiserate later, rather than be a damp blanket from the start.

10 P.M.

I am not sure whether to be a damp blanket or a firework.

It is not Hitler, or Buck Buchanan, or F. Scott, which I suppose I should be less surprised about. But, while we have a name (Donald Hawthorn) and an address (36 Bow Common Road), it's impossible to know who or what he is, unless and until we visit him.

'We could go at once,' I'd said as we sat on a bench in the shade of Somerset House. 'There's plenty of time to get to Mile End and back.'

But Cal, still clutching the slip of paper on which his very existence was printed, declined. 'Not now, Birdy,' he said. 'Just . . . I need some time to think.'

I said nothing else then, mindful of Charlie's chiding. Aware as well that finding out the truth might change everything, mightn't it? Whether he's a spy or just Joe Bloggs, knowing who his father is will alter something about Cal himself, will change the truth of him, his story. Plus it had already been quite the afternoon of revelations, what with the brief appearance (metaphorically) of – I can hardly believe I'm saying this – a sister.

I suppose I should go over the whole messy affair to explain.

We arrived on the Strand to collect the certificate, Cal already in an understandable state of agitation (but trying to deny it), but when the clerk (monk's tonsure haircut, air of efficiency) produced the thing it was he who seemed the more exorcised.

'But you're not a woman,' he said, checking it again.

Cal frowned, as well he might. 'Not when I last looked,' he answered.

The clerk checked the certificate again. 'So you're not Carol Bannister?'

'Cal,' said Cal. 'Well, I think Caleb originally, but only ever Cal out loud. If you see what I mean.'

He was blustering, but I was not. 'Bannister?' I checked. 'That was your surname?'

He nodded. 'Yes. Well, my mother's. And still is. Well, sort of, only Cal Bannister Mannering is a mouthful of silver spoons isn't it? Makes me sound even worse than I am.'

'You're not...worse.' I sighed. 'Could I?' I asked the officious monk, holding out my hand.

The clerk squinted, but did as I asked – being strict with customers had clearly paid off.

'Definitely a girl, which you' – I looked at him again – 'are definitely not.'

'Expect you have the date wrong,' said the clerk. 'Happens a lot. This will be your sister.'

Cal's face went the colour of skimmed milk. 'But I don't *have* a sister.'

'*Had* is probably more accurate,' said the clerk matter-of-factly, as if blankly unaware of the chaos he was conjuring.

I gave him one of my hardest stares. 'Really?' I said.

'Born in 1939,' he carried on, 'and in Mile End. 'Could be the Blitz. Could be malnutrition. Could be—'

'Well, could you check?' Cal this time, and red in the face.

'It's forty-eight hours' notice,' said the clerk, puffing his chest up like a duck.

'Seriously?'

Cal looked as if he might hit the man; I touched his arm. 'You've just told my . . . my friend he might have a long-lost or even . . . even deceased sister. That might be considered a breach of confidence, mightn't it?'

The clerk stared. I stared back.

'Fine,' he said. 'But it'll be another six shillings, and I can't guarantee how long it will take.'

I forced a smile, and scattered some coins on the counter. 'We'll wait.'

And wait we did, for two and a half hours, playing I Spy and hangman to pass the time, though neither of our minds were on the games.

'Thank you,' he said, after one particularly tricky round in which I lost, having failed to guess 'bamboozle'.

'For letting you win?' I asked.

He smiled, but thinly. 'For sitting with me while' – he waved his arms around – 'this happens.'

I nodded. 'You're welcome,' I said.

In that moment I wanted to hug him, to hold him, and I thought he might me, but then he punctured the bubble. 'For the record, I didn't let you win. I just know more words than you.'

I nudged him, and he nudged me back, but that was it until

eventually, at gone four, the clerk returned with two more sheets of paper: Cal's actual birth certificate (the one earmarking Donald Hawthorn) and – oh, it pains me to write it – a death notice for his poor twin sister, just two months after her birth.

'I'm so sorry,' I told him.

He shrugged. 'Can't miss someone you never met.'

I knew this wasn't true – why else was he trying to find his father? On which subject, I suggested we go to Mile End there and then, but Cal had other ideas. He folded the sheets of paper, then stuffed them into his trouser pocket as if they were nothing more than an empty packet or bill. 'French?' he said.

'You hate the French,' I reminded him. 'You only drink beer.'

'Not today,' he said. 'Today I need something stronger.'

He drank what must have been an entire bottle of claret in the end (I stuck to soda water, as the responsible adult), which won't help anything, but at least he's blanked it out for now, asleep on the sofa (Bloomsbury might as well have been Birmingham at closing time).

Tomorrow, I am sure, it will hit him again.

THURSDAY 16 JUNE

7 P.M.

Cal didn't wake until gone lunch and then went straight back to Aster's with not a word to me about yesterday, which I do understand. Though, selfishly, I feel shut out, as if I wasn't part of it, somehow.

Another selfish thought has occurred to me as well. An awful, awful thought: what if I once had a sister as well? Or a brother, of course, in addition to the annoying one I grew up with? Not a twin but someone a little older.

I know I'm prone to 'flights of fancy' as Daddy calls them (or 'absolute madness' if you are listening to Mummy) but I can't stop thinking about that gap between John and I. Seven years is an awfully long time – there's only two years between Felicity and her brother Paul (terrible moustache, low-ranking civil servant), and only one between Gloria and her sister Angela (inexplicably infatuated with John, works in Gamages on the hat counter). And now I think about it, there's a massive gap between Charlie and the next eldest Pakenham. 'There was another one,' she said once, 'but it didn't take.'

What if I'm not an accident or an afterthought? What if the gap is because there was another one of us, but they 'didn't take'? And if so, how on earth has Mummy kept it quiet for so long? Or Daddy, for that matter?

These are questions that demand an answer but I can hardly ask them outright, can I? No, I shall have to find a subtle way of dropping it into conversation (if Mummy ever starts speaking to me again), or engage in some clever detective work. I can't mention it to Charlie (dead babies is hardly an encouraging topic when pregnant), Cal has his own family shenanigans to be dealing with, and Rollo is squeamish about all things labour-related (he has already made Charlie promise not to opt for a home birth; even saying that aloud paled him).

No, I shall just have to stew on it until opportunity makes itself known to me.

SUNDAY 26 JUNE

9 A.M.

I am going to Surbiton for lunch. I may live to regret this decision, as the alternative was a picnic in Regent's Park with Charlie and Aster (who has taken to knitting baby clothes, which, she says, goes against every suffragette bone in her body, and yet she cannot stop herself; there are three boleros and a bonnet already in various shades of lemon, so as to be gender neutral). Plus, my mother is not, to my knowledge, even speaking to me yet, but I am going to turn up on the doorstep and hope for the best. Or at least hope to not make it worse.

7 P.M.

On the bright side, I have not made things any worse than they were, regarding relations with Mummy. Although when she answered the door (she has never let either John or I have a key, and it is a miracle Daddy has one, frankly) she managed to squish her real feelings into a curt, 'I didn't think you were coming.'

'Whyever not?' I said, bustling in, trying to muster 'normality' (although I admit I may have erred towards 'slightly mad' with my out-to-please face). 'Hullo, Pa.'

Daddy had, at this point, wandered forlornly into the hallway in shorts — an outfit Mummy does not countenance except during—

'Wimbledon!' I blurted. 'I'd forgotten!'

I felt terrible as tennis is 'Daddy's missed dream', i.e. he once partnered Bobby Wilson. Only, Mummy persuaded him that dentistry is more dependable and about that she is right. Though the spectre is raised every June, and this year was no exception.

'Still miss it,' he said, performing a half-hearted forehand down the hallway with his imaginary racket and ball.

'People always need dentists,' said Mummy swiftly, as she marched off towards the kitchen. 'Tennis players are a luxury. Like actresses.'

And writers, I thought, but did not say. Thankfully I show no aptitude for tennis or any sport. John has more skill but a tendency to get bored even watching it, much to Daddy's chagrin.

'I'll watch with you later,' I told him.

'Thanks, Birdy,' he said, as he gave me a kiss on my cheek. Then added, 'She'll come round.'

Not if I mess this up, I thought, but again, I managed to keep this silent, as I did through most of the initial lunch discussions, i.e.

1. Gloria is a week overdue, and has gone rogue and eaten a lamb curry to 'bring things on' (a dish of which Mummy does not approve, on grounds of it not having a recipe in *Good Housekeeping* and therefore being of untested quality).
2. Daddy has a new receptionist. It is Angela, i.e. Gloria's sister. Daddy says she is very efficient and less prone to gossip than Mrs Peabody, although she does bang on about John a lot and has asked if there will be a staff party at Christmas and if so, will everyone bring family?
3. Julian has been off school, having been sick during lunch on another boy's plate – apparently after eating fourteen apples. Again, he claims this was a physics experiment. Again, I suspect this is betting madness and Aunt Barbara is fooling herself.

Mummy was just about to say something (probably about apples being brought into disrepute) when the phone rang and on it was John, saying Gloria had started having cramps again, and he would update us as and when a hospital trip was in the offing.

'It's probably wind,' I said without thinking (and unable to keep quiet any longer; it is quite hard when one is a natural chatterbox). 'Charlie has terrible problems, what with that and the heartburn. Though at least the cheese phase is over; that can't have been helping. Not that broccoli is any better.'

'Your mother craved beetroot,' said Daddy, wistfully glancing in the direction of the downstairs lavatory where, thankfully, my mother was ensconced, away from this topic of conversation.

I saw it then, my chance – SNAP! – diamond-bright and beckoning me. 'With all three of us?' I asked.

'Yes,' he said, then shook himself. 'I mean, with both of you.'

But it was too late, I knew it. I knew I was right – there had been another child, somehow, who hadn't worked out. I didn't need to say more, couldn't, as Mummy was back from the lavatory.

'What are you talking about?' She eyed me suspiciously.

'The homosexuality debate in Parliament,' I said, plucking the most controversial topic I could in order to throw her off the scent. 'Cal is thinking about writing an article on it.'

She was suitably appalled. 'Is *he* homosexual?'

'Heavens, no,' I replied. 'At least, not to my knowledge. Charlie is though. And Aster. Oh, and Rollo and Val. Actually, almost everyone I know,' I realised as I spoke. 'How *interesting*.'

Mummy looked more than interested but not in a positive way. 'Are *you* homosexual?'

I sighed. 'No. Though at times I wish I was.'

I did not have time to elaborate on this, probably thankfully, as at that moment John rang again to say that Gloria's waters had broken on the lounge carpet so could Mummy a) come to the hospital and b) recommend a suitable stain remover.

Gloria must be a glutton for punishment, I thought. Mummy is the last person I would want at a birth – all that emphasis on doing things correctly, and little encouragement beyond 'yes, well done, dear'. Although she was present at mine, I suppose; a fact I still find strange.

Anyway, I now have a niece – Geraldine Arbuthnot (much to Daddy's happiness and Mummy's horror) – born just half an hour ago at Kingston General: six pounds and four ounces and everything intact.

And also, I think, a missing sibling. Though what use this information is I don't yet know. I suppose, like Cal, I shall play a waiting game. Perhaps it will matter; perhaps not. But I am glad to know, either way.

JULY
1960

MONDAY
4 JULY

3 P.M.
July, and only three things have been consuming Lexington Street:

1. The infernal heat, which shows no sign of abating any time soon.
2. Charlie's appetite, which is also showing no signs of abating, though has surprised us all by segueing from broccoli to chocolate raisins.
3. The homosexuality debate, which, while it is over, has left a depressing legacy, having been defeated 213 votes to 99.

Rollo is disconsolate, which, on top of his ailing frame, renders him more of an old man than ever. I almost wish he'd take Aster's attitude ('inevitable') or Charlie's ('I wonder if the baby will be gay?').

Cal is, predictably, the most consumed of all of them.

Though mostly because the newspapers are still refusing to take an op-ed piece on it.

'You can hardly blame them,' I said. 'You're neither homosexual nor a journalist. If you subbed under the Mannering name it might be different.'

'Not that again,' he snapped, as we re-stacked the biography section (Rollo's last assistant, Tracy, had shelved them by size and colour, rather than alphabetically. She is now better placed at Debenhams). 'I'm not going to be a nepotist.'

'But isn't nepotism how everything works in the arts?' I pondered. 'Look at those acting dynasties. Look at Ted getting help from Aster. Look at Rollo, for God's sake. His uncle owns the *Herald*, doesn't he?'

'I don't want a ... a pity column, though.'

'"Round Town with Rollo" is not a pity column!' I snapped back. 'Everyone loves him! He gets letters every week.'

'Not now, perhaps. But how do you think he got it in the first place? He's not a writer; he's a shopkeeper, and not even a good one. His uncle, well, let's just say no one else in Rollo's family was talking to him by then, but he "understood".'

'Why does everyone skirt around the issue?' I said then. 'Why is it even an *issue*?'

'Oh, Birdy—'

'Stop "Oh, Birdy"ing me!' I burst out. 'I'm not ... not a child, and I may be from the suburbs but I'm not my bloody mother!'

At that, he baulked, as well he might. I rarely swear and

never in public. 'I'm sorry.' He laid down Barbara Cartland's *We Could Have Danced All Night* atop Anne Frank's diary, an act that felt almost blasphemous. 'You're just so . . . so optimistic, and the world . . . it isn't like that.'

'But it could be,' I replied. 'And I know you think it too or you wouldn't be fighting all the time.'

'I—'

'So why not fight from the inside?' I got in, before he could argue. 'Even if you have to use your name to get there?'

He was silent for a while, then did what Cal always does: shrugged it off. 'I'm not playing that game,' he insisted. 'If I do it, it'll be my way.'

I sighed. There was no point in carrying on with this conversation. At least not now. 'Cup of coffee?' I tried instead.

He nodded and I plodded through the stockroom and upstairs. I knew Rollo could probably do with one, and Ted (who was as addicted as Rollo to espresso so thick you could stand a spoon up in it) was out on a job at the Colony again (their plumbing is infernal; Mummy wouldn't stand for it) so he wasn't around to make it. Charlie is off coffee – she worried it was giving the baby jitters – but I'm making her a chocolate milk (it is too hot for cocoa), and shall find a handful of SunMaid to make it a proper treat before she heads out for work.

7 P.M.

The chocolate milk is congealing on the dressing table, the raisins scattered across the floorboards like mouse droppings. Because when I got to the bedroom, Charlie wasn't reading her script, nor even sewing maternity clothes, which has been her obsession of late. She was sitting, white-faced, on the narrow bed.

'What is it?' I asked, placing the cocoa down carefully. 'Charlie, what's wrong?'

She looked up, and her eyes met mine, and I think I knew in that second before she even said it.

'I'm bleeding,' she said. 'The baby, I—'

'Oh, Charlie.' My hands opened, the raisins lost to the floor as I rushed to hold her.

And now? She is in St Thomas's Hospital, Aster at her side. While we remain on Lexington Street and wait.

And wait.

And wait.

WEDNESDAY 6 JULY

4 P.M.

There is no pretty way to say this. Charlie lost the baby.

How quickly things turn. 'On a sixpence' Daddy always said, and it's true. Yesterday we were all looking forward to the arrival of our 'Soho girl', as Rollo called her. Not that we knew she was a girl for sure, not then. But she was. A tiny, perfect girl. Just 'not viable', the doctor said to Aster. Apparently it happens all the time. More than we think, or at least anyone talks about. But this is of little comfort to anyone.

Rollo is devastated. Aster as well, although she at least is being practical about it, and has told Val he must sign Charlie off work for a week and if there is no one to cover, then she will do it herself or Cal can. I am not sure Cal will make a suitable Juliet, nor wardrobe mistress, but he hasn't complained. Meanwhile, Ted is wandering the house like a lost cat. And I? I am, for once, lost for words. It is as if everything that made me Birdy has been extracted and replaced with a mute. I am awkward and embarrassed and somehow impotent.

Perhaps that is it. Perhaps it is because I know nothing

I can do or say will fix things. Not this time. Not that Charlie seems to need that.

'It's not as if I wanted it,' she snapped when I told her I was sorry. 'And for God's sake, stop it with the long face, it's depressing me.'

She's in her room now with a Georgette Heyer (*Regency Buck*) and a stiff gin. The former was my idea, as I always find Georgette fortifying; Ted tried to protest the latter but she said, 'There's nothing to protect any more, is there?' and none of us could argue with that.

Except, now that I think of it, perhaps it's Charlie that needs protecting.

If only from herself.

FRIDAY
8 JULY

5 P.M.
Charlie is still 'fine, fine, completely fine'. Though she has read six Georgette Heyers in three days, which not even I have managed in my gloomiest of moods (there was an instance when Felicity ditched me for Amanda Horton – enormous glasses, owns a pony – and my only solace was to be found in *The Black Moth* and *Venetia*, until Felicity got thrown into a bed of nettles by Mandy's Shetland, 'Mendelssohn', and horse riding lost its gloss).

Ted is making endless cups of tea in a bid to keep her off the gin, and Rollo has taken to pacing (well, shuffling) the length of the sitting room. He says she is in denial and it will all hit her at some point soon, and then the floodgates will open and it will be us who suffer.

Though not, presumably, as much as she.

SATURDAY
9 JULY

11 A.M.
Charlie is still insisting she is 'right as rain' and will be going in to the Pippin for the matinee.

I have begged her to change her mind but she says there is only so long Doris can cover everything, and besides, there is every chance that Luella Hayes (was once a child extra in *Emergency Ward 10*, barely five foot tall) gets the tummy bug that's doing the rounds and is rendered incapable of going on stage unless it is with a bucket in one hand and a mop in the other, and she doesn't want to miss her chance to be Juliet after all.

3 P.M.
As predicted, Charlie is not right as rain at all. She is home already, having bumped into a woman with a pushchair on Brewer Street (quite literally, it seems) and promptly broken down in tears, and not just at the snag in her nylons.

'It turns out I really did want it after all,' she managed to get out between sobs as she lay on the chaise, her feet in my lap, her head in Rollo's.

'God has a terrible sense of humour,' said Rollo, as he tried to dab at her eyes with his handkerchief.

She swiped it away. 'There is no God,' she snapped. 'You of all people should realise that.'

'I'm sorry,' said Rollo, and he sounded it, ever so.

Well, that set her wailing again.

'Do you . . . do you think you should . . .' I was struggling to get the words out 'We could, that is to say, I could—'

'For God's sake, Birdy, what is it?' she demanded.

'Your mother,' I blurted. 'Shouldn't we let her know what you've been through?'

'Are you mad?' Charlie shot up.

I blinked, willed words to come, but there were none again.

'She'd be relieved,' snapped Charlie. 'Tell me I deserved it for being . . . for being fast, or loose or stupid, or . . . or whatever euphemism she's using these days.'

I shook my head in automatic disbelief, but then stopped myself. Because wouldn't my mother do the same? She'd barely been able to hear Charlie's name once the news was out, and this, well, wouldn't it justify her rancour? There are some things that even today, in 1960, no matter one's background, are considered ill behaviour: being homosexual is one, falling pregnant out of wedlock another. And the two in one fell swoop?

No, Charlie is right. This is best kept to ourselves. I am sure, between us, we can manage.

TUESDAY
12 JULY

4 P.M.
Charlie has barely slept in three nights, what with all the crying, and blowing her nose because of the crying, and getting up for spurious glasses of water (which then have to be checked for gin). I know this because I am sharing her bed (see the gin point again) which may be foolhardy but seems the least I can do given the state of her. We are all pitching in. Ted's been fetching pastries before he goes out to work (which she is stubbornly refusing to eat) and Cal's running the shop single-handedly as I'm too tired and Rollo is too heaven-knows-what these days. Frankly, we need respite care, all of us, and if she can't go to her mother's, then there must be somewhere.

'What about Aster's?' I suggested. 'You could stay there for a couple of days?'

'Norman is pregnant,' she reminded me. 'I couldn't bear it if he had his kittens and I . . .' She didn't finish the sentence and I didn't correct her on Norman's gender. Because another thought had occurred to me.

I said, when it happened, that my mother would be

triumphant somehow about the whole sorry mess, but would she? She may be snobbish, but she's not a monster. And what of the gap – that 'maybe baby' that had never made it to adulthood? Perhaps this could be a connection for her. A catharsis, even. So I had to try, didn't I? For both of their sakes. And I had to do it soon. Now, in fact!

'I know you don't want to see your mother,' I began, 'or tell her anything—'

'No!' she snapped. 'How many times?'

'I hadn't finished!' I told her, impatient myself. 'Let me just say this! So,' I tried again, 'if you don't want to be with your mother, what about mine?'

'Pardon?' she asked, staring at me as if I were stark raving mad.

Perhaps I was, but I was going to say it anyway. 'You don't have to tell her anything. But she's ever so good in a crisis. No nonsense, and all that.'

'But you're always saying she doesn't understand you . . .'

'She doesn't,' I conceded. 'But this is different. You're not me, and besides, I think . . . I just think, as a mother, she'll understand.'

'I . . .'

While Charlie flailed for whatever excuse she could dig up, I snatched at something else. 'Also, her chocolate cake is to die for. Haven't you always said that was the one thing you regretted about not being a deb? That cake at the palace?'

'Well, yes, but—'

'So, have it. Have your cake at last – Mummy bakes ever so well – and have a little holiday in the provinces.'

Charlie frowned. 'Have you even asked her?'

I shook my head. 'Not yet,' I admitted. 'But I just know she'll agree.'

*

Or rather, Daddy would, and did, and I could have flung my arms around him right there and then, but I suppose I shall just have to wait until I arrive. We are getting the train in half an hour – Aster is taking us to the station. She offered to drive us all the way but there is only so much scandal my mother can handle in one day.

As it is, I hope I'm doing the right thing. I suppose we shall both know in a few hours' time.

10 P.M.

If I had hoped to be welcomed with all the tooting ceremony of a prodigal daughter, I was more of a fool than I thought. Daddy answered the door with the look of a man summoned gallows-ward.

'What on earth's happened?' I asked.

He sighed. 'Jam catastrophe.'

He needed say no more. It is Surbiton Show in a week and Mummy and Mrs Tredegar have been locked in an annual jam battle since 1956. Rather like the boat race, it is always one or the other who wins (additional competitors are regarded rather as Johnny-come-latelys) and they are currently even Stevens, so this is a crunch batch. Thankfully Daddy cheered at the sight of Charlie, whom he *did* welcome as the proverbial prodigal, ushering her into the sitting room and offering her a rug for her knees as if she were an invalid or Granny Arbuthnot.

'I'm fine,' Charlie said, 'really.'

But she took the rug anyway, and the cup of tea he gamely made (Daddy can make orange squash and fry an egg, but that really is the limit to his kitchen abilities, largely because Mummy has barred him). She made quite the picture, huddled on the chintz as if it were midwinter, not blistering July. Sort of small, somehow; diminished. She was not fine at all. I knew it, Daddy knew it, and when Mummy finally emerged from the kitchen, in a sugary fug and red-faced from some effort with pectin, she knew it too.

There was a pause as she regarded Charlie and Charlie her, the air thicker than jam itself. I prayed for leniency, for some kind of biblical miracle, and perhaps it was the rigid position, or perhaps Charlie's face – pale as whey with a sheen of sweat from the Welsh blanket – but something seemed to give in Mummy.

She wiped her hands on her apron, and appeared to steel herself. Then, 'Honestly, Gerry,' she said. 'It's far too hot for wool. What she needs is a sheet and a damp flannel. And . . . and a lie down. Come along, dear.'

'But the jam—' began Daddy.

'Oh . . . beggar the jam!' snapped Mummy, which is when we knew she was serious. Then she reached out a hand, and Charlie, apparently entranced, took it, and let herself be led up to my room, where she lay on the lavender candlewick until Mummy took up a supper of cold quiche Lorraine and a vitamin tablet.

'Well, she's lost . . . a lot of blood, hasn't she?' she said when I questioned it (we, much to my disappointment, were still expected to eat at the table).

'So, she can stay?' I checked.

Mummy paused, a forkful of (actually rather crisp and delicious) pastry poised mid-air. 'She can,' she said eventually.

And oh, my heart!

Then ensued a rather tedious conversation that took in Gloria's quest to enter Geraldine in the 'Bonniest Baby' competition at the Surbiton Show (victory unlikely, as she looks like Churchill at the moment), Julian's quest to keep ferrets (again, victory unlikely, on grounds of smell and being 'common'), and the Tredegars' quest for the lead roles in Surbiton Amateur Dramatic Society's Christmas production of *Cat on a Hot Tin Roof* (victory surely impossible on grounds of both age and ability, plus I suspect the accents would make Charlie's Eliza Doolittle look convincing).

Daddy drove me home gone nine, the air still hot even while night began its inky creep from the east.

'How did you know?' he asked as we swung onto the flat expanse of Putney Heath.

'About Mummy?' I checked, snatching a glance at him.

He nodded.

I stared at the tail-lights of an Austin once more, unable to face him suddenly. 'I just . . . did,' I replied. 'I . . . I'm not an accident, am I?' I knew it wasn't really a question, even as I said it.

Daddy laughed – the short, sad kind. 'No, you're long fought-for, my darling.'

A chill passed over me and I shivered. 'What was her name?' I managed. 'Or . . . his?'

Daddy took a deep and loud breath. '*Their* names,' he corrected.

'Oh!' The word burst from me as I imagined it. Imagined poor Mummy. 'I . . . You don't have to tell me . . .'

But he did. 'Three,' he said. 'Two went long before they were born, like poor Charlie's. One . . . well, she survived a few weeks. Alice, she was called.' He paused, then picked up his thread again. 'We'd given up when you came along. So you weren't an accident at all, you were a . . . a bloody miracle.'

I didn't have to look at him to know he was crying quietly, and I thought of Mummy doing the same over all three babies. I jinked, suddenly worried how upsetting she must be finding all this, only . . .

'I did do the right thing, didn't I?' I checked.

BIRDY ARBUTHNOT'S YEAR OF 'YES'

Daddy turned to me briefly, eyes wet, but smiling. 'You did, Birdy, you did.'

WEDNESDAY 13 JULY

10 A.M.
I might have done the right thing by Charlie (although we shall see about that – I suspect she will last barely more than a day once Mummy's myriad 'conditions' (no snacks bar apples, no Thames Television, no gin) have been made apparent) but I have royally messed up when it comes to Rollo. In short, Cal and I forgot we were supposed to review Le Caprice last night and the copy is due in a matter of hours.

'Can't we just cobble something together?' asked Cal. 'I mean, how different can it be to Sheekey's or The Ritz? There'll be steak and some sort of lobster on the menu and we can just call it, I don't know, "predictably brilliant".'

'But what if it isn't?' I said. 'What if the steak is tough as old mutton and the lobster gone off?'

'Val had a pretty poor experience with mussels once,' Rollo pondered. 'Although that might have been Delaney's. Most of the late nineteen-forties sort of blur into one.'

'Well, where *have* you eaten in the last month, then?' Cal demanded.

'Here?' I snorted. 'The Lorelei?'

'Not the Lorelei,' Rollo said, quickly. 'Stav would never forgive me. It's packed in there every shift as it is.'

'Well it's that or the quiche Lorraine I had last night in Magnolia Road,' I snapped, clean out of options. Except . . . 'Actually, why not?' I said then.

Cal frowned at me. 'Why not what?'

'Why not write a review of someone's home cooking for once? It's always menacingly expensive meals, which the average *Herald* reader couldn't possibly dream of. But quiche? Well, that's not out of the realms of most of us.'

Rollo looked mortified. 'I—'

'It's that or the Lorelei,' I threatened. 'Or you come clean and drop the column.'

Rollo held up his hands. 'Quiche it is,' he said. 'God help us if I don't get sacked anyway.'

And so it was that I found myself reviewing Mummy's expertly crisped bacon, the pastry so light it 'must have been kneaded by angels', the accompanying potato salad 'just the right side' of lukewarm (she was trying to rescue the jam and got distracted). I've also noted the 'plain but homely decor', the 'charming company of regular customers', and 'the brisk but efficient manner of the head chef, who is, unusually, a woman'.

'Why is it that men are chefs and woman mere cooks?' Cal wondered aloud as he typed up my dictation (he has, to my disappointment, overtaken my admittedly woeful words per minute, plus his accuracy is immaculate).

I shrugged. 'Because we're not swayed by silly titles?' I suggested. Though I knew this was as pie in the sky as '43 Magnolia Road, Surbiton's newest place to eat and be seen'. 'Perhaps that can be your next battle,' I said eventually.

Cal rolled his eyes, but smiled. 'I'll add it to the list, shall I?' he said, then, having typed the final line – Rollo's habitual sign-off – scanned the page again. 'This is good, you know?'

'It is?'

He nodded. 'I hope your mother's proud when she sees it.'

'If she sees it.' I met his eyes. 'I hope Panther's proud of you.'

He paused, then shot the typewriter carriage back with a slam. 'Perhaps.'

And that was the end of our conversation. He claimed he needed to check on Norman (who is not enjoying pregnancy at all and is using it as an excuse to destroy more matter than usual, including General Eisenhower), but I suspect I had overstepped again. I do make a habit of it.

Oh, I hope Charlie is all right. I hope Mummy isn't bothering her, or Daddy boring her. And I hope to heaven Gloria hasn't shown up with Geraldine. Though perhaps Mummy is tactful enough to put a stop to that at least, even if the baby does look off-putting.

Anyway, I don't have time to surmise anything else as the review needs to be dropped off in Fleet Street by three, and I've to make Rollo tea and toast, and hope he'll eat it this time.

Heavens, being a grown-up never stops, does it? I rather envy Julian, whose problems are still limited to imaginary ferrets and getting locked in the stationery cupboard (he claims it was a mathematical challenge, but even Aunt Barbara says it smells of foul play). Though at least I am not pregnant.

Or bereft.

SATURDAY 16 JULY

10 A.M.
As predicted, Charlie has lasted less than a week with my mother.

'It's all very . . . nice here,' she said when she rang at eight this morning. 'But—'

'Why are you calling so early?' I interrupted, as I staggered across the living room to open the sash.

'Well, precisely,' she said. 'Something about "slug-a-beds", I think?'

It came to me in a horrible flash: Mummy's 'everyone up' rule, even on weekends (lie-ins being responsible for everything from loose morals to gout). 'Oh,' I managed. 'Shall I come to fetch you?' I suggested. 'I can blame it on the shop or something. Or say Val needs you back.'

'Would you?' asked Charlie. 'I mean, I don't want you or her to think I'm ungrateful, because I *am* grateful, very! Only there is only so much dentistry chat one can take. Also your father is trying to get me to take up golf, and I almost caved. If it hadn't been for the fact that I met whatsisname—'

'Mr Tredegar?' I suggested. 'Two doors down. Amateur dramatics.'

'Him,' she agreed. 'Tedious man. Came round last night to borrow a drill bit and didn't leave for three hours. Well, if it wasn't for him then I might be playing a best ball or whatever it is right now.'

'Four-ball better ball.' I sighed, both at the thought and the fact I knew the correct name.

'That's the badger,' she confirmed. 'As it is I had to endure his terrible American accent. Honestly, I nearly gave him lessons on the spot.'

I smiled to myself. 'Say no more. I'm on my way.'

And I am. Just as soon as I can get champion slug-a-bed Rollo up and behind the counter for a couple of hours. I don't know what's wrong with him, but ever since that collapse he's been definitely ailing tummy-wise, and yet has refused to go to the doctor. Says they'll condemn him like a stud thoroughbred gone to seed. I said that was rather braggardly, and if anything, he was more of a mule: a handsome one, but a mule nonetheless. Thankfully he laughed, though he still won't see a GP. Perhaps he needs a dose of my mother as well. She is quicker than the salts to get things moving, it seems.

9 P.M.

Charlie is home, and looking like a new woman. Her skin

is clear, her hair shiny, her nails clipped and free of chipped polish for once. Though she has already had two espressos (coffee is on Mummy's latest proscription list) and run round to the Pippin to beg for her job back from Doris before the show closes for August.

Mummy was sad to see her go, I think. 'You never said she was clever,' she said to me, as Charlie and Daddy took her things to the car.

I frowned. 'I suppose I don't think of her in those terms,' I admitted with a spasm of guilt. 'She's . . . well, she's exciting. Not a bookworm at all.'

'She could make Cambridge as well if she *tried*,' said Mummy. 'She knew the title of every Shakespeare play, and the French for macaroon. We finished the *Times* crossword in minutes. Minutes, I tell you!'

I did not divulge that that was possibly the limit of Charlie's academic ability. That wasn't the point. The point was: 'She doesn't *want* to.'

'Just a suggestion,' she said. 'If this acting thing doesn't work out. She can join you.'

Thankfully, Charlie marched back in again at that point. 'Just sent another lot away, Sheila,' she said to my mother. 'Wanted a table for eight this time.'

Mummy frowned. 'For heaven's sake,' she muttered. 'I'm not a . . . a hotel. Heaven knows what's going on, but this is the third lot since yesterday.'

It came to me in a cold wash, like a slew of gazpacho into the lap. 'I . . . well, I think you might be a sort of . . . restaurant.'

Mummy narrowed her eyes and lips in that synchronised movement that still fills me with terror.

I dug in my pocket and pulled out the review I'd clipped from the *Herald*. 'Here,' I said. 'It was . . . well, it was an emergency.'

'An emergency?' she repeated as she snatched it from my hand and put on the spectacles that hung from a practical strap around her neck.

'It's . . . it's a favour to Rollo,' I explained. 'Cal and I write it but I'd missed our reservation at Le Caprice because of coming here and, well . . . that's it really.'

Daddy, who was reading over her shoulder, grinned. 'This is rather good, Birdy! I like the line about bacon gods.'

I looked to Mummy to see if she might agree with this or any other line. Her face betrayed nothing, then she folded the paper and handed it back with a 'there's a misplaced apostrophe in the third paragraph'.

This, I knew from experience, was her way of saying 'thank you'. Besides, she was right. 'It really was delicious,' I assured her. 'The quiche, I mean. Far better than The Ritz.'

She pulled off her spectacles and patted the rigid set of her hair. 'Nonsense,' she said. 'Anyway, how would you know?'

'I've eaten there,' I assured her. 'And it's true.'

She pinked like a shrimp in a hot pan.

'You'll have to put a sign up,' Daddy said to her then.

'"Reservations full".'

Mummy's mouth twitched, then she shook herself. 'Don't be ridiculous, Gerry. Now get on with you' – she shooed us – 'or you'll get stuck in traffic.'

We didn't get stuck, but we did go the long way so I could show Charlie my school, and Daddy could show her the golf club. And then we persuaded him in for a cup of tea with Rollo and Ted (Cal hasn't shown his face since Wednesday).

'Tell Mummy I'm sorry,' I said, when he left. 'About the review, I mean.'

He smiled. 'She's secretly thrilled,' he said. 'And so she should be. You're turning out to be a nice little writer.'

I bloomed at that, and still felt the syrup sweetness of it as the car pulled off down towards Brewer Street. Tried not to think of the 'and that Cal chap' he'd added as an afterthought.

What Cal is, and who Cal is, are less clear by the day.

At least, who he is to me.

SUNDAY
17 JULY

10 A.M.
I have just reread what I wrote last night, and Cal is no one to me. At least, not in any significant sense. And even if I were considering... *something*, well, I'd be a fool because he's completely unsuitable. Self-pitying and ungracious and, well, too many things to list. I just meant... Oh, I don't know what I meant. It is too hot to think properly, and the door knocker is clonking horribly. Honestly, who is up at ten in the morning on a Sunday in Soho? It's practically sacrilege. Well, they shall just have to deal with me unwashed, unbrushed, and in one of Rollo's cast-off bathrobes, as it is too sweaty to wear anything in bed and I don't have time to dress, still less to keep writing this.

11 A.M.
Of course it was Cal. Of course it was. Because that's exactly the sort of thing I would conjure were I writing a novel. Only, in that version, I would have been immaculate and smelling

of Elizabeth Arden, and would have answered the door with something coquettish or mysterious, rather than the 'for God's sake, I'm coming' that I actually managed. As it is, it is a miracle he didn't turn heel and run off to the Lorelei for sanctuary. Though he did pull quite the look as he took in the dishevelled mess I am, and asked if I had had some sort of accident.

I took a leaf out of Mummy's book and narrowed my eyes. 'Well, if you will call at ungodly hours, what do you expect?' At that he shrank, and I felt a stab of guilt. 'Sorry,' I added. 'It's just . . . it's been a long week.'

'Well, I don't want to add—' he began.

'No, no,' I interrupted. 'Ignore me. Come up to the kitchen. I'll pop the kettle on.'

In the end there was no time for tea as he is a man on mission. He has finally decided to find his father, and we are off to Mile End this very minute. Or at least once I've put something decent on and brushed my hair and teeth.

Oh! I am quite giddy with it. And to think this was my idea! First Charlie and my mother, and now this. Again, if I were writing a novel, there would be a moving reconciliation scene between the men, followed by our own private reconciliation, and—

No, snap out of it, Birdy! And stop bloody writing or nothing will happen at all, least of all . . . that.

10 P.M.

I am a terrible person. Or rather, Cal believes that I'm one, which is more or less the same thing. At least, it feels that way.

I can't even write about it. Not tonight. Perhaps not at all, given that this journal is the very root of it. This sort of thing never happened to Cassandra Mortmain. But then, I expect she kept the Sixpenny Book well-hidden, rather than lying open on the bedspread for all to see.

Oh! I feel nauseated at the thought of it. How I wish I could go back to this morning and rewrite this little bit of my life. Though, if nothing else, this proves that God (or Allah or Mohammed) cannot possibly exist.

That, or they have a very dark sense of humour indeed.

MONDAY
18 JULY

10 P.M.

So I *am* writing about it after all, because I have thought about it long and hard and I don't think I am entirely to blame for the situation. Also because I want to put down for posterity what happened in Mile End as I don't suppose Cal will bother, and one day he might like to recall it, even if it is through my 'frighteningly myopic eyes'. So, here goes nothing.

It started out well enough. We caught an omnibus through Aldgate and Stepney and up towards Bow Road, the dense, elegant architecture giving way to cranes and concrete the further we went into what Mummy still insists on calling 'the slums'.

'I suppose it's progress,' I said. 'Given the damage.' So much had been flattened – still was, the bombs cutting craters into entire neighbourhoods. His included. 'Do you remember any of the war?'

'Nothing,' he replied, his eyes on the tattered awning of an eel and pie shop. 'Not a jot until I was about five and by then, well, my mother was gone and Ickthorpe was . . . permanent. You?'

'Not really,' I admitted. We were taken to Cornwall, to my maternal grandparents, or so Mummy tells me. Daddy stayed in Surbiton, because teeth still needed fixing, I suppose. I don't remember anything until 1945 and only then because Granny Goggins's Jack Russell was sick in my lap on VE Day.

I wondered something though: if perhaps he might feel a sense of connection despite the lack of memory – if the East End was etched in him somehow – and I was about to ask, when the bus pulled to a noisy halt and the driver called out 'Tower Hamlets Cemetery!', a fact that filled me with foreboding, as if death was present already.

'This is us,' he said, and jumped to his feet.

I followed wordlessly, suddenly stoppered at the enormity of it all, at what we might be about to find out. Neither of us spoke as we skirted the graveyard, made our way along Ropery Street to Bow Common Lane.

It was I who broke the silence, as we stared at the plot where Number 36 must have once stood.

'We could ask someone?' I suggested.

He scanned the road. 'The crane operator?' he scoffed. 'The brickies?'

'I just meant . . .' I trailed off. I didn't know what I meant, again. 'I'm sorry,' I said instead. 'There must be someone though. Someone, somewhere who remembers a . . . a Donald Hawthorn.'

And all of a sudden, it coursed through me, hot as a hornet:

determination to sort this, to make this right. I ran across the road and knocked at the door of Number 29.

A woman answered, young – too young to have been around back then. 'I don't suppose your... parents are in?' I tried.

'Parents?' she scoffed. 'Hardly.' A baby cried somewhere down the hallway, and she didn't wait before slamming the door in my face.

'Birdy—' tried Cal.

But I wasn't deterred, refused to be, knocking on every door I could get to, trying 27, 25, 23, then back up to 31, 33 and then 35. And there, finally, was a man around Rollo's age, his hair grey, his skin greyer.

'Thirty-six?' he checked, rubbing a nose that had clearly once been broken. 'Opposite?'

I nodded. 'Donald Hawthorn.'

'Oh yeah, I remember that one, all right. Don, he was. Mouth on him. Gambler, you know? Gee-gees, dogs – anything that raced, basically. Shame the bookies was shut that day. If it'd been open, he might have been spared.'

'You mean—'

'Bomb, obviously. Missed us by the skin of our teeth.'

I glanced at Cal, but his head hung to the ground.

'You relatives or something?' the man carried on.

At that, Cal raised his face. 'No,' he said. 'No relation.'

'Sorry to have bothered you,' I added.

When the man shut the door, Cal turned to me. 'I should

have checked the death certificates, shouldn't I. You'd think, after my... my sister...'

It was his turn to let go of the thread, and without thinking I reached for his hand.

He let me take it. 'Can we go back now?'

I squeezed hard. 'Of course,' I said. 'Of course.'

*

We got off the bus at Tottenham Court Road, still holding hands, a state that remained as we meandered through Sunday Soho, across the Square and then to Lexington Street. As I slipped the key in the lock, something seemed to jump in front of me, bright and glimmering with promise. I seized that too. 'How about I take you for a late lunch at Rules?' I turned to him. 'You can't be gloomy in Rules, Rollo always says that.'

'You can't afford—'

'Daddy slipped me some money for emergencies,' I said. 'And if this isn't one, I don't know what is.'

And then it happened. He touched my cheek and electricity shot through me, a bolt as hot and sharp as lightning itself, but delightful somehow. An exquisite spark!

I felt my cheeks flush with it. 'I-I need to change,' I stammered. 'I'll be quick, though.'

'Can I help you pick?' he asked.

'I... Yes,' I said. 'Of course.'

And that is how he came to be in my bedroom, rifling through the wardrobe that now bustled with Charlie's cast-offs and creations, picking out an emerald dress that shimmered like the carapace of a particularly brilliant beetle. 'Here,' he said. 'This.'

I nodded. He was right. It was perfect. 'I'll just—' I gestured to the screen that Charlie and I had found in a skip on Ingestre Place.

As I slipped behind it, I heard the creak as he sat on my bed, and I cursed myself for not changing the sheets, or at least decreasing them.

'You realise this just means I don't fit anywhere,' he said. 'I've been educated out of the East End but I'm too bloody ill-born for Panther's lot.'

'You can't be angry at Panther,' I said, my heart skittering as I slipped off the rather dowdy brown thing I'd been wearing. 'She did you a kindness. And anyway, that's not true. Aster doesn't think so, and I bet nor do Panther and Freddy.'

'Maybe not them,' he conceded. 'But at school. At univer—'

'You've not even tried university,' I interrupted, as I stepped into the green wiggle dress, pulled it over my hips. 'And Jack manages.'

'Jack's Jack,' he retorted. 'He just mimics the richies—'

'You *are* rich,' I pointed out. 'At least compared to a lot of people. To me, even.'

He didn't reply to that; I assumed at the time he was chastened. But when, a few minutes later I emerged from the screen with a 'ta-dah!' – awaiting a smile, if not exactly the applause I felt the dress deserved – truth slapped sense into me.

He was reading my diary.

This diary.

My stomach plummeted; I didn't know whether to be angry or afraid. 'What . . . what are you doing?'

He looked up at me, his jaw set, his eyes hard and cold. 'Is that what you think?' he asked, shaking the book at me. 'That I'm a . . . a fake. An . . . an angry young man with a – what did you call it? – oh, yes, a "chip on his shoulder"?'

My heart ceased its jinking and seemed to stop dead. 'I never said that,' I pleaded. 'Not exactly, anyway.'

He scoffed. 'I can't believe I almost . . .'

'Almost what?' I asked.

He shook his head, stood.

I panicked, snatched at straws. 'Did you read what else I wrote? That you're . . . you're kind, and . . . inspiring. That I might, I might . . .'

'. . . *like you,*' I didn't finish. Because he was gone. *Is* gone. He hasn't shown up for work, not that I believed he would, and he won't come to the telephone at Aster's. She says he's out, but I suspect her of covering up.

I've told Charlie and she says I must wait it out and that he'll come to his senses soon.

So wait I shall, I suppose.

TUESDAY 19 JULY

11 P.M.
And wait.

FRIDAY
22 JULY

11 P.M.
And wait.

SUNDAY 31 JULY

11 P.M.
And wait.

AUGUST 1960

MONDAY 1 AUGUST

10 A.M.
I have waited patiently for more than a fortnight, but now I am taking this into my own hands. If the mountain will not come to Mohammed then I am jolly well going to the mountain, i.e. I am going to Aster's to have it out with Cal, which, if not quite at Kilimanjaro-summiting levels, is an arduous walk up to Bloomsbury in this heat. At the very least it cannot make things any worse, whatever Charlie says (and she says quite a lot on the matter). Even if we never rekindle whatever it was that happened on the doorstep, then at least we shall be civil again.

Also, it will distract me from the news from Surbiton, which is that, on the back of Rollo Round Town's review of 43 Magnolia Road, Mummy has been offered her own recipe column in the *Herald*. It is to be called 'Winning Ways'.

'Isn't it marvellous?' she said.

I agreed it was, although I admit there was a good deal of pasting on my 'thrilled' face and false platitudes as, really, I am seething green with envy, a condition only aggravated by the fact that Surbiton has the sudden attraction of back gardens and hosepipes and endless lemonade. I know it is only a matter of miles as the crow flies but it might as well be on a different continent in this weather. Where Surbiton is vaguely airy and scented with lavender, Soho is sweaty and fetid. Berwick Street smells terrible, or at least worse than usual, all dropped fruit and rotting fish; the whole effect is of an overfilled saucepan on a raging stove and at any moment the whole lot will boil over.

Perhaps Bloomsbury will offer some relief; it is at least half a mile north, after all.

8 P.M.

Bloomsbury did not offer relief of any kind.

'Oh,' exclaimed a puzzled Aster upon answering the door. 'But Cal's in Essex. Didn't he tell you?'

My face clearly indicated that a) he had not, and b) this was grave news, as within seconds I had been ushered into the drawing room, which is usually an inspirational space – its vertiginous walls filled with mirrors and pictures, many of them Aster's own – but today felt like more human soup, with added cat. (Norman has had the kittens: four of them, all dear little things, though quite definitely not of Boris's Persian lineage, suggesting General Eisenhower did get up to no good after all.) I was, at least, graced with iced tea, laced with some sort of alcohol, which I might usually have refused, but today felt could only fortify my weakening self.

'Spill,' said Aster as she handed me the glass.

I frowned at the glass.

'Not that. The beans!' Aster explained.

'Oh.' I winced. 'He hasn't told you?'

'If he had, I doubt we'd be in this situation.' She sighed, and lifted General Eisenhower into her lap, where he sat scowling at me as if fatherhood – or life – was already too much to bear. 'I assume it's his hot head again?'

'Yes . . . No . . . Oh, I don't know.' I couldn't get a grip on it – on me. 'I'm not really sure. It's all such a . . . a muddle. One minute we were going to Rules—'

'Rules? On your pay packet?' Aster looked horrified, as well she might (I have since checked the menu and Daddy's funds would barely cover lunch for one of us).

'It was an emergency,' I explained. 'Because . . . well, the first bit is his story to tell and I shan't do it for him—'

'His lineage, I assume?' she interrupted.

I flinched but didn't give.

'Sorry, go on,' she nudged.

'Well, I'd left my journal out and he' – I steeled myself – 'read something upsetting. Something I never really intended anyone to see.'

Aster and General Eisenhower regarded me for a moment with something that might have been confusion, and might have been contempt. 'How bad was it?' she asked eventually.

'Pretty bad,' I confirmed. 'Had he read the rest, it might

have made up for it, but . . . well, he didn't.'

Aster nodded. General Eisenhower appeared to do the same.

I glanced away, uneasy under their gaze, caught a portrait above their left shoulders of a blonde in a folly of some sort, gazing over a ha-ha. 'Is that . . . Charlie?' I asked.

Aster glanced up, and – did she jink? 'Her mother,' she said.

I looked up again. 'They're terribly alike.' The same noses. The same eyes. The same way they hold themselves under the eye of their painters – with pride; delight even.

'In some ways,' Aster murmured, still in a reverie. Then she snapped her eyes back to mine. 'But very much not in others.'

I took a chance; after all, I'd confessed to her, hadn't I? Plus, it was a neat change of subject. 'What happened? With you and Daphne, I mean.'

Something passed over her face, leaving a flash of scarlet in its wake. 'I . . . It's a long story.'

But I knew it instantly, recognised it from Charlie herself when Fitz's name was mentioned. 'You and she,' I said in wonder. 'But . . . she married a man.'

Aster laughed, but was unamused. 'Lots of us do.'

'*You* didn't,' I pointed out.

'I always was the bloody-minded one,' she explained. 'Plus, I had the luck of a mother whose only wish was for my happiness.'

'And then you met Topaz.' An eccentric, I knew, who outshone even her literary equivalent.

'And then I met Topaz.' She smiled, guileless this time, and wide, before this slipped. 'Bloody awful, the war,' she added wistfully. Then she stood, General Eisenhower forced floorward; a state that he met with his usual misanthropy. (God knows why Norman suffers him, though perhaps there is someone for everyone, even in cat-land.) 'I'll tell Cal you called for him.'

'I . . . Thank you,' I managed as I shot to my feet, aware this was my cue to exit stage left (pursued, if not by bears, then by a disgruntled feline).

And then, as swiftly as I'd been pulled in, I was out in the swell of Marchmont Street again, my feet sticking to the paving, my dress to my spine, my hair to my forehead. A state I retain as I lie here on the bed wishing – to my absolute surprise – that I were not in Soho at all, nor even in Surbiton, but in the very depths of Essex.

FRIDAY
5 AUGUST

5 P.M.
Bloomsbury has offered relief after all!

Or rather, Aster has. I do believe she has a sixth sense, as she has offered to take us back to Ickthorpe for August. A month in the country! Well, a couple of weeks at least. How terribly Mortmainish after all! Charlie was reluctant at first, as well she might be, given her mother. But, as Aster pointed out, Balfour Hall is several miles out of the village, and she doesn't even have to leave the sanctity of Marigold's if she doesn't want to ('sanctity' said with a pause before it, which I noted, but thankfully Charlie did not. In any case, it is a relief not to be billeted to Panther's and have to share a roof with Cal and, presumably, Jack). Besides, as I pointed out, the Pippin is shut until the next run in September and so she has nothing else to do but mope around Lexington Street complaining about the infernal heat, the recalcitrant plumbing and the continuing presence of Minty Brigham who, while quite delightful in many ways, is hoping to become Ted's latest muse and has taken to wandering stark naked up and down the stairs in a bid to achieve this. None of us need to see that much flesh on a daily basis.

Anyway, in the end she agreed and we are off on Monday, along with Norman, General Eisenhower and their chaotic offspring. Rollo is staying behind on health grounds. I begged him to come but he said he withers anywhere beyond Oxford Street and so, North Essex might actually do for him. Instead, Doris is going to mind the shop, and Val is moving in for a bit.

'But where will he sleep?' I asked without thinking. 'The sofa's awfully uncomfortable for more than a . . . Oh.'

Rollo smiled. 'Such a green little bird. My parakeet.' And he held a dry, slight hand to my face.

I smiled, hiding the twinge of regret I felt – that was Cal's expression, after all – and then the trepidation. After all, in less than twenty-four hours I would be seeing him.

Will be seeing him.

Oh, golly. I do hope he's halfway to forgiving me.

If not, August is going to feel a long, long month indeed.

MONDAY
8 AUGUST

10 A.M.

Essex awaits, and I could not be more thrilled if it were the French Riviera or Paris itself. In fact, Paris is surely only more gruesome stew, whereas Essex will be a breath of fresh air, in every sense. Charlie has promised me river swims, cream teas on lawns and long walks across patchwork fields with 'Marigold's brood', although whether this constitutes children or livestock I failed to ascertain. In any case, I am practically heaving with relief. London is wonderful and Soho *everything*, but it is like any treat: one must steer clear every so often to appreciate it the more. Plus there is only so much smell of drain I can inhale before even a week in Hull might look enticing.

7 P.M.

If I thought Soho was eccentric, Ickthorpe, and, more precisely, the Dower House, home of Marigold and Hugo Launceston and many small Launcestons, is more so.

Marigold is adorable of course, though quite, quite mad. She is mostly dressed in her husband's clothes, as she says skirts are impossible for milking, riding, shearing, shoeing and castrating (this last one said with great aplomb, which I am refusing to think about). Hugo, I assume, dresses more normally, but he is yet to be seen as he commutes into the city by train every day to do something with money, leaving Marigold with the animals (four goats, three sheep, two ponies, a cow, and endless ducks, chickens, rabbits and cats – all of whom seem to wander in and out of the house as and when it pleases them, which is all very well with cats and rabbits but slightly more concerning when it is sheep). On top of that there are the boys: Nesbitt (seven, swarthy, eating mud when we arrived), Andrew (ten, menacing, carries a rabbit with him at all times) and Siegfried (thirteen in a fortnight, mostly melts things and explodes things), named, Marigold told me, after much-missed childhood pets and a 'blacksmith who could spit for Essex'. I thought it best not to interrogate this.

I almost wish I were with Panther at Bridge House, even with Cal not speaking to me. At least there I might be able to change for supper without worrying there is a sheep or a malevolent ten year old watching me. Charlie says I will be used to it all by the morning, and it will be no more than 'happy chaos'.

I do hope so. Right now it is mostly chaos chaos.

TUESDAY
9 AUGUST

10 A.M.
It is definitely still chaos chaos. We awoke to the sound of a cockerel crowing, not from the yard outside, but, rather more shoutingly, from the proximity of our windowsill. More worrying was that Andrew was sitting next to him watching us, like some sort of homunculus.

'How long have you been there?' Charlie demanded as she raised one side of her silk sleep mask.

'Long enough,' he said, ominously, and then disappeared, thankfully taking the cockerel with him.

Charlie let the mask drop, and we were about to go back to sleep when a bleat alerted us to another presence of the livestock variety, and in the end it was just easier to get up and wrangle all non-residents out ourselves.

Breakfast was no less perilous, involving as it did Nesbitt's 'mush' – an experimental recipe which he insisted we try.

'What exactly is in it?' I asked.

'Oats. Malt. Gooseberry jam,' he replied. 'And a secret ingredient.'

This didn't sound too bad and I agreed to a spoonful before passing it to Charlie.

'What exactly *is* the secret ingredient?' she asked as she stared into the gloop.

Marigold provided the answer, swooping in from the scullery with a cry of, 'Don't touch that. It's got fishmeal in it. Duck grade only!'

Too late; I had swallowed. In its defence, it tasted mostly of gooseberries, and Nesbitt assured me it promised 'clear eyes and a deep sheen on feathers'. But I am rather glad we are picnicking for lunch at the river, and are making the sandwiches ourselves. Siegfried begged to come but Marigold reminded him he is barred until he can be trusted not to indulge in a 'repeat of last time' and Andrew isn't coming as he 'has rabbit business to attend to'. We are, however, taking Nesbitt, his water wings, and strict instructions not to let him urinate 'or the other' in the water. But who would do that, I wonder? Surely no one human.

10.15 A.M.
Siegfried, according to Nesbitt. Hence the ban.

5 P.M.
Oh, heavens! The river is silken bliss, just as I imagined, its

banks bulrush-studded, its wide, clear expanse shimmering with sticklebacks and minnows, the air above it alive with the dip and soar of swifts and dragonflies.

The effect was compromised slightly by my swimsuit, which isn't one, i.e. it is a vest and underpants, as I didn't think to bring bathers when I moved from Surbiton – Soho being rather lacking in municipal facilities and me being rather lacking in enthusiasm for chlorinated bowls of hair-studded minestrone. This, though, was as far from the school pool as the Dower House from Lexington Street. Cool, and soothing, and marred only by Nesbitt's determination to imprison several of the river's inhabitants in a plastic bucket.

Though I suppose I should be thankful that he was the only other occupant bar Charlie and me, given the pants debacle. It was that or complete nudity, which both Charlie and Nesbitt mooted several times, but thankfully I managed to dissuade them. I am all for embracing the human form/eschewing embarrassment at our naked states in principle, but not when Cal might be likely to appear from behind an oak tree at any moment. (Not that I was wishing that; if I were, I would be entirely disappointed. Not so much as a glimpse of him or any of the Bridge House lot. Not yet, anyway.)

'Imagine growing up here!' I exclaimed as I attempted what I hoped would appear an elegant breaststroke.

'Dull as anything!' replied Charlie from the bank, where she languished with the script for some new play Valentine is thinking of putting on. 'Summer was the only relief in otherwise frigid torpor.'

I assumed she was exaggerating, but she went on.

'God, I was almost glad of school.'

She had boarded, I knew, at somewhere in Oxfordshire, then gone on to the infamous Cygnets, alma mater of several debs.

I hauled myself up the muddy bank and flopped down next to her, one eye on Nesbitt, who was still scouring the shallows for potential inmates. 'But you're glad to be back, aren't you?' I asked.

She turned onto her side to face me. 'Agreeing to be here isn't quite the same as glad. But, yes, I suppose it's good for me.'

I frowned, aware of the tickle on my skin as the slick of river dissipated in the heat. 'Then why did you come?'

She smiled, laid down her text. 'Oh, Birdy, I know a friend in need when I see one.'

'I—' I went to protest, but cut myself off. She was right, and the realisation sent me pinking. 'It's nothing,' I insisted. 'Really. Just . . . a spat.'

She ignored me. 'If he doesn't show his face later,' she said, 'then we'll call for him tomorrow. It's about time you met Panth properly, anyway.'

'I . . .' But again I gave up. It was useless arguing with Charlie. Besides, I wasn't sure I wanted to.

Thankfully, any confession was interrupted by a caterwaul

from the left bank, where Nesbitt had apparently secured a toad for his collection.

It is called Bob, and is now living in our bedroom in a large jam pan, a situation I tried to amend, but Marigold pointed out that it was an honour, and with such gravity that I was forced to cave.

THURSDAY 11 AUGUST

6 A.M.
Today's oppressive alarm call is Bob, whose croak could awaken the dead (though not, apparently, Charlie, who is still snoring, though marginally less noisily). The wretch is either so alarmed or so delighted to be ensconced in the saucepan that he has been going on about it for an hour already. If he doesn't stop soon, I shall have to remove him to the bathroom sink, which seems a more suitable abode for an amphibian in any case.

6.10 A.M.
I am back from the bathroom, and still very much in possession of a toad. The bathroom may be amphibian-friendly but it is currently also duck-friendly, and I am not at all sure that, in a battle between bird and Bob, the latter would triumph.

6.30 AM
Bob is just going to have to take his chances. If he cannot

defend himself, it is only the will of nature.

6.45 A.M.
After a short, squawking flurry, silence has descended on the East Wing. I fear the worst, but am too exhausted to investigate right now. May the best creature have won.

10 A.M.
Andrew and Nesbitt have descended, demanding to know where Bob is, and why Paul (the ducks are apparently named for the gospels) has been sick on the stairs. I said I would not know, having only just woken. Charlie, thankfully, backed me, but promised a toad hunt once we were dressed and breakfasted. This was met with whooping from Nesbitt, and a severe, meaningful look from Andrew. I am not sure which child I find more disturbing.

11.30AM
It is definitely Andrew. Unsurprisingly Bob is nowhere to be seen, but Andrew says he has 'dissected the sick' and it definitely contains toad residue. I said I couldn't be held responsible if a duck had infiltrated our bedroom in the night. Andrew's look suggested otherwise. And Nesbitt is now delighted as he

thinks Paul can mesmerise himself through walls. It is all too, too much, so Charlie and I are going for a long walk around the village after lunch to escape the menacery.

1 P.M.

Nesbitt is coming with us, along with his plastic bucket. No amount of pleading with either him or Marigold can dissuade them. I fear he is hoping for a replacement toad, despite us insisting we are not going to the river. I can only imagine what he will collect instead.

6 P.M.

We are, once again, replete with amphibian, though this time it is frogs, plural. Personally I cannot tell the difference, but Nesbitt assures me frogs are 'prettier' and, worryingly, 'louder'. Thankfully, they are going to reside in the scullery, which Nesbitt thinks will be mesmeric-duck-proof as Mountbatten (a cat) lives in there. I have warned him that cats and frogs may also 'not mix' but he assure me that Mountbatten 'would not hurt a fly'. All this though is rather beside the point – which is how, exactly, we acquired the frogs – and so I shall begin.

We walked, first, around the Radley Manor estate – former home of Panther, Marigold, Aster et al., but now the property of the National Trust, and open to the public.

'All the stately homes have been opened up,' Charlie explained. 'Blenheim, Chatsworth, Hatfield.'

'Not Balfour Hall though,' I said, referring to her own very definitely stately former home (I had caught a glimpse from the car on the way, and safe to say it makes Radley look like a cottage).

'No. Granny would rather die than let "the commoners" in. Though she may get her wish. The dying I mean. She is eighty-seven, after all.'

'How did you end up here, anyway?' I asked, as we marched across a ha-ha. 'I thought your father owned a mill in Yorkshire?'

'Oh, Daddy was no good at running a business. The mill was an albatross, Mummy said; went under eventually. And then they were just living in the north for no reason, in the cold and the wet.' She paused to gesture at mullioned windows, a garden beset with lupins and hydrangeas. 'The war was a relief I think – at least at first. An excuse to come home. Essex might not be Venice, but it's less wet and London is on the doorstep.'

'What's it like?' I asked. 'Inside, I mean.'

'Radley . . . ?'

'No, Balfour Hall.'

'Oh.' She frowned. 'Horribly ostentatious. All stags' heads and swagged curtains and gilt. Plus, Granny Balfour thinks all men are ghastly and most women too. She prefers the company of dogs, so the smell is terrible.'

Marigold's has a distinctly agricultural smell but I didn't

mention that as Nesbitt was within earshot. 'How many does she have?'

'Eleven at last count.'

'Heavens.' As I have said, pets, and especially dogs, were barred in our house on myriad grounds (smell, shedding, revoltingness of poo). We did briefly foster next door's tortoise, but Mummy was appalled when he became enamoured with a bucket, and he lives in Cornwall now where that sort of thing is clearly more normalised. 'Who else lives there?' I went on, aware that I was needling, but aware as well that she was more amenable than usual; a breakthrough, perhaps!

She shrugged. 'Granny, Mummy, the Bolter perhaps—'

'The Bolter?'

'Aunt Evangeline,' she clarified. 'Beautiful in her youth but knew it, and doomed to pursue unsuitable men. It's a miracle she only has two children really. Calypso and Inigo.' She paused, lost in thought.

'You don't want to see them?' I nudged.

'God, no. Drips, the pair of them. Besides, I can't, can I? Not without upsetting bloody Mummy.' She had soured for a second, appeared almost dour. Then snapped herself out of it. 'Nesbitt! Come along, or we'll be late.'

'Late for what?' I asked, as the boy trotted back from a worrying ditch.

She smiled, her eyes literally twinkling. 'Bridge House. We're expected for tea.'

My heart danced as we walked towards the village, though less waltz and more tarantella. By the time we made it to the eponymous bridge, it was in quite the conniption.

'Isn't it darling?' said Charlie, as I took in the wide, double-fronted St Anne, all red brick and flint.

'I . . . Yes,' I managed. 'Quite . . . darling.'

And, well, it is. The building is handsome, rather than pretty. And practical rather than decorative. Bar the pond, of course – hence the frogs, which kept Nesbitt occupied for the long two hours we stayed there. But who needs bells and whistles when it's the occupants that everyone comes for?

There's Freddy and Panth, both in residence (surgery hours finish at two, and Parliament is in recess) and both as delightful as everyone has painted them. He tall and awkward, in a charming way, she small and confident with curls as defiantly unstyled as she and flaming red to boot. Panther apologized for not introducing herself properly when we'd met briefly before, blaming both the vagaries of Valentine and the press of politics. Apologised, quietly and aside, for Cal as well.

Because, yes, there was him.

He sat, sullen, throughout tea and seed cake on the terrace, only speaking when asked a direct question; a fact Charlie tried her best to take advantage of with myriad pointless queries about everything from the weather forecast to the point of beetroot. In the end he begged to leave the table.

'To do what?' asked Panther, exasperated.

'Does it matter?' he snapped.

I saw Freddy's hand slip to Panther's lap under the table. Saw her collect herself. 'Very well,' she said, adding an apology to Charlie and me once he was safely inside. 'I don't know what's got into him.'

Charlie nudged my leg under the table. I chose not to nudge it back. Besides, this was the very point at which a strange apparition happened. The man who had left the terrace only seconds earlier seemed to reappear, only this time in a running singlet and shorts, his tan torso and forehead dappled with sweat, his eyes as bright as his smile.

'Ma,' he said dipping his head for a kiss from Panth.

'Oh, stop it!' She laughed heartily. 'You're all wet!'

'Ladies.' He grinned at us and I felt heat rise in my cheeks. 'So, you must be the infamous Birdy!'

Thankfully, before I could stammer out a response, Freddy flapped a hand at him. 'Shower!' commanded his father.

'Pond!' responded the apparition. Then promptly pulled off his vest and shoes, and plunged straight into the miniature lake only yards from our vantage point.

'And that,' said Charlie as he bobbed beneath the water, as agile as a seal or a porpoise, 'would be Jack.'

I realised my mouth had been gaping, and promptly shut it. I shook myself. 'Gosh, don't they . . . look alike.'

'That's where the similarities end, I can assure you,' Panther said, a note of something like disappointment in her voice before she snapped out of it. 'Now, more tea, anyone?'

But Panther is right. Even after merely minutes I can tell that, where Cal is all taut, a clenched fist of a man, Jack is ... elastic. Where Cal rails against the world, Jack embraces it. Where Cal sighs and scowls, Jack grins and laughs; a belly sound that carries you with it in its enthusiasm. Was carrying me at that very second, when—

'Nesbitt!'

A yell shook me out of my own reverie, and I caught the boy trying to follow Jack's suit and strip off for the pond, Charlie hot on his tail. Needless to say, within minutes, we were marching back to the Dower House, frogs and bucket in hand.

'He's ... different, isn't he?' I managed. 'Jack, I mean.'

Charlie, one hand in Nesbitt's, turned her eyes to me. 'Don't,' she warned.

'Don't what?' I protested.

'You know exactly what I mean,' she said. 'It would ... it would ruin him.'

I said I was sure I didn't know what on earth she was referring to. But – oh! – I think I do.

It will be perfectly fine, though. I shall just avoid the village altogether. No visits to Bridge House. No ... no anything. I shall confine myself to Marigold's under the pretence of a dicky tummy.

Given Nesbitt's habits, it shan't be hard to muster.

SUNDAY 14 AUGUST

10 A.M.
It has been three days, and if I do not leave the confines of the Dower House – and the menacing presence of Nesbitt, Andrew and Siegfried – I might go quite, quite mad. So far, between them, they have managed to break the refrigerator, flood the downstairs lavatory and cause minor burns to the garage wall. I do not know how Marigold and Hugo cope – not just cope, but seem to embrace the chaos. Although, it is Siegfried's birthday today, and Hugo is worried it will be 'all change'.

'As if he might go to bed an angel and emerge tomorrow as Al Capone,' said Marigold.

However, he is already the latter, so it can't possibly get any worse. Besides, he is only having one friend to tea – Digby, his cousin, who is the son of a woman called 'Bad Harry'. Though on reflection, the 'Bad' bit does not bode well.

In any case, we shall be out. Charlie has finally persuaded me to the river again, and this time in a swimsuit – Aster has mustered one from somewhere; she dropped it round yesterday, along with General Eisenhower. He has apparently taken a profound dislike to his own offspring and she fears murder so Marigold is keeping him. I would protest, but there are already so many animals here as to make it a living menagerie, so I don't suppose we will even notice.

I doubt I shall notice anything, as I am, I admit it, too consumed with the prospect of seeing either Cal or Jack. Or both at once – heavens! Would that be worse? Gosh, yes, I think it might.

I have said nothing to Charlie, though. She has made it quite clear that she disapproves of me even speaking Jack's name.

Jack Mannering. It does have a ring to it, doesn't it? And he seems to know himself, takes his place in the world with joy, with determination. How can one not admire that in a man?

5 P.M.

'Easily,' would be Charlie's answer.

She is seething with me, though I do not see quite what harm I am doing. I only *talked* to the man, for heaven's sake.

And... well, I *did* take his side in an argument. But, in my defence, he had a point, and one both she and I have made to Cal before, though possibly not quite as vociferously.

We were on the bank – Charlie in her slick black one-piece and wearing a massive hat and equally large sunglasses, looking quite the Hepburn-ish heroine; I slightly less chic, but still rather better off in Aster's suit than the cast-off from before, and my hair, newly trimmed, was verging on elfin, and not in a bad way. The men arrived together, which was a surprise in itself, though the argument, already in heated progress, was not.

'I know you want to be a ... a working-class hero, but you just aren't and that's fine.' This, Jack, stripping off his shirt and kicking off his shoes with the same practised movement he'd exercised yesterday.

Cal (in a similar linen shirt and loose trousers but somehow managing to look an inch shorter and a deal scruffier) tried to get a word in. 'It's not—'

'Listen to me for once, little brother.' Jack began to unbuckle his belt – I didn't know where to look, so just carried on staring. 'It doesn't stop you fighting the war. *Use* your privilege. Do something good with it.'

'Like Panther, you mean?' scoffed Cal, thrusting his hands in his pockets just as Jack dropped his own trousers (thankfully revealing swimming trunks underneath). 'Stand for Parliament?'

'If you like.' Jack shrugged. 'Or ... or raise the voices of those who don't have one. Give them space in a newspaper.'

'How?' railed Cal. 'No one will take my articles. Not unless I latch on to the "Mannering" name. They're hardly likely to give me an op-ed as a Bannister.'

Jack laughed. 'And there's privilege talking. You don't start off as Elvis, King of Rock 'n' Roll. You begin as a kid with a guitar.' I think we all looked baffled at that, so he went on. 'Start at the bottom,' he explained. 'Train like everyone else. If you don't want people to see you as special then you have to act like you're not.' He paused, caught my eye. 'Even when you are,' he added.

It is true that at this point I may actually have let out a mew, like one of Norman's kittens. But Jack was polite enough to ignore it and plunge himself, porpoise-like again, into the water. Leaving Cal, Charlie and I rattled on the bank.

'Is he . . . is he always like this?' I managed.

'Yes, worst luck,' said Cal, and slumped down under the willow with a copy of something by Sartre.

'I don't think she meant it that way,' said Charlie, quietly.

I ignored her then, but later, on the way home, this became impossible.

'What's going on?' she demanded. 'I saw the way you looked at Jack. And the way he looked at you!'

'Nothing is going on,' I insisted.

'Well, Jack clearly doesn't think so.'

'What do you mean?' I came to a halt, scattering gravel as I did, and swung round to her.

She lifted her sunglasses. 'Oh, Birdy, come *on*. You were flirting, the pair of you.'

'I . . . I was doing no such thing!' I blurted. 'And nor was he!' I paused, aware I was trembling. 'Was he?'

'Oh, for God's sake.' Charlie dropped her sunglasses, and strode into the distance in a cloud that lingers even now.

Though what it has to do with her, I don't quite understand. It's not as if Jack and I did anything. It's not as if we kissed. He only gave me a ride across the river on his back.

And told me my jokes were 'the bee's bloody knees'.

And asked if I were free for dinner on Friday night, to which I said I was, but only as I am renewed with 'yes' vigour, and also the fayre at Marigold's tends to come with a garnish of animal hair or worse.

Where on earth is the flirting in that?

THURSDAY 18 AUGUST

10 A.M.
I take back my former optimism regarding conditions at the Dower House.

1. One of the frogs has disappeared and General Eisenhower is looking especially smug.
2. Siegfried and Digby got hold of Hugo's port last night and proceeded to throw up in the potato patch. Marigold sent them to bed looking green and weedy and then she and Bad Harry proceeded to drink the last of the bottle between them. I can't say I blame them, but they are both now groaning at the breakfast table and taking it in turns to run to the lavatory. It is like the infamous 'dubious chicken fricassée' incident at Granny's in 1956 all over again, but with more swearing. Siegfried and Digby are, being young, quite fine and have eaten fourteen slices of toast between them.

10 P.M.

Marigold and Bad Harry are not the only ones the worse for wear. Charlie's stew, in which she has festered for the last five days, has deepened. Thankfully, though, this latest plunge has nothing to do with me (or Jack or Cal, who have been billeted by Panther to Radley Farm to help out on the harvest – an act Panther claims is about them 'learning the value of money', and Aster claims is more about 'learning the value of each other'). Instead, the gloom has everything to do with her mother, whom she bumped into at the village shop (on an errand from Marigold to fetch some flour to replace the bag Nesbitt had used for 'ammunition' in his one-boy war against someone called Lump). Or rather, she almost bumped into her, and had to hide behind a display of romantic paperbacks whilst her mother berated Ralph, the postmaster, for mislaying her subscription copy of *The Lady* yet again.

'What did he say?' I asked.

'Something inexplicable about snails,' she snapped. 'But that's hardly the point, is it.'

I shook my head vigorously to agree. 'But . . .' I began, hesitantly. 'What *is* the point?'

She sighed, as if at a tiresome toddler. 'The point is, the countryside is suffocating me. I need to get back to Soho and sharpish. I'm thinking of getting the early train. Will you come? Please say yes, Birdy.'

I had to think, and swiftly. I did not manage it. 'But Friday is our last night,' I protested in desperation. 'And dinner—'

She scoffed. 'Oh, the date with Cal—'

'It's not a date!' I complained. 'It's . . . it's . . . You should come!' I snatched at the only solution I could see. 'You and Cal. It will be . . .' I flailed again. 'Our last hoorah!'

'But my mother—'

'Beggar your mother.' (In my defence, I was desperate.) 'Don't let her stop me— us from enjoying ourselves. Ickthorpe is as much your home as it is hers.'

'Soho is my home,' said Charlie, but her voice had softened slightly and I knew I was winning.

'Please?' I begged. 'For me. I'll make it up to you, I promise. And' – I saw my trump card – 'Aster will be livid if she has to drive the cats back herself. Imagine the carnage!'

A smile tweaked her lips. 'Fine,' she said eventually. 'But . . .' She trailed off.

'What?' I asked.

She shook her head. 'Nothing,' she said. 'None of my business.'

I'm still trying to work out what she was going to say, though I am, at least, distracted by rabbits. Nesbitt has given one each to Charlie and me (David One and David Two). I would protest but actually, they're dear little things, and appear to be the least destructive of all the animal options.

10.30PM
David (which one is unclear, but irrelevant) has weed on an electrical socket and has fused the entire house.

FRIDAY
19 AUGUST

10 A.M.
I would say that what I am about to write is entirely philanthropic, but that would be a lie as I need a distraction from:

1. Rabbit-based catastrophe, i.e. there is no heat or light, and the refrigerator (only just fixed from whatever Nesbitt did to it) is slowly warming up so everyone has been instructed to eat its contents as fast as possible. Siegfried and Nesbitt have taken this as a 'manly challenge' and have commenced with the cheese. I predict one of them will be sick before eleven at this rate, as has Andrew, who has started a book offering strong odds on it being Nesbitt.
2. Dinner tonight, i.e. I am already sweating, and not just down to the continuing heat.

What will I wear? What will I say? Why did I invite Charlie and Cal? How will Jack and I—

No, I must stop that. And anyway, the reason I invited Charlie is obvious: to delay her! And also leads me to my plan: I am going to Balfour Hall to reason with Daphne.

I know this might be foolhardy, particularly given the heat and my absolute lack of navigational sense, but I can hardly not try, can I? Not while I'm here, and the iron (and everything else) is hot etc. And last time – with my own mother – worked out, didn't it? And when I told Aster about Ted? Perhaps it's my fate to be a fixer of things? A sort of modern-day Emma, only with families, not romance.

If only one could monetise it.

SATURDAY 20 AUGUST

10 A.M.
Well, that didn't go according to plan. Though I suppose Austen did warn me; I should have remembered how Emma ended up. But I shall map it out, terrible event by terrible event, as a warning to the future me, should she ever think about interfering in other people's family matters again.

11 A.M.
I depart for Balfour Hall, following Nesbitt's instructions to walk through the village, turn left at the 'very dirty cows' and then right at the 'tree that looks like Lump's mother'. As I don't know Lump, still less his parents, this last instruction was unhelpful, but on I went, undeterred (though without David Two, whom Nesbitt insisted wanted to accompany me, and I suggested might prefer the lawn).

2 P.M.

I arrive at Balfour Hall, via a circuitous route involving four trees, all of which might be taken to resemble mothers of someone called Lump, and introduce myself to some sort of young butler (drawn features, expression of resignation) as 'a friend of Charity'. This met by great alarm, and the summoning of a woman I assume to the housemaid (equally drawn, even greater resignation), but who is revealed as Calypso (the 'butler' being her brother Inigo) by the arrival of Daphne herself.

2.15 P.M.

I explain my presence, and the whole Charlie debacle, leaving out the baby, but making a great deal about the fact she mustn't be made to feel ashamed of her sexuality. 'Look at Aster!' I declare. 'She isn't ashamed. And . . . and I know she misses you even if she won't admit it.'

There is a terrible pause. Then, 'Aster does?' demands Daphne.

'No, Charlie,' I correct (though I have begun to doubt myself at this point, as I fear the sun, and lack of lunch, have rather got to me), and detect an air of disappointment.

2.30 P.M.

Daphne sends me back to the Dower House with strict instructions to mind my own business (though also with a ham sandwich and a bottle of lemonade, for which I am profusely grateful).

4 P.M.

I try to distinguish between dirty cows and very dirty cows.

5 P.M.

I am still trying to distinguish between variations of bovine filth, aware that dinner is a mere two hours away and I am not far off cow-levels of smell myself.

6 P.M.

I am awakened from under 'Lump's mother' by a man (Jack, I decide) hoisting me onto his shoulder. I do not question this, as I am evidently dying.

6.30 P.M.

I am not dying (I am told by Panther) but have mild sunstroke and dehydration, to wit: I am forced to drink a pint of water, and thence hustled into the shower. Dinner is transplanted to Bridge House, and Aster telephones for Charlie. I do not have the energy to contest this rearrangement.

7.30 P.M.

We sit for dinner – Cal and Jack, Charlie and I, Panther, Freddy and Aster. Conversation is a heated debate on the concept of privilege, the ongoing war in Vietnam, and frogs versus toads. Romance does not decorate the air.

9 P.M.

Aster enquires as to where I thought I was going today anyway. I, tiring, heatstruck, and slightly drunk on wine (I was still thirsty!) say, 'It is funny you should ask,' and launch into the story of my encounter with Daphne, my brave declaration of Charlie's sexuality, my rescue by a heroic Jack. This all met by a stony silence.

9.05 P.M.

Stony silence erupts into Charlie shrieking that I had no right, with Aster backing her. Charlie storms off. I storm to the bathroom, deciding I might be sick.

9.15 P.M.

I answer a knock to the bathroom door. Having not been sick after all, I open it. It is Jack (hoorah!).

'Can I come in?' he asks.

I say yes, of course, as I am a woman of 'yes'es. He proceeds to ask if he can tell me something. Assuming it to be a declaration of love, I fling myself at him and proceed to kiss him. We are interrupted by Cal shouting 'for God's sake' at us from the landing.

9.18 P.M.

I realise I am going to be sick after all, and only manage a disastrous mouth to mouth vomit situation by seconds. I proceed to empty my stomach for half an hour. When I emerge from the confines of the toilet bowl, it is no longer Jack by my side, but Cal, who hands me a damp flannel.

'Thank you?' I manage.

He ignores me for several minutes, and we sit on the floor, the both of us, clouded in silence (and the acid tang of bile). 'You shouldn't have done it,' he says eventually. 'Outed her like that.'

'Daphne knew,' I protest. 'She knew about Fitz . . .'

He is quiet for a moment. Then, 'She thought it was a phase,' he explains. 'Nothing more.'

'But . . .' I begin. 'It's . . . it's wrong. To ignore your own daughter because . . . because of who she loves. Especially given she's Sapphic as well.'

He frowns at this. 'Daphne is?'

'With Aster.' I sigh. 'Surely you knew.'

There is another pause. Then he shakes his head. 'Even so. The Balfours are traditional. They toe the line in everything.'

'Charlie doesn't. She does her best not to even see the line.'

'But she knows it's there,' he insists.

'Can we change the subject?' I ask then.

'Fine,' he replies. 'What were you doing with Jack?'

'I . . .' I scrabble for something. 'He rescued me. I might have died,' I add, dramatically.

Cal says nothing.

'And, well' – I feel a confession coming on. A truth – 'everything else was so very messed up, I wanted something to be lovely.'

'And kissing him was supposed to do that?' he snaps.

'Yes . . . No . . . I don't know.' I sigh, emit a tiny sick-smelling belch. 'I think it was more because of a bet I made with myself.' *And because you wouldn't*, I didn't add.

He is silent for a while, then, 'You've got to stop being such a . . . a do-gooder,' he says. 'A fixer. I know you like drama but it only makes things worse.'

'But—'

'No buts,' he interrupts. 'Some of us are . . . happy to stew.'

'I've really beggared everything up,' I realise. 'Haven't I?'

He nods.

'How do I . . . unbeggar it?'

He sighs, and smiles – his special kind that aren't really smiles at all. 'I don't think you do,' he says eventually. 'I think perhaps . . . just let people work things out for themselves.'

'Like Charlie and Daphne?' I ask.

He nods.

'And you and Jack?' I check. 'With Panther and Freddy and the whole parent thing?'

'Yes, but—'

'And me and you?'

He opens his mouth, but nothing comes out, which is more than I can say for mine, which proceeds to chunder a twenty-somethingth time.

Minutes later, I am driven back to Marigold's in disgrace by Aster, who repeats most of what Cal had said, but rather more vociferously.

*

And now? Well, here we are. I have burned my bridges with several friends, and half of Essex as well. Though Marigold's lot have put up a show of despondency at least. Nesbitt has cried twice already, and offered me a sheep, a duck, or a frog of my choice to keep me company in London. I have declined all, and said he must take care of them for me, and I will visit again next year.

I felt terrible lying to him, because the truth is, I doubt I'll see Ickthorpe again.

But I'm glad about one thing: to be returning to Soho. Glad to breathe in filthy air. Glad to trudge through rainbowed puddles, even if I know it's only oil. Glad, above all, to see Rollo –

the one person I haven't mucked things up with. I hope he, at least, can forgive me.

If nothing else, whatever he has to say cannot possibly make things any worse.

5 P.M.

I am more fool than anyone thought. More fool than even I thought.

Rollo has cancer. And it is terminal.

SEPTEMBER 1960

SUNDAY
25 SEPTEMBER

3 P.M.

There is so much to say, and yet all that comes out this month is a stutter. So many times I've tried to pick up my pen and put words to paper that might do justice to how we are all feeling – to how *much* we are feeling – but it seems feeble, pathetic; an empty, selfish gesture. And yet here I am now, trying, again.

Rollo – dear, darling Rollo – says writers' block is common, and I should just document the news, in a factual manner, and perhaps it will come back to me. Valentine agrees, says it is a muscle memory, like riding a bicycle or playing a violin, neither of which I excel at, I admit, but here goes nothing:

1. Soho is still determinedly, wonderfully Soho. Stav pops in every morning with coffee and eggs. Eggs himself bustles in like a pug with gossip gleaned from the French and the Colony. And outside the square mile basks in late summer sunshine, while at night the gutters still glitter and gaze skyward in hope.

2. Also on the bright side, we have acquired one of Norman's kittens. Valentine protested, because of the germs, but Rollo said it was all a bit late for that. The thing dotes on Rollo. 'Marilyn' it's called, after Monroe, of course. Though, in Soho tradition, its gender is irrelevant where naming is concerned; it's a boy.
3. Charlie is in the new thing at the Pippin – a bit part, but still, she has a single line this time ('Christ on a penny farthing, Mavis!') and will understudy the female lead. The play is set in the north of England, which is unfortunate as her Leeds accent is about as convincing as her cockney one. She is happy enough though, convinced this will be the break she's been waiting for. And it is good that she has something to distract her, keep her out of the house, for her sake and mine (she is yet to forgive me, and communicates mostly in monosyllables).
4. Both my birthday and Charlie's have passed without celebration, and, in my case, even reference. Mummy has given me her Olympia, and Daddy ten pounds, but I am yet to collect them, or John and Gloria's offering (talcum powder, I suspect), or Aunt Barbara and Uncle

Roy's (heaven knows; last year it was a book about goats). I don't feel I can leave Soho at all at the moment, as if it might conjure bad luck – much like our departure to Essex.
5. Rollo's column came out last week. Cal did it by himself this time – a review of a new Italian trattoria on Wardour Street, which serves only pizza. He praised it for transcending class, and declared it was set to revolutionise dining, gave it five stars. Rollo was livid, or as livid as one can be from a sick bed – he does not approve of pizza; my mother is in agreement, and rang on the back of it to air her grievances over the impending downfall of society, predicated entirely on Italian bread products. I said nothing, about the review or Cal doing it. It all seems so . . . moot now. The notice will go in the papers, I suppose, and that will be that. No more 'Rollo Round Town'.

No more Rollo at all.

It is impossible to imagine Pennington's without him – Soho without him. Though I suppose we shall have to, and soon. Aster has suggested he transfers to a hospice for these last weeks, but Valentine is refusing. He says as long as he can lift Rollo to the lavatory and bath, then no one is going anywhere, and it is surprisingly hard to argue with Val when he's got his heart set on something. I suppose that's what's kept the Pippin going all this time, despite the small audiences and poor reviews.

We all need something though. To keep us believing. Writing has always been that for me, and . . . yes, I do feel a little better. Perhaps it isn't my calling, but merely therapy. In any case, I shall try to do it a little more often.

OCTOBER 1960

THURSDAY 13 OCTOBER

6 P.M.

Autumn is creeping in. Wind rattles the sashes and rain renders Lexington Street a river of filth. It is as if it has become tired of waiting and now reluctant summer is being ushered into the gutter and swept down the grate. Which I said to Charlie (as it is a nice line, I think) as we both leaned over the back of the chaise and stared out of the living room window at the grey vista of buildings, but she accused me of being overdramatic and told me to put the kettle on again. I did so – not least because it is the most she has said to me in weeks.

Tea and coffee are all that keep us going, it seems. Even the gin and bitters have stayed on the cabinet shelf; impending death is quite literally sobering. Though Charlie has the play to think about as well, I suppose. The director (and playwright), Jennings, is a beast, she has told Rollo, and one needs every wit about them to avoid a shouting. Poor Doris got an earful yesterday (though they may have deserved it – they've been feeding croissant to a pigeon who's taken to nesting in the fly gallery and it managed to defecate on Jennings' hat). It is lucky

Charlie only has the one line to fluff, as her nerves are quite shot with the whole thing, though she makes light of it, and even turned it into a sketch for Rollo's amusement yesterday.

Plus it gets her up and dressed. The rest of us spend the best part of the day in our dressing gowns. Ted says he paints better naked anyway (Minty's idea, apparently) so it's easier to take on and off, and Val barely leaves Rollo's room, though he is sleeping in a cot on the floor now as Rollo has started to have night terrors, and thrashes so much he has given Val a black eye. As for me, I have decided it's my 'thing'. Everyone in Soho needs a 'thing', Rollo once said, to mark them out as eccentric, and mine is to open up shop in a scarlet silk kimono. I'm sure I caught Cal smirking when he plodded through the shop earlier, but even he had the decency to keep his mouth shut. Though, like Charlie, he barely speaks to me anyway these days, so *plus ça change*. Anyway, it's evening, and I'm already dressed for bed, so who's laughing now?

7 P.M.

God (or Allah etc.), apparently (re, the laughing), who has chosen to throw a spanner in the clonking works of 27 Lexington Street in the shape of Jennings. He has fired the leading lady in a disagreement about teacakes (there is a scene involving them in act two, I think, though Doris was almost incomprehensible on the telephone) and so Charlie has her chance at last, and tonight! Needless to say, Val, Ted and I are all putting some actual clothes on (and spraying ourselves liberally with Rollo's cologne as bathing has gone by the wayside as well) to witness her star turn. I have also said a small prayer that she remembers both her lines, and that Leeds and Wales are not the same place (her accent veers across the entire country, occasionally wandering onto the continent).

11 P.M.

My prayer fell on deaf ears, or – one must admit it – a vacant space.

The short story is that the play has closed.

The long story involves a pigeon, and an improvised sketch about the vagaries of men, but I suppose I shall have to start at the beginning to make any sense of it.

It was all going well enough in act one. Charlie's accent stayed vaguely in the Yorkshire triangle, with only one foray into Scots, and she only corpsed once, but Doris (who is on prompt now) threw her the line (something about whippets) and she managed to muster well enough. But it was in act two when it all went awry. What happened, or at least the catalyst, was that the pigeon, possibly not content with messing the set, or eyeing the sofa stage left, decided to join in the performance by landing on an antimacassar during a particularly tricky line about miners.

In Charlie's defence, that would rattle even Redgrave, I think. Though I suspect not even she would have then declared the pigeon definitely male for its insistence on stealing the limelight, and then gone into a whole spiel about the absurdity that merely possessing a penis gives a whole gender a sense of entitlement. Charlie could have stopped at this – *should* have stopped at this – but then came a heckle from the dress circle about whether pigeons even have penises and she took that subject up with gusto for at least a minute before Jennings himself marched her off.

Of course, I bolted backstage, begged him to be gentle. 'There are . . . *circumstances*,' I pleaded. 'Mitigating ones!' I meant Rollo, of course. But Charlie was having none of it.

'Like the director is an unforgivable shit!' she yelled at him.

'How dare you!' he countered.

He clearly doesn't know Charlie. 'I know why you really sacked Marie,' she went on. 'Because she said no to you.'

'What?' (This from Val, who had also appeared in the wings).

'Did you think I'd be easier?' Charlie went on. 'God, I don't even like your lot.'

Jennings smirked. 'Not what Alan Barrow says.'

At that, she slapped him. He went to slap her back, but Val stepped in front and caught the brunt of it himself. Jennings was sacked on the spot, but as it's his play, he took the rights back and so the show is, quite literally, over.

Val insists he doesn't give a fig, that all that matters right now is Rollo. Charlie, at least, is more honest. She says her career has collapsed and she might as well move back to 'bloody Ickthorpe' and become 'the village idiot'.

'It'll all feel less ... terrible in the morning,' I tried.

'Oh ... really?' she snapped. 'And what would you know? Little Miss Do-Gooder.'

I flinched, but steeled myself, knowing this was – at least in part – grief talking: for Rollo and for her role. But even as I wished, again, that I'd stayed away from Daphne, I wanted more for her mother to comfort her. To tell her she's special, whatever she does.

Anyway, someone needs to get through to her, as the gin has disappeared from the cabinet again and her door is locked, and this can only end badly, I think.

FRIDAY
14 OCTOBER

10 A.M.
There is no sign of Charlie.

2 P.M.
There is no sign of Charlie.

4 P.M.
There is still no sign of Charlie. Val has knocked repeatedly, as have I. On the bright side, we know she is alive as she told both of us to 'beggar off'.

6 P.M.
No sign still. Ted said he could unscrew the lock and just let us in, and Cal (on his daily check-in) said, 'Or we could tell her to stop being so bloody self-indulgent. It's not like she's the one who's dying.'

'That's harsh,' I said, quietly.

'You're right,' he said. 'I'm sorry.'

'Although you're right, too,' I admitted. 'She is a little on the self-pitying side.'

If I thought that might kindle some sort of rapprochement, I was wrong; he left within minutes.

Rollo has offered Marilyn to cheer Charlie, but not even he dares enter the lair. I fear this is a job beyond all of us this time.

9 P.M.
Except, perhaps, Aster.

9.45 P.M.
No, I am banned from interfering and 'do-gooding' so I shall just leave well alone.

10 P.M.
Except, she could just say she was here to see Ted, given the exhibition is a matter of weeks away, then she might just 'stumble' upon Charlie and give her one of her talking-tos.

10.10 P.M.

I have telephoned. Aster is coming tomorrow! Until then, she says, I must leave Charlie some hot buttered toast outside the door, a cup of tea, and two aspirin.

I have done so, and knocked to tell her. She told me to 'beggar off and stop interfering' again, but when I checked again, not two minutes later, the toast and tea and pills have gone. Now, it is down to Aster to work her Mannering magic.

That or I shall have burned every bridge I ever had.

SATURDAY 15 OCTOBER

11 A.M.
Like a hotel maid, I have cleared the empty plate from the landing and delivered a second batch of hot tea and toast, and now practically itch with anticipation, as Aster is due at any moment! Or rather, she is due today, and I am choosing to assume it will be this morning, because she is very much a morning sort of person – a lark, like me! That is, I used to be very lark-like under Mummy's jurisdiction, but admittedly have become more of a slug-a-bed in Soho, where the owls and nightingales hoot and sing so loudly and so late into the night that it is hard to get to sleep before two. Plus Rollo's rest is fitful at best, and he takes it where he can; morphine helps, he says, but then his wits are knocked for six, which compromises his determination to rage against the dying of the light etc.. Though now that death – Dylan Thomas's 'good night' – is facing us, I can rather see the attraction in 'going gentle'. Raging seems rather pointless, given everything, plus it is awfully loud when he does it. Still, it is his last wishes that matter, and we are doing our best to meet all of them, however spurious. I feel

sure that cheering Charlie would be one of them, were he awake right now.

On which point, where is Aster? Oh, I do hope that she manages something when she gets here. For Charlie's sake and, I admit it, for mine. I know I've messed up horribly with her over the whole Daphne thing and I miss her. I miss her terribly. Isn't it odd how one can be just feet away from someone – share rooms, a fridge, a bottle of milk, even – and yet feel bereft of them, feel so terribly alone?

12 P.M.

There is no sign of Aster.

1 P.M.

There is still no sign of Aster. I suppose she does operate on her own terms at all times (she says it is vital for women to set their conditions and stick to them, or people – she means men – will only take advantage).

I have taken Charlie up some hot soup and fresh bread from Maison Bertaux, and empty plates were delivered to the landing within minutes, so unless she is tipping it out the window or feeding that wretched pigeon (whom I blame for everything) then this, at least, is positive.

2 P.M.
The door! Thank heaven. I shall report back shortly, and hopefully with good news.

2.10 P.M.
It was only Cal (on Rollo duty), who said Aster left the house on Marchmont Street at eight this morning and hasn't been seen since.

'But how could she?' I snapped. 'This is . . . this is Charlie's entire life we're talking about.'

Cal rolled his eyes. 'It's a play. Let her stew for a few days. She's eating now, isn't she?'

'Yes, but—'

'Stay out of it, Birdy. You're . . .' He trailed off.

'I'm what?' I demanded.

'Nothing,' he finished, his voice, I am sure, tinged with sadness. But I couldn't check as by then he'd trolled off to Rollo's room.

Anyway, he is wrong. I am taking things into my own hands, i.e. I am going to channel Aster and give Charlie the talking-to myself. It cannot be that hard. I shall just muster steely detachment and drop my voice an octave like Topaz Mortmain.

10 P.M.

It *is* that hard. For a start, if I lower my voice I do not gain gravitas, I just sound like a madwoman. As Charlie pointed out.

'Hello?' I asked in my best Aster alto.

'Oh, beggar off, Birdy!' she snapped. 'How many times?'

'It's not Birdy,' I insisted, still in disguise. 'It's Aster. Or at least you have to imagine it so.'

She groaned. 'You sound quite, quite mad.'

'Well, that may be true, but . . . just listen anyway,' I begged (this in my normal voice). 'Please?'

She said nothing to this, so I assumed a yes and sat on the floor by the door, and thought very hard: *What would Aster do?*

And – poof! – there it was: a gleaming emerald for the taking.

'You mustn't let one incident put you off,' I said, voice low again. 'It's like . . . knitting. At first, it's all dropped stitches and whatnot, but you'll get better at it eventually.'

There was a pause, then my heart jumped, hare-happy.

'I've been trying for two years now,' she replied, 'and I can still barely muster bloody garter stitch.'

I wasn't entirely sure this was metaphorical, but chose to believe so as I have never even seen her with needles. 'So . . . re-ravel the wool, and try again. You can't give up just because . . . because something's difficult.'

Another pause. Then, 'You sound like my mother.'

I shook myself. Was this positive or not? I chose the former.

'Well . . . perhaps that's a good thing,' I suggested. 'Though I *was* going for Aster.'

I was sure I could see the smile through solid oak. I would have asked then to come in, but the front door sounded again (finally).

'Shouldn't you get that?' she said, when it became evident I hadn't moved.

'Cal will,' I said. 'And anyway, I think perhaps she'll— it will be redundant now.'

There was a pause, then a sigh. 'Who did you call?' she asked. 'Be honest.'

I jinked, perfectly ready to lie, then thought better of it. 'Aster,' I admitted. 'But I assumed she'd forgotten, hence the impression.'

'Aster forgets nothing,' Charlie said, with another heavy sigh.

But if I was expecting a telling-off, I was to be surprised, because instead I heard a scramble, then footsteps, then the bedroom door opened, a dishevelled Charlie in a soup-stained slip framed in the entrance.

'I suppose I should at least brush my hair,' she said.

'And teeth?' I suggested, smiling now, my eyes pricking with salt. Hot with embarrassment, I wiped them away. But I needn't have bothered; Charlie wasn't looking at me. She was looking over my shoulder at whoever had appeared at the top of the stairs.

I swung round. 'Aster—?'

But it wasn't her at all.

'Charity?' she said, with an air of disbelief. 'What on earth has happened?'

'I . . .' Charlie tried to set her jaw, but I could see it tremble with emotion. 'I . . . oh, Mummy!'

*

I don't know what, precisely, was said in the bedroom, but when Daphne finally left, nearly two hours later, there was a hug. Perfunctory, but a hug nonetheless.

'She admitted she understands,' said Charlie when she emerged not twenty minutes later – washed and dressed, I am thankful to say.

'Good, I—'

'No, *really* understands.'

'Oh? *Ohhh*.' I realised her meaning. Too much of her meaning. 'Because she and Aster are Sapphic?' I said without thinking.

'You knew?' Her face had clouded over again, and my insides slipped, scared I had sent us straight back into the mess whence we came.

'I'm sorry!' I blurted. 'I . . . I guessed and Aster confirmed it. I should have—'

'It's fine.' And she smiled – thinly, but, like the hug, still very much there. 'Besides, I'd guessed myself a long while ago. Why do you think I was so livid with her?'

'I thought . . . I thought you assumed she was narrow-minded?'

'That might have been easier. But to have someone *like* me dismiss it as "sinful"? Well, that stung. Made it all seem . . . impossible.'

Words stoppered in me, too tangled with feelings. 'Oh, Charlie,' I managed. And then . . . then we were hugging, so tightly and rightly, it felt almost as if we were one person.

'I'm sorry,' I sobbed into her shoulder.

'It's fine.' She kissed the top of my hair, then pulled back and frowned. 'This really does need a trim,' she said. 'Shall I fetch the scissors?'

I was about to say an enthusiastic 'yes!' (I would have let her shear me entirely bald at that point) when the door went *again*.

'Probably Aster at last,' I said. 'Shall I tell her to go?'

Charlie grinned. 'Let her in,' she said. 'I'll put the kettle on.'

I retreated again to the shop floor, and opened the door, and, well, it is hard not to believe in God (or whoever) at this point, because, yet again, it wasn't Aster.

It wasn't a woman at all.

'We're closed,' I said to the (admittedly dashing) man in the hat. 'Illness in the family.'

He looked puzzled. 'I'm not after books, doll,' he told me, his accent pure Frank Sinatra.

I admit, I was briefly flattered (I find all Americans hopelessly romantic), but remembered Aster's warnings swiftly enough. 'I'm nobody's doll,' I insisted, as brusquely as I could manage. Then frowned. 'Are you a friend of Rollo?' I asked. 'Because if so, you should know he's ... incapacitated.'

It was his turn to frown. 'Who the hell is Rollo? Charlie's father?'

'Charlie's father's dead,' I snapped. 'And *everyone* knows Rollo!'

If he was put off, he didn't show it. Just grinned widely. 'Well, not me. But I do know talent when I see it, and, my God, I see it in Charlie Pakenham.'

I'm ashamed to say I grasped the door frame at this point. 'Wait. You're—'

'Randy Garret.' He grasped my hand and shook it. 'Agent to the stars.'

Well, what could I do but let him in?

There ensued a ten-minute spiel about how he loved the whole 'act' at the Pippin, and that she was a slapstick star in the making. 'You have a touch of the Lucys about you,' he told the enraptured Charlie.

'Who's Lucy?' I asked, picturing the singular Lucy I knew – a sturdy girl two years below me, who could fit an entire orange in her mouth, and often did.

'Lucille Ball!' Rollo shot (we had all gathered in his room for this – Charlie and I, Ted and Minty, Val and Cal; Val tried to argue, but Rollo was insistent, and made it another 'dying wish', which he knows we cannot refuse).

Still I shrugged.

'*I Love Lucy?*' tried Cal. 'It's a television series. American.'

'Oh, that explains it,' I said. 'Mummy bans all things American in our house. On account of their butchering of the mother tongue. Also creamed corn.'

Randy just rolled his eyes. 'Well, imagine Princess Margaret crossed with a ballsy American redhead and that's our Charlie.'

'It's Charity, actually,' she said.

We all frowned at her.

She held up her hands. 'Mummy reminded me about Daddy choosing it and, well, I think I like it after all.'

'Me too,' agreed Randy. 'And the Yanks are going to love it. I can see the headlines now: "Sweet Charity takes the U-S by storm!"'

'The Yanks?' (Cal this time.)

'Oh, didn't I say?' He turned to Charlie (Charity?), his smile practically an advertisement for Aquafresh. 'You're going to Hollywood, baby.'

Well, *that* shook the room. I suspect all of us, including Charlie, wanted to protest. But we all knew, too, that *this* was her chance, her throw of the dice.

'You've got to do it,' I told her. 'I shan't . . . I shan't speak to you again if you don't.'

'Some chance!' She laughed.

'And I won't . . . ask you to marry me again?' offered Ted.

'Well, that *would* be a shame,' Charlie said faux-soberly.

'Though I think you could have picked "paint me" for better effect.'

Ted laughed, slipped his arm around Minty.

'It's the least you owe me,' said Val. 'After everything. Become a star and make me proud.'

Charlie, truly sober now, nodded.

'And, it is my dying wish that you go!' announced Rollo. 'So that's that.'

Charlie smiled, laid a hand on his. 'Then I shall go.'

Thankfully at that point, the door went again. We were still laughing when we bundled Aster up the stairs.

'What?' she demanded, quite huffily. 'What on earth is so funny?'

'Nothing!' I whooped.

'Nothing, my darling aunt!' Charlie agreed with a yelp. 'Absolutely nothing.'

And I think I shall leave it there for the day. There is little else to say after all: Charlie – sorry, Charity – is going to America. Rollo is going further and for good. And Soho won't be the same for any of us now.

So we must make the most of it while we can, I suppose.

SUNDAY 16 OCTOBER

8 A.M.

I couldn't sleep, and, as I suspected, nor could Rollo, so at little after six, I slipped to the kitchen and made us both cocoa.

Val was asleep on his cot, but Rollo ushered me to the edge of the bed, where I perched, taut as stretched elastic, sipping on my drink and trying not to think about it all.

'You remind me of me,' he said after a while.

I set my cup down on the nightstand. 'In what way?' I asked, though with eagerness, I might add; being compared to Rollo – to anyone in this house – was as good as being a Mortmain, I knew now.

I saw him smile in the weak light that seeped through the gap in his curtain. 'You live in that happiest of states.'

'Which is?'

'Anticipation,' he said. 'The very best place to be, before reality tarnishes the glint.'

I thought for a moment. 'I think it's because of the tigers.'

He frowned.

'From that Hodgson poem. It's in my favourite book as well:

I Capture the Castle.'

He nodded, but still looked confused.

'"Tamed", Hodgson calls them. "Shabby." And I know it's about poor dear animals in circuses, but I see them as people. The sort of people I don't want to be.' I paused. Was I going to admit it? Yes, yes I was. 'Like my parents, I suppose. Bit parts, you know?' *Nobodies*, I didn't say.

He placed a hand on mine – cold and frailer than ever – and went on to surprise me more than he ever had before. 'I don't think they're that,' he said. 'Your parents. Not shabby, anyway. None of them are – in the suburbs, in the villages, wherever. They're just doing their best, like all of us.' He paused to cough, and took another sip of drink. 'Besides,' he went on. 'Better that than everyone wanting to be the protagonist, isn't it? That's the trouble with Soho. Too many leading ladies. Not enough audience.'

'I'm not one of those,' I said quickly. 'I'm more of a spectator. And I like it, as long as it's all interesting, because I can write about it. Anyway' – I squeezed his hand gently – 'isn't Soho the leading lady?'

'Touché,' he said. 'Clever girl. Just promise me something?'

'What's that?'

'Don't do what I've done. Don't spend so much time in pubs and clubs jawing about the great things you're going to do that you never actually do them.'

I went to protest. 'But—'

'Promise me,' he insisted. 'My dying wish!'

That trick. But it worked. 'I shan't,' I promised, and laughed. A laugh that turned quickly into a sob and I found myself in Rollo's arms, being held as if he really were my own father after all.

'And another thing,' he said into my hair. 'Once you get famous you must leave, do you hear me? This is a place for the want-to-bes and not-quite-yets.' He sighed. 'And maybe-never-wills.'

I brought my head up. 'You were something – *are* something,' I insisted. 'You're a . . . a saviour. You've saved Ted, Charity, Cal, me. Even Val.'

At that, the body on the floor seemed to snore in approval.

'I . . .' began Rollo. But he trailed off; it was his time to cry.

We stayed there until the light from the streetlamp began to wash into the morning's own. Until now. And in a moment I will catch up on sleep (I am due in Surbiton at two, after all) but, just for a while, the windows are flung open and I am letting all Soho in – the sound, the smells, the everything.

And making a promise to Rollo and myself. A promise I intend to keep.

NOVEMBER 1960

THURSDAY 10 NOVEMBER

10 A.M.
Rollo's list of 'Dying Wishes' is reaching *War and Peace* proportions. This week alone, he has added:

1. Be immortalised in oil paint.
2. Grow an obscenely large moustache.
3. Read *Lady Chatterley's Lover*, the 'dirty' version.

Ted is fixing the first, and the second, well – that's the business of Rollo's follicles and Val, who is in charge of shaving equipment since an incident in which I nicked Rollo's chin and ruined his second-best dress shirt. I did point out that perhaps he shouldn't be wearing Gieves and Hawkes in bed, but he replied, 'If not now, when?' which sent me into floods of tears. So of course I am eager to make amends with number three, but given the censors only lost their case in court a week ago, I feel this is a long shot. Besides which, if anyone can fulfil it, it's Rollo himself.

'You're a bookseller,' I said, 'surely you can just . . . buy one from the publisher?'

'Our credit with Penguin is . . . less than healthy,' he explained. 'So you'll have to try Foyles. That's the closest. If not there, then' – he paused to sigh – 'it will have to be Hatchards.' He shuddered.

'But—' I began (knowing how deep his rivalry with the Piccadilly store ran).

'I'll do it.' Cal stepped in.

'I shall!' I rattled back. 'I wasn't refusing, just . . . confirming details.'

'You can both do it.' Rollo raised his eyebrows meaningfully, and I knew he would not brook any argument. That is the only advantage of dying, I think: people tend to do as you ask for once.

So a morning with Cal awaits. I feel I need to steel myself as much for this as for the whole Rollo situation: paste on my blithe 'I'm fine!' face, and pretend that everything is utterly normal. Nothing to see here at all . . .

5 P.M.

It was worse than I anticipated: a morning became a day and what a waste it was. For a start, the man at Foyles (gaunt face, air of a haunted pencil) laughed at us. 'Should have been here at nine on the dot,' he said. 'The print run was meagre and the few we had sold out within minutes.'

It was the same story at Hatchards, Atkins and Hilton's; there was not one copy left along the entire length of Cecil Court.

'Now what?' I snapped at Cal.

'I don't know why you're shirty with me,' he said. 'It's hardly my fault if the book-buying public is more interested in filth than in literature.'

'I think it's literature as well,' I said. 'Just . . . racy.'

Cal shrugged. 'Lawrence was at it for years, but throw in a gamekeeper and a Lady and some . . . some rumpy-pumpy in a potting shed and suddenly every Tom, Dick and . . . whoever wants in.'

'Rumpy-pumpy?' I had to stifle a smirk.

'You know what I mean.'

He'd reddened, so I let it go. 'That's it though, isn't it?' I suggested instead. 'It's not the . . . the *you know what* so much as the fact they're not seen as equals.'

'Exactly,' said Cal. 'But I bet none of the readers will give a fig. It will be school all over again: skim over the political bits and mark up the anatomical.'

'Speak for yourself,' I said. 'We did nothing of the sort.' This was a lie – Felicity's copy of *The Captain and I* was so well-thumbed that several pages fell out when I finally got my turn.

Cal had the sense, or grace, not to question me. 'What do we tell Rollo?' he asked.

I shrugged. 'Maybe we say "it's in hand" and try harder to

come up with something. Surely someone we know will have got one? Aster knows half of London, for God's sake. Panther probably knows Lawrence himself.'

Cal frowned. 'You do know Lawrence is dead?'

I did not. But I didn't let on, other than pink as much as he had a second ago. 'I meant... relatives. Aster, then. You can ask her later.'

We trudged back to Lexington Street in abject silence but for the damp slap of our shoes on wet pavement; the inches of air between us were thick enough to slice. But if we hoped that would be the last of the joint missions, we were to be sorely disappointed.

'Excellent,' said Rollo, when I'd told him he'd have a copy within the week. 'Today, Piccadilly, tomorrow Fleet Street!'

'Pardon?' I asked.

Rollo smiled, with the air of someone who knew exactly what he was doing. 'I'm tidying up my affairs,' he said. 'And it's time to forewarn the *Herald* that Rollo will be around town no more.'

'I can take over!' Cal protested.

'I can!' I matched him.

But Rollo held up his hands. 'No,' he said, tight and precise. 'It's time to stop this nonsense. I've written a letter and I'd like you to deliver it to the editor for me.'

'Why?' I asked.

Cal, for once, was in agreement. 'Couldn't you just *send* it?' he demanded.

Rollo ignored him. 'Ten o'clock tomorrow,' he said. 'One hundred and three Fleet Street. Take a curriculum vitae and ask for Derry.'

'Derry?' I repeated.

'Runs things for my uncle,' Rollo explained. 'He'll be expecting you.'

I felt something in me shimmer for a second, and I turned to catch Cal, a flicker of something kindling in him as well.

'See you tomorrow, I suppose,' he said.

I nodded. 'See you tomorrow. Don't be late!' I added.

He let his lips slip into a grin, if only for a second. Then straightened his face. 'As if.' Then he clattered out and down the stairs, and back, I assume, to Aster and Chatterley.

I wish I'd asked now what jobs were in prospect; what Rollo meant when he said, 'May the best one win.'

I suppose it will all come out in the morning. These things always do. I just hope it isn't another sixpence-swivel. I know I wished for Life with a capital L, but I wouldn't mind a little reliability for a while. There is only so much change one can take – so much carousel-spin and big-dipper – before one begins to get travel sick.

FRIDAY
11 NOVEMBER

10 A.M.
Charity says I am not to mind Cal, he will come round (from what and to what, I did not ask), and it is Derry I should be worried about.

'Whatever for?' I enquired, as she straightened the seam of my stockings for me and smoothed the skirt of the Worth dress.

'He has a reputation,' she warned me. 'Bit of a – oh, for heaven's sake, hold still.'

'I am!' I insisted, wriggling. 'Bit of a what?'

'A bully,' she finished. 'And a snob. Not that it stopped him ... you know. Had a thing with the Bolter once upon a time.'

'Your aunt?' I checked.

She stood, nodded as she neatened my hair. 'There was a rumour that Calypso was his,' she went on. 'Thankfully not true. Not that the actual progenitor is much better. Absolute cad. Rich, mind – which suits Evangeline to a "t".' She looked me up and down, smiled. 'Perfect.'

I smiled back at the time, but now, as I sit in the fust of the bookshop, awaiting Cal, I wonder, *For what, though? For what?*

5 P.M.

Charity was right: Edwin Derry (too many free lunches, too much brilliantine) is a bully and a snob and a hundred other things besides. But – heavens! – I want to work for him.

'So you're the little ghosts, then,' he said as he dropped the letter on his desk, leaned back in his leather chair, and assessed the pair of us.

I jinked; had Rollo told him everything? 'I don't know—'

'That's me,' Cal interrupted.

'And me!' I added.

'Well, not the pizza place,' Cal hissed. 'Or the Wolseley. You were ... otherwise engaged.'

'I was looking after Rollo!' I pointed out. 'And the review of Magnolia Road was ...' but I trailed off, remembering where I was, and with whom.

Derry snorted, clearly amused, but something else too. 'Nine out of ten for mimicry then,' he said.

'Only nine?' I bristled.

'Old Rollo would never have used the word "serviette".' He flapped a hand at the air as if swatting an invisible fly. 'A sub had to scrub it.'

'Even though it would have been understood,' Cal pointed out.

'But looked down upon,' Derry returned. 'Our readers expect' – he flapped that hand again – '*standards* when it comes to certain voices.'

I bristled again, but he was right. I hadn't known all the rules, and Cal? Cal hated them.

'I take it that means you won't be hiring either of us then.' Cal stuck his hands in his pockets, jutted his chest, the angry young man back in a flash.

Derry didn't flinch. 'You remind me of your mother,' he said. 'Well, your adoptive one. Panther always gives me a run for my money as well.'

'I . . . You know?' Cal checked. 'Did Rollo—'

Derry interrupted him. 'I've always known. You've been on the radar of the paper for a while. All the placard-wavers are. None of them quite as articulate as you though. Or as . . . interesting.'

'Then . . . then why not give me the job?' blustered Cal.

'Or me!' I tried, though I knew mine was the lost cause. I wasn't posh, not even by adoption.

'Come on,' Derry scoffed, 'admit it. Neither of you gives a jot about lobster or steak tartare.'

'I . . .' But I trailed off again. He was right: food was Mummy's bag, not mine. Not really. Or at least, not the ten-pounds-a-plate sort.

'So, what then?' snapped Cal. 'That's it? Thanks, but no thanks?'

Derry sighed. 'So terribly trigger-happy, aren't you. So very sure the world is against you.'

Cal went to retaliate but I grasped his arm, held tight to it.

Derry nodded at me, went on. 'There's a job coming up in the new year. Cub reporter. I think you should apply.' He eyed me again, added, 'Both of you.'

My heart soared, only to be swiped at by Cal.

'Both of us? But—'

I yanked at him again. He stilled. 'Thank you,' I said. '*We* will.'

Our time up, Derry gestured at the door; I pulled Cal towards it.

'Oh, one more thing,' added Derry.

I looked over my shoulder.

'Keep that fire in you.' He smiled. 'You're going to need it.'

*

So now I know, at least, what Rollo was talking about. Though I'm not sure I stand a chance. Cal has the background, the connections, the . . . everything. I have, what? A certificate in typing proficiency, and, when it's put to the test, which surely it will be, Cal will best me at that as well, and at shorthand.

I wish I'd listened to Miss Beveridge. Or I wish . . . I wish I'd been born a Mannering, or . . . a Mortmain. And I wish above everything that Rollo may live.

That Charity may stay.

That Cal may forgive me.

But if wishes were horses, beggars would ride; that's what Mummy always says.

I just hadn't realised quite how very 'beggar' I was until now.

WEDNESDAY 23 NOVEMBER

11 A.M.
At last there is something to take my mind off my own misfortune: Ted's exhibition, which opens in Mayfair tomorrow. Aster is in and out of Lexington Street like a bluebottle in June, Ted is panicking in the attic with Minty, and the whole house seems to quiver in anticipation. As well it might: everyone will be there – the great and the good, the famous and infamous, the old money and new. Aster says Eggs has promised to show his face, as has Lucian, and, 'If we're lucky, the Fitzpatricks might deign to grace us with their presence.'

I said I hoped not, for Charity's sake, but Aster pointed out that they are madly rich and like to squire shiny new artists, of which Ted is the newest and shiniest, so Charity will just have to put her feelings aside for a while. 'Besides,' she went on, 'she's going to America. She'll be knee-deep in women in a week.'

The image was startling. 'Isn't it . . . frowned upon there as well?' I checked.

'You've not heard of the Sewing Circle?' Aster looked aghast.

In truth, I *had* heard of these women – Garbo and Dietrich among them – for whom the euphemistic term was used to cover their more Sapphic activity, but had dismissed it as impossible. 'It's not just a rumour, then?'

Aster laughed – guttural and guileless. 'Oh, you are such a sweet thing. Cal is right about you.'

'Cal?' What on earth had he said? Something about me being green, I assumed. But whatever it was, I was not about to find out.

Aster flapped a hand. 'No time for that now. You two will just have to sort it out between you.'

Then she swept back upstairs to bark at the removal firm who were manhandling the paintings – the nude of me among them; a fact I realised with a jolt. How Charity can be so devil-may-care about the whole thing is baffling, if terribly impressive.

'Oh, don't be so . . . Surbiton about it!' she snapped at me when I voiced concern that half of London was about to bear witness to my naked frame.

'I'm not!' I insisted. 'It's just that . . .'

But what was the point? She was right – *is* right. I *am* being 'Surbiton' about it – being tamed and shabby after all – when really I'm Soho now, or should be. Why should I be ashamed of my body? It's a sturdy, useful thing, despite its slightness. And it's not as if Mummy and Daddy will show up, or Aunt Barbara, or any of the golf club lot. It will be the usual suspects from the Colony and Gargoyle, and a bunch of drunk aristocrats.

5 P.M.

Mummy has telephoned to let me know how excited she is for the 'little art show'.

I demanded to know how she had heard about it – assuming a leak from Charity – but she said the notice was to the left of 'Winning Ways with Quiche' last week and she was surprised I hadn't let her know earlier. I said we'd all been a little preoccupied lately, given *things*.

'Oh, yes,' she said, then promptly hung up (she does not like to discuss death, unless it's of a celebrity or a politician of whom she disapproves).

I suppose at the very least it will be a change from the Women's Guild annual art fair, which is mainly Beryl Tredegar's appalling watercolours (dogs, the fruit bowl, an unidentifiable bird) and Aunt Barbara's oils of menacing horses. Besides which, I have my legs crossed and am barely recognisable, given that Ted mainly painted me in his Picasso phase, so hopefully she will skim past me and on to the triptych of Charity in the bath, one of which lacks even a strategically placed flannel.

THURSDAY 24 NOVEMBER

10 P.M.

I was not 'unrecognisable'. According to Mummy (and Daddy, and Aunt Barbara, and Julian, who seemed glued to the thing) I have a 'telltale mole' on my shoulder, which meant she could spot me immediately despite my 'wonky' face and arms.

'What will the Tredegars say?' she demanded, her face puce.

'Nothing,' I pointed out hotly. 'Unless you tell them about it. This is Cork Street, not the village hall. And I did offer you the chance to preview it, but you refused, citing golf. Now do have some more wine.' I pressed on her another glass of Chardonnay.

'Don't worry too much,' Daddy said when she had gone to the ladies. 'It's all just new to her.'

'I'm not,' I said. 'I don't have time, what with Rollo.' *And Cal, and Charity leaving*, I didn't add.

'You can always come home for a bit,' Daddy said then. 'If it would make it easier?'

I shook my head. 'I can't. I can't leave them.' I bit back tears, and he squeezed my arm.

'Your turn for some Dutch courage,' he suggested, and grasped a glass of champagne from a passing waiter – a glass I clutched until it had turned quite lukewarm, my parents had left for the suburbs again, and the room had settled back into chatter.

I was standing, my spine against a doorframe, happy to play wallflower for a while, when a voice over my shoulder barked, 'Excellent breasts.'

I swung round, my hand flattened into a slap, only to find Marigold, hands on her hips, deadly serious.

'Proportions as fine as an ox,' she continued, waving at the painting in question. 'Of course, you're too slight for livestock, but, still... admirable, frankly.'

'I... Thank you?' I managed. 'I didn't realise you'd be coming.'

'I wasn't going to bother, but Andrew and Nesbitt wanted to visit the Natural History Museum so I've left them at Aster's for the evening.'

The thought of what they might be doing to the apartment – to Norman – was terrifying. I was only glad the kittens had all been farmed out. 'I didn't know art was your bag,' I said.

'Oh, yes.' She nodded furiously. 'Quite the Whistler in my youth. But farming rather sucks up one's time.'

I nodded, as if I were quite *au fait* with ploughing and scattering and all that. 'Is Panther here yet?' I asked.

She nodded towards a corner where I caught a glimpse of her and Freddy – her curls in signature disarray, her dress barely containing her. She looked magnificent, as ever, and never more in love with the man on her arm.

But they weren't the only couple to catch my attention. To the left, under a six-foot square canvas of Charity in the window seat, stood Aster, with none other than the subject's mother. 'Daphne!' I exclaimed.

'Oh, yes.' Marigold's line of sight met mine. 'Of course, we're all thankful for old Pakey, even if he did have a cheese face, because without him, there would be no Charity. But really Aster was always her destiny. Even at nine, I knew it.'

'Do you think—'

'I doubt it.' She cut me off. 'Too much water under the old bridge. Especially in Ickthorpe. But friends, well – isn't that something?'

I watched then, as Aster laughed at whatever Daphne had said, placed a hand on her arm, while Daphne's face flashed pink, her lips tipping into a smile. Would they just be friends? Could they be? Could Cal and I? Could Charity and Fitz . . . ?

I scanned the room quickly, my eyes alighting on Lady Caroline – willowy in a silver shift dress. I scanned again, saw Charity at the opposite side, deep in something heated with Cal. My insides flinched, but I couldn't think about that. I had a chance, if I took it now. A chance to do something good, and right. And, yes, it was meddling, but what did I have to lose? Charity was leaving for America anyway. We'd all be leaving, wouldn't we? The house would be sold on, and well, I might never see any of these people – Charity, Marigold, Aster, Panther, Val, Daphne . . . Cal – again. And the thought was a wash of cold slop on me, while the thought of what I might achieve a shot of something hot and invigorating. 'Yes,' I said, to my own question. 'Yes, you shall.'

And I did. And perhaps it will pay off, perhaps not. But I can't think about that now, because of what happened next.

'There you are, Birdy,' said a voice – a man's voice this time.

I knew without turning it was him; my whole body felt it. 'Cal,' I said, as I met his eyes, smiled, more tightly than I felt.

He, however, was grinning as he held something up in front of me.

I focused, saw what it was. '*Lady Chatterley*!' I exclaimed. 'You found it!' I didn't care that it was he who'd managed it; Rollo's last dying wish would be met, and that was all mattered.

'Marigold had brought a copy for the train,' he explained. 'So I nabbed it.'

'And she didn't mind?' I asked.

'Said I was welcome to it. That it was nothing she hadn't seen or done before.'

'Lawks.' It was my turn to flush, but I mustered swiftly. 'I have to give it to him,' I said then. 'I can take it back straight after this.'

'*I* could—' Cal suggested.

I jinked again at the emphasis. 'Of course. You found it. You should be the one—'

'I meant together,' he blurted. 'I could come with you. *We* could go.'

I wasn't sure if this meant he'd forgiven me; I wasn't sure I'd met whatever conditions that required, although the fact Daphne and Aster were still laughing, their camaraderie – and whatever else might be glimmering – lighting up the far side of the gallery, perhaps bore me out. I wasn't going to question it in any case – beggars (and remember, I am very beggar) can't be choosers, after all. 'Yes!' I said again.

And so we left, grabbing our Macintoshes from the cloakroom and then clattering and splashing down the cobbles behind Bond Street, across a rain-slicked Regent Street and into the square mile of home.

We shook ourselves like dogs when we burst through the door of the shop.

'You're soaked,' he said. 'Your hair.' He went to touch the sodden mop that clung to my head like an oilskin cap then stopped himself. 'Sorry, I . . . I'm not sure—'

I was sure, but I couldn't say it. Not yet. 'The book,' I blurted. 'Is it wet as well?'

He snapped to, fished into the pocket of his coat and pulled it out. 'A bit damp,' he said, flicking through the pages. 'But nothing irreparable.'

'Thank heaven,' I said.

There was another pause, one ripe and singing. Then, 'Come on,' he said. And this time, when he reached for me – for my hand – he didn't stop himself, and I let him.

And I have never been more thankful that I did. Because when we got to the top of the stairs, we were met by a tear-stained Valentine.

'What?' I asked. But I knew; clearly we both did, as Cal's fingers tightened in mine.

'It's . . . it's Rollo,' Val answered, his voice as broken as he. 'He's gone.'

DECEMBER 1960

FRIDAY
2 DECEMBER

10 A.M.
I recall it now: something he said the day of the exhibition – Rollo, I mean – only I didn't listen at the time, or not to the subtext anyway. 'I burned bright once, but now I'm down to a nub of wick. I am guttering,' he said. 'Ready to be snuffed out.'

And now the light is gone.

He knew it; Rollo knew he was leaving. But we all, somehow, believed – in the face of overwhelming evidence – that we still had time, still had days, weeks, maybe even months with him.

What fools, we.

If nothing else it is a reminder, I suppose, to seize things when they are in front of you; to say things when they must be said rather than fold them up and file them away for 'the right time'.

But of course, Cal dropped my hand, and it was Val who held me as I sobbed, and then I, Charity, when she staggered in gone midnight. And I've not seen Cal since, not once among the stream of Soho faces – the Roberts, Doris, Eggs, everyone – coming to offer condolences, or more often apologies for not paying off debts. At one point, I think, the whole of the French had decamped to our living room, Charity and I buzzing among them with the last of wine from Rollo's 'cellar', i.e. the cupboard under the stairs, where also languished an old hockey stick, oars, a black and white photograph of smart boys on benches in front of their house at Harrow – vestiges from that more orthodox life he couldn't quite leave behind.

But now he is leaving both. The funeral is at noon at St Paul's on Bedford Street – the Actors' Church, Charity says, more forgiving of 'difference'; the wake at Aster's at three.

And then?

I can't think about it. The world must surely, like Rollo, gutter and snuff out.

MONDAY
5 DECEMBER

10 A.M.
Of course, the world did not snuff out, however I might have wished it on the day. Life, as determined as a dandelion weed in a crack of concrete, pushes through, persists. Though it has taken this long to be able to write about it.

Can a funeral be a fine thing? A few days ago, I would have shaken my head, thought whoever proposed such a thing must be quite, quite delusional. And yet now I believe that, given the right place, the right congregation, perhaps it can. Because this was as fine an occasion as one might wish for oneself. If I had worried that Rollo lacked a family, that the pews would be sparsely populated, if populated at all, I was mistaken. Every wooden seat, every kneeler was taken; there was standing room only at the back. Not his blood relatives, of course, bar his uncle – they, if they are living still, have no truck with him, or with any of 'the likes of us' as Valentine put it. I was glad, then, not to see the shame on their faces, endure their – what? Pity, perhaps? Glad that the family he found, rather than was born to, filled St Paul's with their song, with their eulogies, with their unfettered love; the Mannerings – every one of them: Panther and Freddy, Jack and Cal, Marigold and her lot, Val, Aster and, yes, Daphne as well, whom Charity clung to through 'Jerusalem'.

I did not cling to my own mother, though she was, to my pride, among the mourners. She and Daddy didn't warn me they were coming, but must have snuck in, as it was only as I turned to watch Rollo's coffin pass down the nave – ported high by Cal, Ted, Val, and their chess friends from the French – that I caught sight of her hat (it is unmissable – an atrocity that more resembles a dead cormorant than headwear) among those in the back pews. I found, again to my surprise, that when I had wended my way to her, through the clusters of painters, poets, waiters, market traders that made up the rest of Rollo's faithful, I was glad to see her.

She did not hug me (Mummy does not do hugs; I assume she regards them as inefficient), but she did smile fondly as she asked, 'And how are you bearing up?'

'Fine,' I lied, as I buried my face in the familiar knit of Daddy's jumper. (He is as generous with his affections as she is miserly.)

Daddy pulled back, looked at me. 'Not fine at all, are you, Birdy? But you will be, I promise.'

I smiled faintly, too bruised to believe it possible yet knowing he had lived through the loss of his own father and two uncles, so must know a little of this. My thoughts were interrupted by a metaphorical slap from Mummy.

'I expect you'll be coming home early now,' she said. 'Given' – she waved her hands at the sea of ink-black we swam in – 'everything.'

'I...'

Would I go home?

Should I?

27 Lexington Street will be sold, I assume, its occupants scattering like crows from a farmer's shotgun. Charity is already set on America, Ted on St Ives 'for the light' – he and Minty leave in the new year. Plus I have no home now, no guaranteed job; my friends are leaving or gone. What is left for me in Soho? No, it should be Surbiton for me, and then, if I can manage it, Cambridge. And yet...

I have no answer now, just as none I had then.

'I don't know,' I told Mummy. 'We'll see.'

'But Cambridge,' she reminded me.

That, I ignored, but it seems only a matter of time, surely. We go to the solicitors on Dover Street at two for the reading of the will, and then I shall pack my bags, I suppose, call Daddy to fetch me at the weekend. What point taking up space when the estate agent would rather us gone, swept out with the rest of the dust and clutter. Besides, Mummy only gave me a year and that year is nearly up.

Perhaps Rollo was right: better to move on before one tires of Soho, or it of us. Before we become like the laggers at the back of the Colony: living on nothing but stories and cigarettes and blagged gin.

5 P.M.

I could witter on for sentences about what happened at Hubert and Briggs. Could lament the sallowness of the reception area, the dark-panelled anteroom into which we were ushered as if into the bowel of the building itself, the fact that Edwin Briggs ('junior', he informed us) more resembled a cadaver than a man. But no, I will get to the point: 27 Lexington Street is ours. And when I say 'our' I mean Charity, Ted and I.

Reading this back now I remain as flabbergasted as I was at the time, though at least now, in the privacy of my bedroom – yes, on Lexington Street – it matters not if I yelp.

'To my partner, Valentine, and our adopted children . . .' began Briggs.

'That means you three,' added Val. 'In case you weren't sure.'

My heart jinked; Charity and I glanced at each other. Ted, as resolute as ever, stared at a stain on the wall.

Briggs sighed tightly. 'Can I finish now?'

Valentine held up his hands, apologised.

'. . . I leave the residence at twenty-seven Lexington Street.'

There came the yelp; I felt the world teeter and tip, as if somehow had shoved it off-kilter. But there was more.

'A lease on the ground floor, known as "Pennington's",

to be taken up by Aster Mannering.'

'Will she?' Charity turned to Val. 'Aster, I mean. Take over at Pennington's?'

He nodded, with a quiet smile. 'We've been talking about it for a while. She wants to open a bookshop for women. I think it was your mother's idea.'

Charity's eyes filled with bright tears.

Ours were not far behind. It was only when we got back to the shop – where Aster and Cal were waiting with tea and fruit cake; more welcome than I could have imagined – that we managed to dry our eyes long enough to talk about the enormity of it all.

'But how?' I asked. 'How will we manage? I'm due back in Surbiton to sit for wretched Cambridge. I can't live in two places. And I shan't have any income.'

Val shrugged. 'I honestly don't know. I told Rollo we hadn't the means but he said we'd find a way.'

'You could always sell,' said Aster, with the kind of smile that suggested she was pot stirring, not serious. 'I hear Paul Raymond is on the scout for locations.'

'The strip club fellow?' asked Cal.

'No,' I said, full-stop sure of myself in this, if nothing else. 'We're not selling. Not to a . . . a pornographer.'

'Then I'll stay,' Charity said.

'Pardon?' I asked.

'You heard me.' She jutted her chin. 'I shan't go. I *can't* go.'

'Whyever not?' asked Cal.

'Not after ... everything. I can't abandon you. And I shan't be able to pay rent here as well as America.'

'You won't need to pay rent—'

'The building's falling down,' she pointed out. 'Or hadn't you noticed?'

I glanced quickly at the damp patch on the ceiling, the paper peeling off the back wall.

'We all need to pay something,' she went on. 'Ted as well. Not even Aster's lease will raise a new roof.'

'We can rent out your room,' I said. 'Ted's too.'

Charlie frowned. 'But you can't want to live with strangers,' she continued.

'*You* were all strangers,' I pointed out. 'Besides. I don't think I'll be staying. Not if I get into Cambridge.'

Charity went quiet for a while. Then grasped my arm. 'Come with me!'

It wasn't a question, more one of her whimsical demands. But for once, I was immune. 'My life is in England,' I told her. 'At least for now.'

'But—'

'Go!' I insisted. 'Whatever happens, I'll be fine. We all will. The rooms will be rented and ... well, then we'll see.'

Her face fell, then lit as bright as the neon sign on the Revue Bar. 'Oh my goodness!' she shrieked. 'I'm going to America! I'm going to America!' Then, as quickly as she'd brimmed, she shrank back. 'Oh, God. I'm so sorry, I shouldn't have, not with Rollo—'

'Nonsense,' said Val. 'This is exactly what Rollo would want.'

'So is this,' said Cal, when he and I went down to the kitchen to put the rusty kettle on again, fetch milk from the weary fridge, rattle the recalcitrant boiler.

I looked at the hand he held out to me, realised quickly, and with a spasm of embarrassment that he didn't mean the hand itself, but the newspaper clipping gripped in it.

'What is it?' I asked.

He waved it again, bade me take it.

I did so. '"Cub reporter wanted for the *Herald* news desk",' I read. '"Requirements: a nose for a capital story, attention to detail, shorthand. Typing proficiency preferable. Open test, including a pitch for a feature article, to be held at ten a.m. on the sixth of Dec—" Wait. That's tomorrow!' I realised with a jolt. 'How long have you known about this?'

Cal shook his head. 'Two weeks. But I knew if I said anything . . .' He seemed to steel himself. 'You were distracted. You had . . . Rollo to concentrate on.'

Bitterness consumed me. 'What if . . . what if I wanted a distraction from the distraction? Or did you just want to keep it to yourself and now you feel – what? Guilty?'

He shook his head, his face red now. 'I didn't mean to keep it from you. I meant to . . . to protect you.'

'I don't need protecting,' I snapped. 'This isn't a . . . a storybook. I'm not a damsel in distress.'

'I know—' he tried.

But I wasn't listening. 'I'll see you at Fleet Street,' I said.

'Where are you going?' he asked. 'We're meant to be making tea?'

'You do it,' I snapped back. 'Seeing as I'm *distracted*.'

'Birdy, I'm sorry—'

'I'm going for a walk,' I said, before he could try to stop me.

And I did. I walked the streets of this square mile – Berwick, Beak, Poland, Greek; the grid that strings between Charing Cross Road and Regent Street like a dew-dappled spider's web – and I didn't stop until the red-hot anger had faded to embers.

But the fire? The fire is in me still, waiting to be kindled into flame again. Because now I have a home in Soho. And a job prospect tomorrow.

And I know what I shall write about, too.

TUESDAY 6 DECEMBER

5 P.M.

There were ten of us in the end: nine men in their teens and twenties – some in three-piece suits, others in threadbare shirts and mismatched jackets – one, I am sure, in his adoptive father's demob suit – but I the only woman.

'Typing pool's that way,' joked one of them. At least, I assumed it was a joke at first, but when I refused to budge he nudged the acne-pocked kid next to him. 'Women at the *Herald*? Derry'd die before that happens.'

'Recipes, then, is it?' asked another.

My face flashed with heat, despite the freezing air that wafted into the foyer with each swing of the brass-edged doors. I opened my mouth to snap back but a hand stayed me.

'Ignore them,' Cal said, his breath on my neck. 'You're worth ten of them and you know it.'

Every cell of me wanted to lean into him, to feel his arms close around me, but that would be conceding defeat, wouldn't it? I shook him off. 'I do know,' I said. And I found that it wasn't a lie. I *was* worth more than them, with their backwards attitudes and their sly eyes. What sort of reporters would they make? The conniving kind, I decided; the kind that finagles their way into someone's trust, then abuses it for six inches of print.

A flood of something rushed me then – not Cal's flattering words, but my own belief in myself: a solid thing, and strong too. And over the course of the morning – through the blur of shorthand, and transcription tests, the tour of the building with its whirr and clank of the presses, the thick fug of cigarette smoke, the click-click-click of typewriter keys – it only became more iron-like, so that when I handed in my feature pitch as we were leaving, it was with a flourish.

'When will we hear?' I asked the secretary (severe spectacles, air of grim efficiency) who was collecting them.

'I doubt it will be until after Christmas now.' She glanced around, then leaned in. 'Between you and me, he's off to Spain for three weeks.'

'Golf?' I asked.

She sighed. 'While the rest of us run the bloody ship.'

I nodded. 'Thank you.'

'Best of luck,' she said. 'And good for you. Be nice to have a woman in the newsroom. I'm Jeanie, by the way.'

'Birdy,' I replied. 'Well, Margaret, but—'

'Ten to one,' said a man who had loomed beside me, thrusting his own sheets into Jeanie's hand. 'Not promising odds, love.'

I watched as Jeanie shuffled his feature to the bottom of the pile. 'Thanks, *love*,' she replied.

We both smirked as she met my eyes.

*

Perhaps I will get the job; perhaps not. Cal certainly deserves it as much as I, and maybe even that man, with his slick hair and pity, can write a pretty line. But I knew in that second that, even with Rollo gone, with Charity and Ted elsewhere, with Cal and I at odds, I will find friends in London: sisters who understand me, will boost me no matter what the cost to them. Will hold me up, and I them, against the men who would cut each other – cut us – down.

Oh, I know not all men. Daddy is a wonder; Val, too. Even Cal . . . Especially Cal.

But I do think that Charity has it right; I only hope the Sewing Circle welcomes her as warmly as it has, apparently, so many others.

SATURDAY 24 DECEMBER

4 P.M.

I wasn't going to write until tomorrow, as a sort of gloom has consumed 27 Lexington Street for the past week. Or rather, one more melancholy than the general Rollo-less torpor. Charity says it is the thought of Christmas without him, and I suspect she is right. The house seems to rattle even more than normal, and unsurprisingly, given that Ted has left already for Chipping Norton – he's ensconced at the Brighams' country residence for the festive season, now that he's the darling of the art world – and Val for Ickthorpe with Aster, and Cal, I presume. Daphne begged Charity to come up to Essex, but she said she's not spending her last British Christmas in the 'back of beyond', besides which we've already offered to cook lunch for Doris, as the oven in their garret above the Pippin has been on the blink since 1957.

Mummy is livid, of course.

'Not. Coming. Home?' Her words were punctuated with ire. 'But—'

'Boxing Day!' I offered. 'I'll come on Boxing Day when Aunt

Barbara and Uncle Roy are there. I'll even occupy Julian!' This was a generous offer, and she knew it.

'Boxing Day,' she conceded. 'But this has to be . . .' Her voice caught, like a scratch on a gramophone record. 'This is the end to this nonsense. Do you understand? This is your—'

I made a noise to suggest the line was bad and hung up. This is not the time for that conversation, not yet. Besides, I was – *am* – preoccupied, because Charity has a visitor.

Yes, it is Fitz! And thus, the torpor has been punctured by the slice of possibility. Of course, there is the chance that any minute now she will be booted out, but it's been an hour so far, there have been no raised voices, no slams of doors, and I can hear the sound of Billie Holiday filtering down through the floorboards, which can only be a good sign, I think.

7 P.M.
Fitz is still here.

8 P.M.
Fitz is still here!

9 P.M.
Fitz is still here and, what's more, is *staying*.

'For how long?' I asked, delighted, when the pair finally descended, in mismatched silk dressing gowns, and identical tousled hair.

They looked at each other, grinned. 'Well, for good,' said Fitz. 'I think.'

'Through Christmas,' clarified Charity. 'And then, well . . .' She grasped Fitz's hand. 'She's coming with me to Hollywood.'

Every inch of me glimmered. 'You are?'

Fitz nodded, her dark eyes glimmering. 'I am,' she said, as if realising the brilliance of this only now. 'I really am!'

It was my turn to be grasped as they headed for the bedroom again with their cheese and biscuits – a lovers' supper if ever there was one.

'Thank you,' said Fitz, who had run back down quickly. 'For what you said at the exhibition.'

I glanced up to see Charity waiting, her eyes on me kind. So she knew, then, that this was my doing. Relief rushed me – a welcome wash of warm syrup. 'You're welcome,' I said. 'You're . . . meant to be.'

'I'm not sure I believe in fate,' said Fitz. 'Or "meant-to-be"s. But I do believe in rightness. And we are *right* together.'

'You are,' I said, with every bit of gusto I could muster, while the rest of me tamped down the thought that perhaps I might be *right* with someone too.

Still, Christmas tomorrow, and that will distract me. I only hope the chicken can stretch to four after all.

SUNDAY
25 DECEMBER

11 A.M.
Five. Cal is here.

'Room for one more?' he asked, forlornly, from the doorstep.

I pulled my robe tighter around me against the chill wind. 'I thought you'd gone to Essex.'

He shook his head. 'Norman's pregnant again. Boris, I assume.'

This was better than her own brother, at least, though I didn't say so.

'Anyway, she's taken up residence in the airing cupboard and won't be moved. Someone had to stay and feed her.'

My lips were desperate to pull into a smile, but I refused them. 'Then you'd better come in,' I conceded. 'I don't want you getting frostbite and poor Norman starving.'

'Thanks,' he said, as he hung up his peacoat – Freddy's as well? – in the hall behind the shop. 'I didn't even know if you'd still be here. You know, with Surbiton.'

'Tomorrow.' I curtailed a wince at the thought. 'Anyway, Charity would have been. Though, well, she's not . . . alone.'

He frowned, then let his mouth gape. 'God, not Alan?'

'Heavens, no!' I smiled this time, full and wide – how could I not? 'Fitz.'

I don't know what I expected, but it wasn't the hug I found myself enveloped in, if only briefly.

'God, sorry,' he said and pulled back, as if aware, suddenly, of what he was doing. 'I should have asked. I know it's not . . . we're not . . .'

I did not know what, exactly, we weren't, but I shrugged, folded my arms. 'It's fine.' I smiled, willing away the heat in my cheeks. 'And it *is* good news, isn't it?'

'The best,' he said. 'Well, perhaps not as good as . . .' But again he trailed off, before he could tell me what it was that might trump it. Instead, a second later, he snapped from whatever reverie he'd slipped into and said, 'Kettle?'

I nodded, glad of something to do – to occupy my hands if not my mind. Though in fact it is him making tea, while I write this and sip the sherry he insisted on pouring me ('festive spirit'), and wait for Doris to get here, for Charity and Fitz to get up, and for Christmas to officially begin.

2 P.M.

There has been a hitch – or perhaps a giant spanner – in the works. Or rather, if we had a spanner, and someone to wield it, perhaps there wouldn't be a hitch. Or . . . actually, I shall just write it plainly, because I am not capturing the catastrophe at all well – the oven has joined the boiler in its resolute refusal to work when required. No doubt, like the boiler again, it will come on in the middle of the night, or in the searing heat of July, and clank its merry tune, but right now, on a Christmas Day as arctic as Wenceslas's, it is stubbornly silent, and quite, quite cold.

'We should never have let Ted leave,' said Charity. 'He would know what to do.'

'Don't look at me!' Doris held up their hands. 'I can do your mascara, darling, but a wrench is men's work.'

'That's terribly old-fashioned,' I pointed out.

'Can you do it, then?' Fitz asked me, her voice replete with belief.

'I . . . No,' I admitted.

'I like how none of you think I might be able to do it,' Cal added. 'Charming.'

'Can you?' I asked.

There was a pause. 'No,' he said. 'But that's not the point.'

'It is literally the point,' said Charity. 'We don't need' – she threw her hands up – 'political gestures. We need the bloody oven to work so we can cook the chicken, otherwise it's cheese and biscuits.'

'Well, just the biscuits,' Fitz said shyly. 'I'm afraid I'm a bit of a cheese fiend.' She pulled a face. 'I ate most of it last night.'

If Charity minded, she didn't show it. 'Piglet,' she said, and kissed her.

'So it's biscuits for Christmas dinner then?' said Cal. 'I think even Tiny Tim had better.'

'Tiny Tim had a goose,' sighed Doris.

'Yes, but that was after Scrooge had a change of heart,' said Cal. 'Before that—'

'Can we quit with the Dickens?' demanded Charity. 'We need to think.'

It came to me then, ready-made, as if on a plate. 'I have an idea,' I offered.

All eyes were on me, as expectant as a five year old's on Christmas Eve.

'Surbiton,' I said. 'Mummy always has a turkey that could feed Jesus's five thousand. And she's seething that I didn't go home as it is.'

'But won't she object to the rest of us?' Cal was frowning.

I thought of her then, at Rollo's funeral. How she had packed away her own prejudices and done a good thing, for my sake. 'No,' I said. 'She won't.'

But when I rang her, she went one better. 'We'll come to you!' she said.

'But, John and Gloria—'

'Have got a tummy bug and so Daddy has banned them. He's got a crunch four-ball in the morning and he can't be coming down with something, not when the captaincy is up for grabs.'

'It is?'

'Gordon Rawlingson is defecting to Kingston.' This said with an air of resignation.

This, I knew, was more important than life or death. More important, even, than completing the *Times* crossword. 'But we can—'

'There won't be trains,' she went on. 'And none of you has a car.'

This, I had to admit, was true.

'It's settled,' she said with the snap of finality. Then, 'Gerry!' she called down the hallway. 'Fetch the foil! We're going to Soho!'

And so it is. Surbiton is coming to Soho for Christmas – a sixpence-turn again.

I wonder how many more of those we shall we see before the season is through?

MONDAY
26 DECEMBER

1 A.M.

The sixpences have spun myriad times, and so swift that I am giddy with it.

But I know from every book I have read, every film I have witnessed that one cannot just come in with the crunch scene; there must be build-up, context, tension.

Or at least my mother, wittering on about the parakeets eating all the seed she's put out for the greenfinches.

'Parakeets?' checked Doris, as we ploughed through Mummy's turkey – a little cooler than one might have liked, but not in the slightest bit dry.

'Oh, yes,' said Daddy, pleased to be able to touch on one of his specialist subjects. 'There's been a flock of them in Richmond Park for a while but they've started venturing into the conurbations as well.'

'The thieves,' added Mummy.

'I think it's exotic,' said Fitz. 'Parakeets in Surbiton.'

I smiled to myself, remembering when Rollo had called me just that.

'I suppose it is rather,' said Daddy, even more puffed up.

'Hardly,' said Mummy. 'They're vultures,' she went on. 'But green.'

'But greenfinches are green,' I pointed out.

'Not the same,' she said. 'Greenfinch green is tasteful. Parakeet green has ideas above its station. Parakeet green—'

'Presents!' I said then, remembering something. 'We haven't done presents.'

Charity clapped a hand on her mouth. 'But I haven't got Fitz one.' She turned to her ... girlfriend? 'I'm so sorry. I didn't know—'

But Fitz shook her head. 'This is all the present I need,' she said, and took her hand.

I glanced at my mother who reddened but, to her credit, said nothing.

'Yours are back at the house,' admitted Daddy to me then. 'We forgot them in the rush.'

'Well yours are here,' I said. 'Under the tree.'

*

And so, lunch done, we decamped from table to tree – if one could call it that; Valentine had got it out of the prop store for us, its plastic branches quite bent, its baubles rather suffering from the attentions of Marilyn – sat in the corner of the room, the light from Lexington Street catching my foil star on its topmost reach.

I reached under it, pulled out six soft packages. 'There's

one for everyone,' I said. 'Doris and Fitz, you too.' In truth, Fitz's had been meant for Rollo, but I knew, wherever he was watching from, he would approve.

'A scarf!' Mummy exclaimed, holding up the soft, moss-stitched cashmere, hers in a beige I knew couldn't possibly offend her.

'I love it,' said Daddy, wrapping his yellow-striped one – golf club colours – around his neck immediately (possibly in self-defence as the room is as cold as the oven).

'When did you do this?' asked Charity, her neck adorned in scarlet mohair, contrasting nicely with Fitz and Doris's cornflower blue.

I winced. 'On Rollo watch,' I said. 'And then... after. Writing was so hard and well, Mummy taught me when I was small and I've never had a use for it until now.'

At that, Mummy seemed to bloom.

I glanced, then, at the last recipient, who was on the stool in the corner, holding his opened package as if terrified.

I went over to him, sat down. 'It won't bite,' I assured him. 'It's not poisoned, or charmed.'

'It's just...' He looked up at me. 'I didn't get you anything. I didn't think... given, well, everything.'

I shook my head. 'I don't give just to get back.'

'I know, but... I'm sorry,' he said then. 'For everything. For... for reading your diary, for trying to take credit for the column, for all of it. I've been a cad. A spoiled brat.'

'It's fine, really—'

'No, it's not. And I . . . I'll make it up to you.' He wound the scarf round his neck then, the emerald setting off his eyes, just as I knew it would. 'It's beautiful,' he said. 'Thank you.'

'It is,' I agreed, loudly.

You are, I whispered to myself. I caught Charity's eye but looked away; I didn't need her egging me on, not now – not with my parents, of all people, here. But, oh God, how I wanted him. Even if he didn't feel the same. Even if this wasn't the right time for confessions, even if he was so inclined. But then, when would be? Perhaps I should say something anyway, I thought. Perhaps—

'What *is* that?' Mummy said, as if listening in to my thoughts. 'That noise.'

We all paused, listened.

Fitz shrugged. 'Fire engine, I think,' she said.

'On Christmas Day?' I asked.

Cal rolled his eyes. 'It'll be someone drunk and left their oven on.'

'Lucky beggars,' I said. 'To have an oven that works.'

'Poor beggars,' said Daddy. 'Imagine the chaos.'

I winced at my ignorance, just as Doris's eyes widened.

'I . . . Oh, bloody hell,' they said.

If Mummy disapproved at the swearing, I didn't have time to check, as I realised the implications at the same time as Charity.

'The Pippin?' we yelped.

'Oh, Christ,' said Cal. 'Get your coats.'

We didn't need telling, were already down the stairs – Doris and Fitz, Daddy and Mummy in hot pursuit (Mummy running back briefly to check our own oven was firmly in the off position, despite its frigid state).

But by the time we arrived on Beak Street and had pushed through the crowd, there was nothing we could do but stand and watch as the flames ate what was left of the little theatre – of Doris's home, of Charity's past, of Valentine's entire life.

'Someone will have to telephone him,' said Cal eventually.

'I will,' said Doris, sadly. 'My doing.'

'No, it isn't,' Cal insisted. 'Anyway, the Pippin has had its day. Like Soho. He knows that.'

My mind flicked to the *Herald* and my feature pitch. 'Soho will never have had its day,' I insisted.

'At least there will be insurance,' said Daddy, practically. 'A big payout on prime land like this.'

'Perhaps he can sell *that* to Paul Raymond,' sneered Charity.

Cal groaned. 'God, don't give him ideas.'

'I don't think standing here is helping,' said Mummy then. 'A cup of tea is what we need. Come along, all of you.'

Like the Pied Piper, she led us – Daddy and I, Doris and Cal, Charity and Fitz: waifs and strays all – in a solemn column back to Pennington's, where she boiled the kettle, checked the boiler, and – miracle of miracles – fixed the oven after all.

'How did you do that?' I asked.

'Loose wire,' she said, wiping her hands on a tea towel. 'How do you think I coped in the war? Right, time to be off.'

My insides slipped. I knew what I should do, but I couldn't. 'Don't ask me to come home,' I begged. 'I will, I promise. Just not tonight.'

But Mummy shook her head. And then, against every bone in her that couldn't abide sentimentality – that put it all on a par with whimsical pictures of kittens – she touched my shoulder. 'This is your home now, isn't it?' she said. 'I know you think I don't understand, but I do. If you want to sit for Cambridge, then I shall help you all I can. But if not, well . . . that will be up to you. It's your life, not mine, I realise now.'

I went to open my mouth but before I could say thank you – say anything – the warmth in her expression had been replaced with the usual determination. She dropped her hand and pulled on her gloves with gusto. 'Come along, Gerry,' she called. 'Home. Before the roads ice over.'

*

We sat for hours after that. Talking about everything and nothing – Rollo, the Pippin, the dog at the Lorelei; Bacon's latest paintings and how they compared to Ted's, whether the French would ever serve beer, the job at the *Herald*.

'When will you hear?' asked Charity, Fitz in her lap, fast asleep.

I glanced at Cal.

'Any day,' he said, his eyes staying on mine. Then he seemed to shake himself. 'I should go,' he said. 'It's been, well, a hell of a day.'

'We should go to bed too,' said Charlie, nudging Fitz up. 'Doris, I'll show you Ted's room. It's yours for as long as you need.'

Doris smiled, their eyes bright with tears; there were hugs as they and the others made their way upstairs.

Then it was just Cal and I, beached in the sitting room. 'I . . . I'll see myself out,' he said.

Then I was seized with it. It was now, I realised. Time. Before one of us got the job and it all got complicated again – or more complicated. 'I was an idiot,' I blurted.

He frowned. 'I don't—'

'With the "yes" thing,' I explained. 'All that' – I flapped a hand at invisible moths – 'nonsense with Jack. That was the only reason I kissed him, and even when I did, I wished—'

Oh, God, was I going to say it? I looked at my shoes for courage.

'You wished what?' he pushed.

I looked up, saw the green of his eyes, my scarf – found the courage, the guts I'd been looking for. 'I wished it had been you.'

There was a pause, as taut and tense as stretched elastic, and then, in the next second, I felt at last what Charity had with Fitz, what Val had with Rollo, Aster with Daphne – because as our lips met, as electricity crackled around us, at the centre was something solid, something . . . *right*.

I don't know how long we stayed like that – our lips, our minds somehow melded. I only know, as we at last parted, we were both laughing.

'I really do have to go,' he said, his feet cemented to the floorboards. 'Norman will be going spare.'

'You do,' I agreed, immoveable. 'You really do.'

When we finally made it to the doorstep, it was to the sound of the bells at St Anne's ringing in Boxing Day.

'Goodbye, then,' I said into the warm wool of his peacoat.

He kissed the top of my head. 'You're not a comma, you know.'

I looked up, confused. 'Pardon?' I asked.

'In the diary, remember? You said you were a comma and Charlie an exclamation mark. That's just not true.'

I got it, nodded. 'And I don't think you're a fake,' I said. 'I think ... I think you're bloody wonderful.'

Needless to say, we kissed again.

And again.

And again.

But now I am in bed, Doris snoring from the attic, Charity and Fitz doing ... what I wish I were doing, two doors along.

But that will come. I know it now.

And I know, too, that I *am* an exclamation mark. And that this, all of it, is Life with that capital L.

SATURDAY 31 DECEMBER

10 A.M.

The letter from the *Herald* is here, sitting staidly on the kitchen table, sort of taunting me – a Schrödinger's cat of a thing. Because right now I both have and haven't got the job, but once I open it then, well, whatever it is becomes concrete. Either my joy and Cal's disappointment, or his triumph and my wretched defeat.

Neither, of course, is appealing. Which is why I am up here in my room, avoiding the issue, while Cal (who arrived at the same time as the letter, having performed morning Norman duty) placates Charity and Fitz, who are leaving for America later this morning, and are so far from packed as to be catastrophic.

Perhaps I shall wait until they have gone; having to paste on my pleased-as-punch face if Cal gets it might be easier without an audience, after all.

I only wish he had received his letter first – then we could have avoided all this wretched tension and got on with the big farewell instead.

11 A.M.

Charity is packed, and has given me three minutes to come down or she says she is going to open it herself and then telephone my mother. I wish this were an empty threat, but I suspect she will happily go through with it.

Oh, heavens! Here comes another sixpence-spin, and there is nothing I can do to change it now.

9 P.M.

The deed is done.

And Charity has gone.

And I am at the kitchen table writing, because it is the only way I know to make sense of things. Because retelling it will help me, I've realised. Not just to become a better journalist – though I think, truly, that writing is a muscle memory, like playing the violin or practising javelin – but to become a better me.

So here they are: the final scenes of this year – my year of 'yes'. My year of living differently. Of living dangerously.

*

Picture the kitchen – the boiler clanging unhelpfully, the radiator rattling in concert, Charity and Fitz clamouring at me as Cal took my hand.

'You've got to rip it open,' said Fitz.

'Like a plaster,' agreed Charity.

Cal concurred. 'It's the only way,' he said, squeezing my fingers.

I stared at the thing again – my name and address in neat italics, the *Herald*'s stamp in the upper left corner. 'You could open yours first,' I said. 'Then we'd both know.'

'That would require me going back to Aster's,' he pointed out. 'And I've only just come from there.'

'I don't know why you don't just move in,' Charity suggested then. 'You're back here every day as it is. Bring Norman with you if you must. Marilyn will be glad of the company.'

I reddened, felt my hand slick with sweat in his. 'I . . . I'm not sure Cal wants—'

'Well, I—' Cal started.

'Someone will need to take Rollo's room,' she went on. 'It can't sit there like a bloody shrine until Kingdom Come. Not now Val isn't coming back.'

Val was staying on in Ickthorpe, he'd decided, now that Rollo and the Pippin had gone. Soho *had* had its day after all, at least for one of us.

'Anyway, not the point!' Charity snapped me from my thoughts. 'We've a flight to catch at five. Just bloody open it, would you?'

I dropped Cal's hand, wiped the sheen of my own sweat on my trouser leg. 'Oh, heavens.' I took a breath.

'May the best writer win— What?' Cal added when Charity grimaced. 'Isn't that the point of this?'

'Not to me,' I said, sharply. Then softened. 'Not any more. We're both good enough. We both deserve it. It's just . . .'

'Only one of us can get it,' Cal finished. He smiled, and I felt that shimmer in me again. Whatever happened, it would be all right. *We* would be all right. As long as—'

'Right, that's it,' snapped Charity and grabbed the letter herself, tore off the top. 'Do you want to read this or shall I?'

I snatched it back. '*I* shall.'

I grasped the metaphorical plaster and pulled the letter out of its pocket – the vellum heavy, as if with the weight of its contents; unfolded it.

Then I read the first line. '*I am happy to inform . . .*'

The rest of it blurred, my eyes brimming, my heart rabbit-fast. 'I . . . I'm so sorry,' I stammered.

Cal threw his arms round me and held me, tightly. 'I'm not,' he said. 'It was always going to be you.'

My insides were a whirligig – half delighted, half desperate. Nothing and everything made sense, suddenly. I had a job; one I'd longed for, but one that this man – a man I was beginning to think . . . no, not think, *know* that I loved – seemed destined for as well.

'Well, this is awkward,' observed Charity, reading my mind. 'But' – she brandished her watch – 'if we don't leave now, we'll miss the aeroplane. An aeroplane! How thrilling.'

I was glad of the distraction, wiped my eyes and nose, and thrust the letter into the pocket of my Fair Isle cardigan. 'Are you coming?' I asked Cal, tentatively.

His face, which had been oddly blank – as if paused in time –

suddenly reanimated. 'Of course I am.' He smiled. 'Wouldn't miss it for the world.'

Nor, apparently, would Daphne, who arrived with Aster in the Jaguar. 'Taxi for Pakenham!' she called from the door.

'Mummy?' Charity's mouth gaped, then lit into a grin. 'You came!'

'Aster brought me down this morning,' she explained. 'It's bad enough we missed you at Christmas, but not to see you off as well...'

'Oh, God.' Charity suddenly peered over Daphne's shoulder. 'You didn't bring the terrible twosome, did you?'

Daphne laughed. 'Calypso and Inigo? Hardly. They're with one of your sisters and a vicar for a week. I can't remember which. Everything's been' – she glanced at Aster – 'so very up in the air lately.' She turned to Fitz then. 'I'm sorry your mother isn't here, dear. I know it's 1960 – almost '61 – but... well, for some of us, it can take a while to catch up.'

Charity and Fitz both hugged her then, until she protested she might cease breathing, and Aster reminded them of the time.

How they managed to cram into the motorcar with all eight of their suitcases is a miracle, but perhaps, I reflect, as I think about Charity and Fitz, about Daphne and Aster, about Cal – gallant Cal! – and I, it is a day for those. But back to the story...

'*In fide vade!*' called Daphne, as she clambered into the front seat.

'What on earth is that?' I asked.

'Didn't you do Latin in Surbiton?' Cal asked. 'You surprise me.'

I pulled a face. 'I mean, I *did*, but Felicity and I didn't exactly listen. We mainly looked at the pictures of naked statues.'

He smiled. "Twas ever thus. "Go forth in faith",' he explained. 'It's the Balfour family motto.'

I frowned. 'I'm pretty sure Charity doesn't believe in God,' I said.

'But she believes in herself,' he said. He took my hand. 'And you should start too.'

I wanted to kiss him then and there, but Charity took that moment to stick her head out of the window. 'What are you doing out on the pavement?'

'Me?' I checked.

'Yes, you. Get in!'

And so I did. And I shall not write about the airport, for it was every bit as wonderful and awful as you imagine. There was not a dry eye among us.

*

It was two hours later when Aster dropped me back off at Lexington Street, and to Cal, before her return to Essex with Daphne.

'Give my love to Mum and Dad,' said Cal through the window, before they pitched off into the inky evening.

At that – that casual acceptance, that embrace of his family – I felt my heart squeeze and gripped his hand as I pulled him back towards the door.

But instead of coming in, Cal lingered on the pavement.

'What's happening?' I asked. Then I felt the crackle of the letter in my cardigan pocket. 'Oh.' My heart plunged. He'd realised the weight of it at last, I realised. Decided he couldn't face me, not any more. My eyes pricked with the sting of tears; I steeled myself for whatever he had to say.

'Birdy?' He touched a hand to my face.

'It's fine,' I lied. 'You go. This is' – I wiped an eye – 'just Charity leaving.'

He laughed.

Wait, was he mocking me? Was this the old sarcastic Cal that I'd met outside Morley College all those months ago. Was—

'Oh, Birdy, no.' He had seen my face. 'I'm just going to fetch Norman.'

'I . . . Pardon?'

He smiled, kind, and every bit the Cal I knew now. 'Charity was right.' He grinned. 'I spend most of my time here. And you need the rent. So I'm moving in. If you'll have me, of course.'

I thought for a moment. We did need the rent. And he did practically live here.

But neither of those are the point, are they? The point is, I want him. I want *us*.

'Yes!' I said. 'Very definitely, yes.'

The last 'yes' of 1960. And one of the best.

*

And so he has gone to get the cat, and I am here, writing – not in the kitchen sink, but by candlelight. And, on top of the last 'yes', this, I think, will be my last entry, at least for a while; I shall be writing all day, every day soon, albeit (I assume) the most basic of columns; the safest of jobs. But there is energy left in me, and ink in my pen enough to at least set down my next set of resolutions.

In no particular order, I resolve to:

1. Give the copy of *Mrs Dalloway* to Aster to sell.
2. Finish *Lady Chatterley's Lover*.
3. Do something with my hair, now I no longer have Charity to rely on.
4. Write to Charity every week.
5. Go home for Sunday lunch every month, and be pleased to see John and his lot if they're there.
6. Make Mummy proud again, for next year's round robin (this year she used the word 'admirable', which for her, is gushing).
7. Take Cal to see the parakeets.
8. Try not to meddle in other people's affairs, unless it is essential.
9. Say 'yes' only after I have thought carefully about whatever it is.
10. Stop wishing I were Cassandra Mortmain.

The last shan't be hard, at least. Because why on earth would I want to be her, or anyone else, for that matter?

I want to be me, Birdy Arbuthnot.

And I want to be here, in Soho, on Lexington Street, for ever.

THE HERALD

September 1st 1961

*New Life in Old Soho
by Birdy Arbuthnot, Junior News Reporter*

'Soho's changing hands,' comes the lament from the French.

'It's not what it was,' cry the Colony members, propped up by the bar – or do *they* prop *it*?

The complaints are the same, whichever club or pub you drop into, at whatever time – from early-morning espresso at the Lorelei or Bar Italia, to last orders at the Crown and Two: the fanfare arrival of chain stores ('how tawdry!') on Carnaby Street; the quiet creep of sex, as a certain Mr Raymond expands the empire that was founded just three years ago in the old Doric Ballroom; the rise in rents and flight of those who have called Soho home ever since they were forced to flee less-welcoming places for what has always been London's foundling borough. And yet, not every rat is jumping. So this ship, surely, is not sinking yet?

Despite the concerns of some of its regulars, the Colony Room on Dean Street and its steadfast owner, Muriel Belcher – feared and revered in equal measure – show no sign of shutting up shop. Nor, either, does the Mandrake on Meard Street, or, round the corner, the Gargoyle, despite its new daytime guise of 'strip club'. Painters 'Eggs' Bacon and Freud can still be found, several lunchtimes a month, shucking oysters at their habitual table at Wheeler's; jazz singer George Melly and actor Barry Humphries at the Caves du France or the Gay Hussar. While Pennington's, the long-standing bookshop, named for its late owner Rollo, eldest son of the Earl of Buckingham, is enjoying a revival at the hands of fashion designer and portrait artist Aster Mannering, who, along with her business partner and close friend Lady Daphne Pakenham, promotes the work of women and minoritised writers above all others.

Yes, Soho is home to some those in the suburbs may quake at: the seedy and illegal; the drifters and grifters and those who have, perhaps, seen better times. But there is life, it seems, in the old dog yet, and all Life at that, with a capital L. So, every week, on page 10 of your Herald, my cub colleague, Cal Mannering, and I will be taking a snapshot of our Soho home, bringing you a new gem or an old favourite, and inviting you to walk with us around this square mile – not of vice (as my mother – the indomitable Mrs Arbuthnot, of page 11's 'Winning Ways', once amusingly derided it), but of life.

ACKNOWLEDGEMENTS

Birdy began as a very different character in a very different novel: a mere bit part, but one whose back story seemed determined to shunt its way into the limelight. And so, eventually, that book was put to one side to give Birdy her chance to shine, and what better place than Soho, and in the orbit of the Mannerings. But she brings with her, too, many of the ideas I was working through in that earlier work – the issue of class, the pitfalls of "social climbing", the problem of being a woman even in a decade as famously progressive as the 1960s.

So my first thanks go to my publisher Hazel Holmes, my editor Emma Roberts, and all at UCLan, who have championed both *A Calamity of Mannerings* and *Birdy Arbuthnot's Year of 'Yes'* from first glimmer of an idea to the last lines.

To my agent Julia Churchill, who has always encouraged me to write what I love, no matter the genre or age banding.

To my late friend and neighbour Joe Roberts, who mourned the loss of the "old Soho", and to whom this book is dedicated.

To Hannah Rials, writer and bookseller extraordinaire at Mr B's Emporium, for the dozens of copies of *Calamity* she has hand-sold, and for the introduction to Laura Wood, whose own feminist, historical novels are an ongoing inspiration.

To my Monday BTP Writers Club booth-mates, whom I have had the privilege to pen and witter alongside for years now, and the London Writers Salon, whose four-daily Writers Hours gave me space, time and accountability to write.

To the Placers, who are always there with virtual tea and sympathy, and Anna Wilson and the Boskenna gang with actual tea and sympathy, as well as scones and swimming.

Lastly to Millie and Paul, who encourage the worlds that take shape in my head and don't mind when I want to go off and play there for days.

IF YOU LIKED THIS, YOU'LL LOVE . . .

'What an absolute hoot! Set in 1924, and galloping with coming-of-age giddiness, and the promise of parties and life-changing romance . . . simply brims with vim.'
LOVEREADING4KIDS

'Masterful, beautiful and utterly compelling.'
CATHERINE BRUTON

NOMINATED FOR THE CARNEGIE MEDAL FOR WRITING 2025

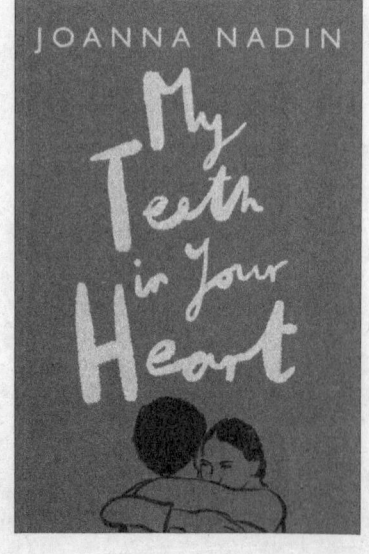